PRAISE FOR SHOLES & MOORE'S
AWARD WINNING BESTSELLING THRILLERS

THE BLADE

"Sholes & Moore are at the top of their game in this dark, chilling cat-and-mouse race to stop an unimaginable act of terrorism. THE BLADE is full-throttle thriller writing." -- David Morrell, *New York Times* bestselling author of MURDER AS A FINE ART.

"Completely kept me guessing. THE BLADE delivers a razor edge of suspense. As fast as you think you know what's going on, you're wrong. An absolute thrill ride." -- Lisa Gardner, #1 *New York Times* bestselling author of CATCH ME

"History and suspense entangle from page one, forming a plot rife with deceit and deception. Sholes & Moore write with a confident, assured hand --- always keeping the reader primed and ready for the gut punch. This is another terrific outing. I highly recommend that you sink your claws into this entertaining nugget." -- Steve Berry, *New York Times* bestselling author of THE COLUMBUS AFFAIR

"THE BLADE by Sholes & Moore is an epic thriller, combining contemporary suspense and historical mystery. From the opening scene in Iraq to the final explosion at Big Bear Lake in Colorado, this is one hell of a thrill ride. Well-crafted, with vivid settings and a premise that will blow your mind, this thriller is not to be missed! Highly recommended." -- Douglas Preston, #1 *New York Times* bestselling author of THE MONSTER OF FLORENCE

"Fast. Fresh. Fascinating. THE BLADE is another razor-sharp thriller from one of my favorite writing teams!" -- Brad Thor, #1 *New York Times* bestselling author of BLACK LIST

"You will need THE BLADE to cut the tension as you turn the pages to the shocking climax. Sholes & Moore have painted a stunning portrait of suspense that leaves you wanting their next collaboration." -- *Suspense Magazine*

THE PHOENIX APOSTLES

"Fast-paced, exciting story that grips the audience." -- *The Mystery Gazette*

"Once again, Lynn Sholes & Joe Moore have produced a novel that is as revelatory as it is packed with action and suspense. THE PHOENIX APOSTLES takes their talent to new heights in a story that will leave readers breathless and wanting more. Bold, taut, and masterfully told, here is a book that demands to be read in one sitting." -- James Rollins, *New York Times* bestselling author of THE DOOMSDAY KEY

"A fascinating, compelling page-turner. Lynn Sholes & Joe Moore hit all the right notes with THE PHOENIX APOSTLES!" -- Carla Neggers, *New York Times* bestselling author of COLD DAWN

"Lynn Sholes & Joe Moore have created a knockout apocalyptic thriller with THE PHOENIX APOSTLES. An epic tale of gold, archaeology, mass murder, ancient prophecy and terrorism, it propels the reader at light speed from its opening chapters to its stunning climax. An outstanding read!" -- Douglas Preston, #1 *New York Times* bestselling author of IMPACT and THE MONSTER OF FLORENCE

"An ingenious thriller with an audacious plot. Awesome; a reminder why fiction is fun." -- *Library Journal*

"What do you get when you cross Indiana Jones with THE DA VINCI CODE? THE PHOENIX APOSTLES, a rollicking thrill ride with so many twists and turns that you won't have time to catch your breath!" -- Tess Gerritsen, *New York Times* bestselling author of ICE COLD

"Sholes and Moore have been writing stellar thrillers that use religious themes for some time, and their fifth effort, the first to feature archaeologist Seneca Hunt, is their best yet. Hunt and her fiancé are on a dig near Mexico City when explosions rock the site. Hunt is the only survivor. Still grieving, she teams up with a journalist who has evidence that the explosion was meant to cover up a robbery. All over the world, tombs are being invaded and bodies stolen, while valuable jewels and gold are left behind. Who are the thieves, and do all the missing bodies belong to infamous mass murderers throughout history? The breakneck pace and sharp characterizations immerse the reader into a surprising and frightening story that posits what the future might look like if science is allowed to run amok. Fans of historical thrillers and mysteries with a religious tint will devour this one while eagerly awaiting the next Seneca Hunt adventure." – *Booklist*

THE GRAIL CONSPIRACY
#1 Bestselling Kindle Book on Amazon

ForeWord Magazine Book-Of-The-Year

Independent Publisher IPPY Award Nominee

"Cotten Stone is a heroine for the ages." ~ Douglas Preston, #1 *New York Times* bestselling co-author of RELIC

"Action-packed, twenty-first century Indiana Jones." ~ Harriet Klausner, ReviewCentre

"If you love books by Steve Berry and Dan Brown, you will love this one, too. The search for the Holy Grail is an exciting adventure and definitely worth reading." ~ Bookreporter.com

"In this time of Dan Brown, here are fresh voices. THE GRAIL CONSPIRACY is everything a mystery should be." ~ Stuart Hecht, The Book Vault

"Gripping!" ~ *Mystery Scene Magazine*

"Spellbinding!" ~ *BookSense*

THE LAST SECRET
"Sholes & Moore have the magical ability to keep you on the edge of your seat. From the first page to the last, you won't be able to put it down." ~ ReaderViews

"Skillfully crafted page-turner." ~ Debra Hamel, Book-Blog.com

"A blend of international thriller and religious fiction, it's an attention-grabber that kept me up at night feverishly turning pages because I just had to know what would happen next. (THE LAST SECRET is) one for those who want a really good "DA VINCI CODE"-esque read." ~ Lelia Taylor, Creatures 'n Crooks Bookshoppe

"Superb thriller. Sholes & Moore write some of the best apocalyptical thrillers on the market today." ~ Harriet Klausner, ReviewCentre

"Demonic possession, strange suicides, and Biblical prophecy collide in THE LAST SECRET, an intelligent religious thriller with bite. Once again, Cotten Stone proves herself to be a heroine for the new millennium. A female Indiana Jones with a press pass! Insightful, engrossing...but more importantly, a suspenseful thriller from first page to last!" ~ James Rollins, *New York Times* bestselling author of BLACK ORDER

"Fascinating and breathless, THE LAST SECRET will leave you glued to your chair. The story sweeps across centuries in a quest for the secret key to surviving Armageddon. Sholes & Moore are true story-tellers with unerring eyes and the souls of artists. You'll love this one!" ~ Gayle Lynds, *New York Times* bestselling author of THE LAST SPYMASTER

"THE LAST SECRET grabs you and won't let go. This is a page-turner with an awesomely creative premise and a surprise around every corner." ~ Lewis Perdue, *New York Times* bestselling author of DAUGHTER OF GOD

"Engaging. Sholes & Moore are experienced authors whose expertise is evident. THE LAST SECRET is entertaining and recommended." ~ BookPleasures

THE HADES PROJECT

"THE HADES PROJECT is an exceptional novel, a dark labyrinth of suspense, international intrigue and apocalyptic horror. The characters, the pacing and the amazing premise of this series are all first-rate. Sholes & Moore are very talented writers indeed." ~ Douglas Preston, #1 *New York Times* bestselling co-author of RELIC

"Short chapters and a pulsating storyline make this a quick read, and those looking for well-drawn characters will be pleased as well. Fans of religious-themed thrillers like THE DA VINCI CODE will enjoy. Recommended for all public libraries." ~ *Library Journal*

"A compelling thriller!" ~ Harriet Klausner *The Mystery Gazette*

"Smoothly-written, nicely paced page-turner." ~ Book-Blog

". . . the tension builds as Stone and her mortal and otherworldly allies race to avert catastrophe." ~ *Publishers Weekly*

"THE HADES PROJECT is a briskly-paced read combining Christian fantasy with mystery. Fans of THE DA VINCI CODE should find THE HADES PROJECT a satisfying read. ~ *Mystery Scene Magazine*

THE 731 LEGACY

"Sholes & Moore are the new Preston & Child. From the very first chapter, THE 731 LEGACY wraps a rope around your neck, pulls it tight, and never lets go! This is what masterful storytelling is all about!" ~ Brad Thor, #1 *New York Times* bestselling author of THE LAST PATRIOT

"What an outrageous and terrifying read. I can't get enough of Cotten Stone!" ~ Lincoln Child, #1 *New York Times* bestselling author of DEEP STORM

"A superb blend of science, myth, history, and imagination. Strap yourself to the chair and get ready for a heart-thumping ride. Sholes & Moore are clearly ahead of the pack, able to satisfy even the most finicky of reader. THE 731 LEGACY is a labyrinth of mystery, crisply plotted and paced, with throat-grabbing twists." ~ Steve Berry, *New York Times* bestselling author of THE TEMPLAR LEGACY

THE 731 LEGACY "has a bit of everything found in popular thrillers: destruction of civilization, ancient religious lore, modern science, and non-stop action. It could be entitled Angels and Demons, and is far superior to the book that bears that title." ~ *Mystery Scene Magazine*

THE SHIELD

LYNN SHOLES & JOE MOORE

THE SHIELD

Published by Stone Creek Books
Edited by Jodie Renner (www.jodierennerediting.com)
Interior design by Joe Moore
Cover design by Joe Moore
Cover image © 2014

Excerpt from THE BLADE
© 2013 by Lynn Sholes & Joe Moore
Published by Stone Creek Books

ISBN: 0692223118
ISBN-13: 978-0692223116

DEDICATION

For Sebastian
~ Lynn Sholes

For Carol
~Joe Moore

"The presence of unidentified spacecraft flying in our atmosphere is now accepted as de facto by the military."
Relationship with Inhabitants of Celestial Bodies (June 1947)

~ Dr. J. Robert Oppenheimer
Director of Advanced Studies
Princeton, New Jersey
&
~ Professor Albert Einstein
Princeton, New Jersey

AUTHORS NOTE

Are we alone? That question has mystified the mind ever since the first human gazed up into the night sky. If we're not alone, why would life from another world want to visit us? How could they survive the journey?

Two historical events, Tunguska and Roswell, and one article published in the *Arizona Gazette* in 1909 intrigued your authors enough to inspire THE SHIELD. In writing this tale, we think we may have touched on the possible answers to the age-old questions of life on other worlds.

Will we ever untangle truth and fact from fiction and opinion regarding the remarkable crash on a summer night in the desert near Roswell, New Mexico? Or the massive explosion above the Siberian swamps near Tunguska in 1908? Or whether G.E. Kincaid really discovered a mysterious citadel built into the wall of the Grand Canyon? Maybe. Maybe not. We may never really know.

But what great fodder it is for our story.

Lynn Sholes & Joe Moore

CHAPTER 1 - NIGHT VISITOR
Big Bear Lake, Colorado

I sat up, startled from sleep. My first muddled thought was earthquake. The walls and windows of my cabin shuddered, shaking a picture off the wall. But then I quickly recognized the thunderous roar of a turbojet helicopter. A beam of bright light shone through the window blinds. Instinct kicked in and I rolled to my side and snatched the SIG Sauer from the nightstand drawer.

The chopper's spotlight swept away and I used the opportunity to run to the living room with both hands locked on the 9mm's grip.

From the light seeping through curtains and blinds I could tell my entire front yard and surrounding area were lit up as if the sun had kicked the moon to the curb. The sound of the helicopter landing was unmistakable.

I stood flush against the wall, gun still gripped with both clammy hands.

A rap on the door made me flinch, and I took aim. I'd already been shot twice in my life and had no intention of this being number three.

"Maxine Decker?"

Another strident knock.

"Agent Decker?"

"Who's there? What do you want?"

"I need to speak with you regarding important government business."

I edged my way to stand beside the door and pulled on a

slat in the sidelight mini-blinds for a view of the porch. Backlit by the brilliance of the chopper's spotlight was a man of medium height and trim build. Other than that, he was nothing but a silhouette.

"Identify yourself," I yelled over the noise of the rotors.

"Peter Kepner. I'm with the government and I need to speak to you right away."

"You must be out of the loop, Kepner. I'm no longer a federal agent. I retired from OSI."

"I'm not OSI. I'm an emissary from Beowulf."

"Never heard of it. And if you're not OSI, then why do you want to talk to me?"

"In times of national security issues, Beowulf has executive authority to recruit CIA, FBI, NSA, even Air Force Office of Special Investigations agents. Retired or otherwise."

"Tell the pilot to kill the light and shut down the engine. And tell anyone else on board to stay put. Do it now."

The man relayed my demand through hand signals and his radio. The spotlight dimmed and the rotors trimmed down to a slow idle.

I switched on the front porch light and pulled back the blinds on the sidelight. "Turn around slowly."

Kepner did a 360.

"Show me some ID. And remember I have my weapon pointed at you."

"Got it. But for security reasons, I don't carry any special identification. I can show you my driver's license and a couple of credit cards."

"I'm not Walmart, so you're gonna have to come up with something better than that."

He pulled an envelope from his back pocket. "Agent Decker, I have something for you. I'm sliding it under the door."

I let the blinds snap back and saw the end of the envelope poke through. I picked it up and switched on the lamp on the foyer table. My curiosity was aroused by the embossed seal—the image of a fire-breathing dragon. *Beowulf.* I remembered the ancient epic poem I'd had to study in high school.

I checked to see that Kepner was still there. Then with a zip of my finger I slit the envelope.

I withdrew the stationery, shook it open, and held it close to the light. Seeing the letterhead, I whipped around and glared at the door.

CHAPTER 2 - THE LIGHT BRIGADE
Big Bear Lake, Colorado

My eyes swept the length of the paper. At the top of the stationery was the official White House letterhead. At the bottom was the supposed signature of Guy LeClaire, President of the United States.

Slowly I read the contents, then took a moment to digest it. I retrieved my cell phone from the charger on my nightstand and returned to the living room.

"You still out there, Kepner?" I called.

"Still here."

I did a quick Google search and came up with the phone number I needed to dial according to the instructions in the letter—the White House switchboard. When my call was answered, I continued to follow the directions I was given in the letter. "I'd like to speak with Tennyson."

"One moment, please," the operator said.

A few seconds later, a synthesized voicemail told me to leave a message. I glanced at the letter to make sure I would reply exactly right. "I have read *The Charge of the Light Brigade*."

Then I hung up and waited.

In a moment, my cell rang. "Maxine Decker," I answered.

"Ms. Decker, this is Guy LeClaire."

His words were steady and unmistakable with that distinctive, crisp Boston accent.

My voice had a small tremor in it, both because I was speaking with the President of the United States and because I knew that whatever the reason for Kepner's visit, it was of utmost importance. "Yes, Mr. President?"

"I apologize for this late-night visit and call. We have a critical matter that requires swift and efficient measures. You're needed to participate in a special assignment. Please invite Mr. Kepner inside so he can speak to you. He'll give you more details."

Before I could say anything else, he thanked me once more and ended the call. I stood there a minute trying to absorb what just happened. I unlocked the front door, thankful I wasn't the sheer nightie type, instead wearing long flannel pajama bottoms and a loose-fitting tee.

With a wave of my arm, I invited Peter Kepner inside. I decided to claim the overstuffed chair and leave the sofa to him. Even though I felt confident that the visitor was legitimate, I conspicuously rested the SIG on my lap, one hand atop it. With the kind of business I'd been in for so many years, if I'd learned one thing, it was never to let my guard down. Being betrayed by my partner a few years back had clinched that for me.

I gestured for my visitor to take a seat on the couch opposite me.

Kepner sat, eyed the gun, then looked squarely at me.

"Why the personal visit, Mr. Kepner? Why not a phone call? And why couldn't it have waited until morning? For drama's sake?"

Other than a condescending smile, Kepner didn't react to my jab. "What I'm about to disclose is top secret, and I can't emphasize that enough. As with all electronic communication, there is the outside possibility of unwanted surveillance. That explains my personal visit. And, we need to move on this ASAP. Waiting until the morning would delay our response."

Kepner leaned forward, his elbows on his thighs, fingers laced. "You were a hell of a civilian OSI agent. Top in the antiquities black market. That's why you're Beowulf's choice for this project."

"Like I said, I've never heard of Beowulf."

"And that's a good thing—the way it's supposed to be,

Agent Decker."

He wasn't going to let go of the *agent* title no matter how many times I said I was retired.

Kepner steepled his fingers then aimed them at me. "Here's the deal. There's been a serious breach of security at the Beowulf headquarters."

"Excuse me, but first would you elaborate a little more on what exactly Beowulf is? What's the function or mission?"

"I can't give you any more explanation until we are in a protected and secure environment. All I can do at this point is echo the request from the President that your assistance is needed to help with a potentially grave threat to our national security. The United States and its allies are at risk. I would like for you to get ready and leave with me as quickly as you can."

I'd promised myself I wouldn't return to my old occupation in any fashion. I'd consulted on one job after retiring and it had nearly gotten me killed. But this . . . this sounded like something critical that truly put the nation in peril. I felt my resolve softening.

"Where are we going?" I asked.

"I'm sorry, but I can't say."

"So you want me to take off with you to an undisclosed location to help with an undisclosed mission involving a government operation I've never heard of? Right now, in the middle of the night?" I plastered a *you've-got-to-be-kidding-me* expression on my face.

"That's about it."

I chuckled. "Who said the government doesn't have a sense of humor."

His expression quickly reverted to somber and so did mine. This was obviously a no-bullshit situation.

"Just one more thing. Don't pack a bag—no clothes or toiletries. But bring your ID, including your passport. Everything else will be provided for you."

I thought the request to take my passport was strange, especially since he carried so little. "Why my passport?"

"This may eventually require international travel."

I stood, holding the 9mm at my side.
He pointed to it. "And no guns."

CHAPTER 3 - BROKEN PIECES
Five days earlier. JFK International, New York City

The TSA officer watched the travelers passing through the international security checkpoint. A passenger had been asked to step aside after her shoulder bag was X-rayed. Apparently, something had attracted the attention of one of his inspectors. He observed the strikingly beautiful blonde in a fashionable business suit follow the inspector to a side table. There she placed her bag down and stood back while he unzipped it.

The officer wandered over to stand beside the woman and witness the bag search. The inspector was new on the job and the TSA officer wanted to make sure the search was being conducted by the book.

The bag, a leather satchel with a shoulder strap, contained an e-book reader, notepads and pens, some basic office supplies, and a loose-leaf binder full of what looked like design layouts for an advertising brochure.

While the inspector carefully checked the contents, the officer said, "May I see your passport, please?"

With a warm smile, the woman reached inside her purse and removed it—a Canadian passport in the name of Patricia Barney.

"What's your destination, Ms. Barney?" the officer asked.

"Amsterdam."

"Beautiful city."

"Yes, it is. Very European."

"Ma'am," the inspector said, "can you tell me what this is?" He held up a plastic baggie containing three small objects rolled in bubble wrap. He opened the bag and peeled back the bubble wrap. The objects looked identical—triangular in shape, slightly convex, and cream colored. Each was about five centimeters across.

"Those are pieces of a broken porcelain vase. I'm taking them to a specialist in the Netherlands while I visit friends, in hopes he can match the color so I can have a replica made. It belonged to my grandmother, and my goal is to have the new one made before she discovers it was broken." As the woman spoke, she calmly glanced from the officer to the inspector.

The officer took the package from his associate, examined the contents, and then rebundled it. After putting it back in the Ziploc, he held up the bag and jiggled it.

Patricia Barney flinched.

Then he gave it back to the inspector. "Sorry for the delay, Ms. Barney. Sometimes the sensors set off alerts randomly or if an object isn't recognized." He gave a slight nod to the other man and watched as the baggie was returned to the satchel.

"Good luck with finding that replacement," the inspector said as he handed the satchel to her.

"Have a nice day," the officer said. They both watched her rejoin the rest of the passengers and head for the KLM gate. When he returned to his station, he felt a slight tingle in his right hand. Shaking it seemed to make the tingle lessen. As he watched the line of travelers snake toward the metal detectors, he shook his hand again. Probably nothing, he thought, and turned his attention to the next passenger in line.

CHAPTER 4 - NIGHT FLIGHT
Big Bear Lake, Colorado

Did I have some kind of death wish? That was the question buzzing around in my head like a nuisance fly. Brushing my teeth before leaving with Kepner, I glanced in the mirror. What was I thinking to agree to this? I'd been enjoying my retirement. Life was good. The nightmares had dwindled, and I wasn't awakening in the middle of the night in a sweat, my heart exploding in my chest.

Even as I attempted to talk some sense into my brain, I found myself in the closet slipping into khaki pants followed by a pullover sweater and jacket. Next came my high-top hiking boots. As far as Kepner was concerned, I'd be leaving my SIG behind. He didn't need to know about my Walther PPK that I slid inside my boot.

Fully dressed, I emerged into the living room. "All set." I shoved my license and other ID in my pants' pocket and slipped my cell into the inside pocket of my jacket.

Kepner opened the front door. "Let's go."

Stepping onto the porch, I felt the chilly Colorado night air. It was August and the mountains had the loveliest cool temps once the sun went down. I took a big fat lungful of air, knowing I was going to miss it.

Kepner signaled the helicopter's pilot and before we reached it, the turbos spun up and the rotors quickly approached full rotation.

I climbed in, followed by Kepner. He handed me a headset, put one on himself, and adjusted the mic.

The rotors roared and we were airborne.

"Where are we headed?" I asked.

"Grand Junction. Walker Field, to be exact. But that's all you need to know right now. Be patient, Agent Decker."

"Sure." I *was* being patient. What did he expect? I'd been dragged out of bed in the middle of the night because the President said I was needed. But that was basically all I'd been told. If they wanted me so badly, why couldn't they divulge more about *why* they needed me? From all the mystery surrounding tonight's event, I had drawn the single most obvious conclusion. Beowulf was black ops.

Something else was obvious. Kepner wasn't going to call me by my first name. During twenty years as an OSI agent, I never got completely comfortable with the military environment. After all, I was a civilian agent—a trained archaeologist—working on the fringe of the Air Force machine. My job was to locate and identify artifacts, relics, art objects, and antiquities suspected of being stolen or smuggled by military personnel. I did my job better than anyone else, and that's why my less-than-straight-and-narrow attitude was tolerated. Despite my frequent nonconformist approaches, they always kept sending me back into the field to track down the bad guys. And that's what I would still be doing on a regular basis had I not decided I was allergic to lead from one too many bullets. I'd finally had enough and retired to my remote Colorado cabin. But now, here I was. Again.

Thinking about the past, I started to get that old queasiness in my gut. And what made it worse was the dark feeling that the Beowulf operation was blacker than anything I'd come across before.

———

Just over an hour passed before we reached a private aviation area at the northwest corner of Grand Junction Airport at Walker Field. After jumping onto the tarmac, we walked a short distance to a small Lear business jet, its engines spinning at idle, the strobes and navigation lights washing the immediate area with color and flashes. As we approached, someone inside opened the side hatch and let it drop down, forming steps.

"Our ride," Kepner said.

I tried to pry more information about our destination but he wouldn't budge. "I'll fill you in once we're in the air," was all he offered.

Kepner's long paces and fast gait were difficult for me to keep up with. I double-stepped to almost each of his strides.

"Come on. Give me a break. I feel like a puppy at the heels of his master and I don't like it. Tell me what the mission is all about."

He turned and looked at me. "You are a persistent one."

"So brief me."

"I'm not sure you're going to like it."

CHAPTER 5 - FULL DISCLOSURE
Grand Junction, Colorado

I settled into one of the six leather seats in the small Learjet while Kepner sat across the narrow aisle from me. The pilot and copilot looked like recruiting posters for military fighter pilots—tall, with close-cropped hair, square jaws, and serious expressions. They acknowledged us as we boarded, and then briefly updated Kepner on the status of the plane, weather, and flying time, which would be just under an hour.

Within minutes, the jet screamed down the runway and pulled into a steep climb. One of my Air Force buddies had once told me that small business jets like this one were as close to a fighter as a private civilian could own. I believed it as we rapidly left the lights of Grand Junction behind and shot into the black Colorado night.

"I'm afraid there won't be an in-flight movie or cocktails served, Agent Decker," Kepner said as we quickly reached cruising altitude.

"Tight budget?" My question caused him to smile for the first time.

"I think you'll soon find that we spend our money where we can get the most bang for the buck."

"And where would that be?" As we banked left, I glanced out of the window and spotted the Big Dipper and Polaris swinging past. I knew we were on a southwest heading.

Kepner saw me establishing our direction. "The next leg of our journey ends in Flagstaff."

"Is that our destination?"

"No, only one more hop after that."

I peered back out the window at the sprinkling of lights from small farm communities interspersed with a black landscape. "I'm still waiting to hear what this is all about. And why me?"

Kepner seemed to consider my question.

"You can at least tell me something about Beowulf," I added. "Even if your prediction is right and I don't like it."

Kepner blinked and cocked his head to the side, then looked back at me. "All right," he finally said. "Let me start with this. The organization has been around in one form or another since the mid-1980s. It was one of the many offshoots of Star Wars."

"The Strategic Defense Initiative—Reagan's program?"

"Correct. One of many byproducts of SDI. Beowulf is probably the last one standing."

"Probably?"

He nodded. "The handful of other programs I knew about are all gone."

"So, you've been with Beowulf for, what, twenty-eight years?"

"No, I came onboard in 1993 when SDI was 'dissolved'." He formed quotes in the air with his fingers.

"You mean Star Wars went on even though the public thought it was shut down?"

"SDI didn't continue, but some of the darker programs did."

"Beowulf is a 'dark' program." I repeated his quote gesture. "I kind of figured that out on my own."

"We've covered as much as we need to for now."

"What do you do for Beowulf?"

Again, he seemed to ponder the question.

"Come on. Are you the boss or the night watchman? I at least deserve to know that much."

"Head of security."

"See, that wasn't so hard, was it? Would you like to know anything about me?"

"No need, Agent Decker. I know everything about you."

This ruffled my feathers a bit. "That doesn't seem fair."

"We don't recruit anyone without full disclosure of their history. You've been thoroughly vetted."

"Then you know all about my sordid past?"

In a dry, deadpan delivery, he said, "I know you grew up in Albuquerque alongside your twin sister, Francine. Your mother was a real estate agent and your father taught Economics at the University of New Mexico. You were president of your high school senior class and graduated with honors. You went on to study archaeology and got your masters in the same field. Your sister became an RN and later got involved with global disaster relief organizations.

"Nearing graduation, one of your professors suggested you become a civilian agent for the Air Force Office of Special Investigations. While in civil service, you met and married Kenneth Gates, a fellow OSI agent and computer forensics expert. The marriage ended in divorce. All told, you spent twenty years as an OSI agent before suffering serious gunshot wounds in Iraq—an event in which you shot and supposedly killed your partner, Special Agent Aaron Knox."

At this point I turned back to the window. My chest tightened at the thoughts of Francine and shooting Aaron.

"After recovering from your wounds, you retired to a mountain cabin until your ex-husband brought you back to OSI as a consultant to assist in tracking down an ancient relic called the Blade of Abraham. You wound up stopping a terrorist threat on the city of Las Vegas."

Kepner fell silent for a moment. As I turned back to him, he said, "Did I leave anything out?"

"You've covered enough." It was considerate of him not to mention how Francine died.

"The reason we need you is your talent for finding things that have gone missing, just as you did with the Blade of Abraham and so many other rare, stolen objects. You are one of the best at what you do, and we are on an important journey, one that could change the course of history."

CHAPTER 6 - THE ABYSS
Four days earlier. RAI Center, Amsterdam, The Netherlands

Patricia Barney walked across the sprawling entrance hall, had her ID badge barcode scanned at the security checkpoint, and proceeded along what seemed like endless carpeted aisles separating the hundreds of exhibits. Each interconnected building contained different areas of technology—television production, computers, internet, telecommunications, gaming, and others. The names ranged from the giants of technology like Sony, Harris, Panasonic, and Apple all the way down to small software developers and hardware manufacturers vying for attention. The booth Patricia sought was in Hall 4, companies dedicated to communication. She spotted the modest corner exhibit with its brightly colored sign that read Red Star Innovations.

Three Red Star employees, in matching polo shirts and slacks, were putting the final touches on the various product displays as she approached. The man she was to meet—in his late fifties with a dark, close-cropped beard, and dark eyes—saw her and stepped away from the others. He met her with a polite kiss on each cheek. As he did so, he whispered, "Were you followed?"

She shook her head.

"And you have them?"

"Yes."

"One moment." He grabbed a briefcase from behind a display counter and then waved to the two co-workers. "I shall return shortly."

A few moments later, they sat at a small table in the far corner of the food court silently sipping Douwe Egberts dark roast. His eyes roamed the area around them as if taking a mental picture of the hundreds of attendees moving in steady streams throughout the exhibition hall.

Finally, he placed his cup down. "Any complications?"

"The handoff at the motel went just as planned. My bag was inspected at JFK, but it raised no suspicion." Now it was Patricia's turn to scan the crowd of food court patrons.

"Is there any evidence of your meeting with him?"

"This was a small motel in a small Arizona town, so I doubt it."

"You are very good, Patricia." The man gave a sly grin.

"I believe that's why you hired me."

"So," he said, glancing around again, "it's time to finalize our business." He pointed at the satchel still hanging over her shoulder. "Shall we?"

She slipped it off and placed it next to his feet. At the same time, he reached into his briefcase, removed an envelope, and laid it on the table.

"In euros?"

He nodded.

"I don't suppose you'll tell me what the objects are in the parcel and why you have gone to such extreme measures to get them?" She watched him remove the baggie of triangular objects from the satchel and place it in his briefcase.

"You will be better off not knowing."

"Of course. How about this, then? The Beowulf staff has an exceptionally high level of security clearance. How did you get someone to smuggle the pieces out of the facility?"

"Everyone has skeletons in his closet, as the Americans like to say. Threatening to expose them is more than enough motivation."

"Those pesky skeletons." They both laughed as she retrieved the satchel. "I've been thinking about leaving the game."

"I can see why." He patted the envelope just before she

took it. "Is this the most you've made on a single job?"

She dropped the envelope in her bag and slid the strap back onto her shoulder. "If you call me for anything else and I don't return the call, don't be offended. I'm either on a beach somewhere in the South Pacific or . . ."

"Dead? You're much too beautiful and smart to be caught. Plus, you will get bored on that beach."

She winked. "Depends on who I have snuggled up beside me."

Patricia stood and started to leave but paused. "By the way, be careful how you handle the objects. They make your skin tingle."

"Good to know."

She made her way through the crowds on the long walk back to the entrance hall. Outside to the right was the taxi queue with a few people in line. Judging from their conversations, they were mostly booth-setup crews heading back to their hotels during show hours after working all night. A few businessmen and exhibitors also stood in line.

Patricia took the place at the end of the queue and waited her turn for a taxi. A few others came to stand behind her. The line moved along quickly and she soon found herself at the front. The taxi pulled up and she opened the door and slid into the back seat. She felt someone push in right behind her and slam the door shut.

Patricia turned to complain just as the taxi pulled from the curb. "What are you doing?" she asked the man in the suit next to her. "This is my—"

She knew in an instant she had just made the biggest mistake of her life. She was supposed to be a professional and yet she had let her guard down. So enchanted by the amount of money in her satchel and her new life on some tropical isle, she had neglected to scrutinize those waiting in the taxi queue. How convenient that the taxi had pulled into line ahead of the others. Full of her triumph, she didn't even notice the classic setup. Now she stared at the man pressing his hand against her neck. Patricia knew there was no point in fighting. A second after the sting of the needle, she felt herself surrender to the abyss.

CHAPTER 7 - THE EAST RIM
Flagstaff, Arizona

The jet touched down in the darkness of Flagstaff Pulliam Airport just after 4:00 AM and quickly steered to a collection of hangars south of the main passenger terminal.

Our *Top Gun* pilots taxied the Learjet off the single main runway onto the tarmac. As soon as we came to a halt, one copilot emerged from the cockpit, opened the hatch, and lowered it. Kepner motioned for me to get off. He followed.

He placed his hand at my elbow and hurried me to a helicopter parked around sixty meters away, its rotors spinning, its skin painted midnight black. As soon as we climbed in and buckled up, we lifted off. I saw that our Learjet was already racing down the runway. The whole transfer from jet touchdown to helicopter liftoff couldn't have taken more than three minutes.

Kepner slipped on a set of headphones and pointed to a pair hanging nearby. Once I had them on, I said into the mic, "I really wanted to hit the Flagstaff gift shop during our layover."

He gave me his now-famous blank stare

"How far this leg?" I asked.

"About seventy miles."

I estimated that we were heading northwest. Seventy miles would put us . . . "We're going to the Grand Canyon?"

"Very good. We're headed to a remote area on the East Rim."

"I've always wanted to see it by helicopter."

"Unfortunately, Agent Decker, you won't this trip."

———

Thirty minutes later, we landed. I couldn't see much except what the full moon illuminated. I noticed that before putting us down, the pilot slipped on what looked like a night vision device. This guy set the bird down with as much assurance as if he were pulling his car into his garage for the hundredth time.

Kepner slid open the side door and jumped out with me right behind. We ducked under the spinning rotors and walked briskly away from the helicopter across hard-packed sand and small stones. Once we were at a safe distance, the black machine rose, banked, and roared back in the direction we had come.

After the sand blasting from the rotor wash blew past, the night surrounded us like a cloak—moonlight swept across a brilliant, starry sky. A whisper of wind cleared the air of the dust from the aircraft's takeoff.

As my eyes became adjusted to the dark, I realized we were standing on a flat expanse of land. In the distance before us ran a dark zigzagging scar gouging the landscape. I assumed it was the Grand Canyon. Not far away in shadow sat a one-story structure the size of a neighborhood 7-Eleven.

"This way." Kepner started toward the building.

As we cut the distance in half, a number of high-intensity floods transformed our surroundings into daylight.

"One second," Kepner said, taking my arm.

We halted and stood silently in the bath of light for ten or fifteen seconds. Then the lamps blinked off, leaving us again wrapped in the blanket of night.

After a moment to let our eyes readjust, we continued on until we came to the front of the building. Even in the muted light I could make out a front porch built of rustic logs and rough-hewn lumber. Strange, I thought, there were no windows. As we stood on the porch, a light over our heads turned on. A plaque with the arrowhead-shaped emblem of the National Park Service was fastened to the wall next to the door. And below it, a sign read "Closed. No Admittance."

"Get many tourists up here?" I asked.

"It's restricted."

Kepner placed his face against the wall beside the door. I wondered what the hell he was doing, and then realized he had aligned his left eye with an iris scanner. An electronic buzz sounded and he pushed the door open. We entered a room about the size of a two-car garage. Fluorescent lights flooded the space.

The room was empty except for a small bare office desk and chair in the corner. I looked across the room. "Are those elevator doors?"

Because he didn't answer, I decided Kepner liked screwing with my head. Either that, or he was just an arrogant dick who didn't feel it necessary to answer my questions. It wouldn't be long before he really pissed me off and I'd bail on this whole deal, presidential request or not.

"Come on," Kepner said. As we walked toward the doors, I heard the click of the lock behind us. The front entrance was secured.

Kepner pushed the *down* button and the elevator doors parted. We stepped inside and he pressed the number 3 button on the control panel, the lowest of the levels. The lift motor spun to life and we dropped. I had no way of knowing how far we descended, but I guessed at least sixty meters, maybe more.

The elevator came to a smooth stop and the doors slid open. What lay before me caused me to take in a sharp breath.

Kepner stepped out, turned, and said, "Welcome to Beowulf."

CHAPTER 8 - CHAUCER
Beowulf Headquarters

Exiting the elevator, I noticed a security checkpoint manned by two ominous-looking men holding assault rifles. The Beowulf insignia patch adorned the breast pockets of their black jumpsuits. The floor, walls, and ceiling were a polished gray material illuminated with indirect lighting. A number of small black globes suspended from above told me we were under video surveillance.

Kepner led me past the two sentries and we entered a hallway like those in a modern corporate office, with a slight dissimilarity. The workstations and terminals that sat dark and empty weren't separated by the conventional portable partitions. Instead, they were divided by glass panels. This was very different from my old stomping grounds at DC3, the OSI headquarters at the Department of Defense Cyber Crime Center in Maryland. To carve this facility out of solid rock had to have been an amazing feat. Money had not been spared.

I assumed that whatever staff occupied these stations would be coming in later, since it was still an hour before dawn. I suppressed a yawn, thinking I should still be home, snug in my bed.

We stopped in front of a set of sculptured stainless-steel double doors that bore the now-familiar Beowulf shield. The nameplate read: Director.

"The director will take it from here. I have some other things to attend to. I'll check in with you later when I get back." Kepner tapped once then opened the door and gestured for me to enter. As I did so, I sensed that he stayed behind. I turned to check. Kepner was gone and the door softly clicked closed.

"Good morning, Agent Decker."

The greeting had come from a man sitting behind a glass and stainless-steel desk. I assumed the 50ish, silver-templed man was the director. He wore a jumpsuit similar to the security guards'. Other than the leather chairs, all the furniture and appointments in the office were also stainless and glass. I wondered what was up with the decor. *Fetish or functionality?*

"It hasn't been that good of a morning," I said. My adrenalin hadn't slowed much since Kepner arrived at my cabin. The shock of it all and lack of sleep were taking a toll.

He came from around his desk and shook my hand. Above the Beowulf patch was a nametag: Chaucer. As I tried to decide whether that was his first or last name, he picked up on my dilemma.

"Please, call me Chaucer."

I acknowledged.

"It's nice to meet you, Agent Decker. You have quite a reputation. All good, by the way."

He returned to his high-back chair, and with a wave of his hand invited me to sit in one of the chairs across the desk from him.

I thanked him for the compliment and sat.

"I have to say, Chaucer, your operation works fast. I feel like I zip lined here."

"Once we set upon a course of action, we waste no time in getting underway." He laid his hands palm down on his desk. "I'm sure you have lots of questions, but maybe I can answer most before you ask."

"Thank god," I said. "Your head of security stonewalled me."

"I apologize. He's very cautious not to give out too much info. Let me see if I can help you out. I'll start with my name. Chaucer isn't my given name. It's a code name."

An English poet. "Like Tennyson for the President?"

"Beowulf deals with extremely sensitive matters and is answerable only to Tennyson. We never reference the President or use his name. Because of the necessity to operate with ultimate covertness, we are different from other black operations. Congress is not even aware that we exist." He paused a moment, letting that settle in.

"Then how are you funded? Doesn't Congress have to appropriate funds even for black ops?"

"Yes. But not Beowulf. Before I continue, I need to impress upon you that what you are going to learn about Beowulf and our project must be regarded with the highest degree of discretion and confidentiality. Any suspicion of a lack thereof will result in the harshest of responses. You've been selected for your skills and for your character. Two other things were factored in. You don't break under even the most intense situations. And when it isn't easy, you do what you have to do."

I knew what he was referring to—the tragic death of my sister at my own hands, and when I'd been forced to shoot my partner.

"Do you clearly understand what I have just said?"

I gave an affirmative nod.

"Good, because if you can't agree with that, we won't go any further. Look me in the eyes."

Chaucer held my gaze and then continued. "Your help is needed in a critical matter, vital to this country's and others' security and safety. There may be times when you are on your own and things get dicey. I want you to be aware of that. So, if you're going to back out, do it now, not later. Once you're in, you're in."

"You mean I can't decide after you explain what the project is?"

"No."

Whatever the critical matter was, everyone had made it abundantly clear that it was a global-changing issue. If my country needed me that badly, how could I turn my back? My brain urged me to check out now, but my gut said *no way*. I had too many years of service with OSI embedded in me so my loyalty must have become part of my DNA.

"All right. I've come this far. It's a long walk home."

"That means you're agreeing?"

"Yes."

"Okay, Agent Decker. Glad to have you. First, I'll tell you we are a crew of only ten. The fewer who have knowledge of Beowulf, the more secure it remains. There will be no non-disclosure contract for you to sign. There'll be no paper trail that will connect us. This is a verbal agreement only. Please be reminded one last time that any violation will provoke serious measures."

Chaucer sat back in his chair, his eyes fixed on mine.

I got the picture. "Crystal clear."

"Then we'll proceed."

I heard my breath come out in a noticeable sigh. I'd been on some hazardous assignments in my time, but already I knew this was way beyond anything I'd ever been involved in.

"You asked about funding. I'll address that briefly, even though it is irrelevant."

I'd just been reprimanded. For now, I'd shut up and listen. This guy was no candy-ass, and this was no candy-ass operation.

"Every year the Department of Defense has single-line items in their budgets represented by a series of numbers and letters along with a code name—it might read Operation Dragonfly with a vague general description. These line items are simply covers for a black budget. It's a type of slush fund set up by the DoD. It keeps Congress's nose out of the DoD's business—in other words, no congressional oversight. Suppose 2.6 million is budgeted for Operation Dragonfly. But really only 1.2 million actually gets to that project. The rest is funneled to a blacker-than-black op like Beowulf. We are considered beyond black. We arrange to skim enough from each of those line items and, voilà, we have our funding."

"Sounds like government money laundering."

"If looking at it that way helps you understand Beowulf's

magnitude and the seriousness of what you'll be working on, then it'll benefit us both."

Chaucer rose and strolled over to a side credenza where a pitcher of ice water and glasses sat. "Would you like some?"

I declined.

He poured a glass and took a deep swallow before returning to lean against the side of his desk.

"Agent Decker, tell me what you know about the Roswell UFO Incident in 1947."

CHAPTER 9 - BIGFOOT
Beowulf Headquarters

"I don't know what's true and what's fiction."

"Then I take it you *have* heard of the Roswell Incident?"

"Sure. Who hasn't? Try surfing the cable channels without running into a documentary on UFOs." I wiggled my fingers near my temples and imitated the Twilight Zone's theme music. "Little gray men with big black eyes."

"I assure you, Agent Decker, that I am deadly serious and I think you should be as well. The situation we face is not a joke. I understand you don't know all the details yet, but you need to be open. And your attitude needs to be less flippant. Now, let's try it again. What can you tell me about what happened in Roswell, New Mexico, in the summer of 1947?"

I hated to admit it, but I deserved his admonishment. My remarks didn't serve me well. Referencing little gray men didn't illustrate the professionalism I'd spent years polishing and exemplifying during my career. Bewilderment was no excuse. For god's sake, the President of the United States had personally called me. Maybe when the director got down to the nitty-gritty, I'd have greater appreciation of the situation. "I stand corrected. You're right."

I paused a moment to think of what I did know about Roswell. "Let me start again. Most of what I know about the incident comes from what seems like an endless supply of programs on TV about UFOs, alien technology, whether visitors from other planets helped build the pyramids, and those types of topics. Supposedly, there's still a controversy over whether or not an alien spacecraft really crashed in the New Mexico desert. There were reports of witnesses who saw the debris field and even collected some of the wreckage. I never paid much attention, but I recall seeing photos of the military showing off a piece of it. There were claims the material had some very unusual characteristics. And there were some people who even claimed bodies were recovered. Didn't the Army issue a statement that they had found the wreckage of a UFO, but then retracted it and said what they recovered in the desert were the remnants of a weather balloon?"

"That's accurate." Chaucer returned to his chair. "Anything else?"

"I believe that's it." But then I remembered one last thing. "Oh, back when I was in college, a video was going around that supposedly documented an autopsy of an alien body recovered at the Roswell site."

"Tell me, Agent Decker, what is your impression? What do you believe happened in Roswell that summer in 1947?"

"I haven't spent much time thinking about it, other than it probably ranks up there with Bigfoot stories. Makes for good ratings for the Sci-Fi Channel, and I suppose it continues to fuel government cover-up conspiracy theorists. But since you've specifically asked me about it, I'm assuming there's more to it."

Chaucer stared intently at me. Had all the Beowulf guys taken a special course in deadpanning? He sat there as if waiting for me to say more. I caved to the pressure of the silence and added, "I guess the curiosity about Roswell wouldn't have continued this long if there wasn't a bit of fact to it."

"The alien autopsy video, which technically should probably have been called a necropsy, was a hoax. Even though the cameraman confessed, he still contended that he had seen the original footage but over the years it had degraded. He said that in the fake film he had embedded a few salvaged original clips, but he never said which ones."

"So there was no truth in that at all?"

"None."

The director appeared amused by the autopsy story and he continued, "Was it a weather balloon? No. Did an alien spacecraft crash in Roswell, New Mexico, in 1947?"

He paused, and I thought I saw the slightest break in his expressionless stare.

"The answer," Chaucer said, "is yes. Twenty-five miles from Roswell, to be exact. Did the Army collect the craft debris? Yes. Were two bodies recovered? Yes. One was sacrificed for a necropsy, the other cryogenically frozen. Neither of which appeared in that video you mentioned. That was a fraud."

A few hundred questions flooded my head as I stared at Chaucer. I made every effort to sound calm, as if he had just told me my car needed an oil change. "What happened to all that evidence of the crash?"

"Everything was transported to Fort Worth, then to Wright Field, then to Groom Lake—Area 51—and finally here to the Beowulf facility."

I reeled from all the information. I'd just heard the answer to one of the biggest questions mankind has ever faced—are we alone? In my wildest dreams I wouldn't have anticipated something like what Chaucer had just revealed. But even if it was true, why was I brought here? What did any of that have to do with me or my previous line of work?

"What do you need from me?" I asked with a dry mouth and clammy palms.

The director took another gulp of water, and I wished now I hadn't declined a glass.

"Logical question. Let's take a walk, Agent Decker."

————

I tried to slow my racing mind as Chaucer led me out of his office and into the belly of Beowulf. The facility opened up into a modest expanse of glass-partitioned work stations around a central hub.

The director threw a switch, and the sparse night lighting

was instantly replaced with a flood of brilliant light.

I'd seen a lot of technology over the years, but what I now observed was phenomenal. I didn't recognize half of the equipment. The non-porous theme continued to play out. The glass partitions of the working areas reminded me of the CTU headquarters in the television series, *24*, which had been one of my favorite shows years back. Beowulf was on a smaller scale than *24*'s Counter Terrorism Unit, from what I could tell, but maybe what I saw was only a minuscule portion of the facility.

I fell behind Chaucer, ogling everything. He allowed me a moment to take it in, but then he quickly refocused my attention.

"Over here, Agent."

I came to stand by his side, looking through a glass panel.

"Do you know what that is?"

I peered through the glass, trying hard to make something spectacular out of what was on the other side. It looked to me like a desktop computer sitting on another glass and stainless desk. But the way he had asked me the question, I was sure my answer would be lame. "Evidently it's not just a computer."

"Good perception, Agent."

"Can you call me Maxine or Max? I'm not fond of *agent* anymore."

Chaucer smiled. "Beowulf has very strict protocols. We establish only professional relationships with our colleagues. Calling one by his or her first name fosters a personal relationship. Even though our small staff is lodged here on another floor in single-room dormitory-style apartments, we all still respect the rule." He gestured once again to the table and the computer. "So, Agent, do you know what you are looking at?"

At this point, I wasn't even sure what planet I was on. "I guess you're going to have to tell me."

CHAPTER 10 - INCREDIBLE
Beowulf Headquarters

My curiosity about the computer must have registered in my expression. Chaucer's eyes brightened.

"Outside of Tennyson and the staff, few know of its existence. As far as we are aware, it is the only quantum computer on the planet."

That took my breath away. I'd been around my ex, the OSI computer forensics guru, long enough to appreciate the magnitude of what I was seeing. Many times, Kenny had told me a quantum computer was the ultimate—its power boggled the mind. He said super computers are basically powerful PCs with massive processing and memory resources, while a quantum computer uses molecules to do its calculations. Then he went on to talk about quantum mechanical phenomena like superposition and entanglement, and I remember my eyes glazing over. It probably had nothing to do with the Johnny Walker I was sipping at the time, but I do remember him saying that encryption and decryption were the keys to quantum computing. If data is protected under super heavy encryption, theoretically, any computer can break it. The question is how long it would take. It could take hundreds, even thousands of years for current super computers to decrypt most of the military's encrypted information. A quantum computer could do the same job in microseconds, perhaps nanoseconds.

I turned to Chaucer. "But I thought a fully functioning quantum computer was still years away?"

"That's what the rest of the world believes. We want to keep it that way."

"Why here? Seems a strange location for a facility like this."

"Secrecy and security were paramount when we chose this location. It was constructed in anticipation of building the world's first quantum computer. I helped design the computer, and I alone operate it."

"So you're a hands-on director?"

"Very much so."

The place seemed like overkill to me, but I wanted to stay on Chaucer's good side. "It's such an exceptional accomplishment to construct something like this when there are plenty of secure government compounds that already exist. You had an amazing vision."

I hoped Chaucer would provide more information, but he didn't bite. He just moved down the hall. I followed, the question *why here* still hanging in my mind. I decided to let the director reveal as much as he was willing and at his own rate before I asked any more questions.

"While I explain," he said, "I want you to see something." We turned right and climbed a set of open stairs to a second level. The director stopped in front of a fairly large workroom—like all the others, it was housed in glass partitions. Transparency meant exactly that at Beowulf. Everybody could see what everybody else was up to. His office was the only exception I'd noticed so far.

"In there, Agent Decker." He guided me into the room. "Take your time and look around. What you see are working documents and photographs of the items recovered from the Roswell crash site."

The glass walls were covered with schematics, photographs, diagrams, spreadsheets filled with numbers, data charts, all encased in laminating film that retained traces of the remains of dry erase markers. Some displays were as large as six feet by six feet—others as small as a traditional five by seven photograph. At one end of the room a portion of the wall was opaque white and served as a projection screen. In the center of the room was a long glass conference table with ten chairs positioned about it. Atop the table, in front of each chair, sat three computer monitors arranged in a squared-off U-shape. Nothing spectacular about that, I thought, but on closer inspection I shook my head in amazement. Built right into the glass of the conference table were all the computer components as well as the touch-screen keyboards and track pads.

I dragged my finger across the smooth surface, careful not to touch any of the virtual keys and controls. "Incredible."

Chaucer didn't utter a word so I continued to browse the room. I approached one of the largest of the blown-up glossy photos. It looked like a picture of some type of I-beam, like those used in construction. Then I noticed the dimensions written in metric at the bottom. I rounded them off and did a rough conversion in my head—18 inches long, 3/8 inch wide with 1/16 inch ridges running its length. The inside surface had a purplish violet hue and appeared to be metallic. And there was writing—like Egyptian hieroglyphs, but not exactly. I studied the glyphs. No, definitely not Egyptian. There weren't any animals—no vultures, owls, snakes. No beetles. Those were common in Egyptian text. These were all geometric figures like cubes, spheres, cylinders, pyramids, and combinations of geometric shapes. They weren't line drawings, but solid 3-D forms. There were perhaps thirty of the figures placed close together.

I circled the room, seeing more photos of similar I-beams. I stopped in front of a photo of something that looked like monofilament fishing line, but by now I knew better.

"Not monofilament?"

"Correct. We think it might be advanced fiber optics," Chaucer told me. "Nothing like we know of today."

"Hmmm. Interesting. And this?" I pointed to some photos of a material similar to aluminum foil except it was burnished, not shiny or reflective like the Reynolds Wrap in my kitchen.

Chaucer anticipated my reaction. "No, it's not aluminum foil. It's much lighter—and it has memory. You can fold it up, and when released, it goes back to its original shape. Pretty close to indestructible, too. A sledge hammer does no damage."

"That's pretty impressive." I moved to some photos of objects that looked like porcelain shards. "Not as remarkable as the other photos."

"Don't be fooled by their simplicity. Those three fragments are embedded with an advanced propulsion technology, one that's not of this world. Or if they are, their conductivity, magnetism, and other characteristics have been altered. I ask you to make special mental note of those unimpressive pieces. They're why you're here."

I took a moment to study the picture of the three objects. Then my attention fell on a large photograph of what looked like a giant donut standing upright. At the base, a slice of the donut was removed. Inserted in the space was a transparent chamber. Judging from the handful of technicians nearby, the chamber could hold two or three people.

"What's the big Krispy Kreme?"

"Something we call a displacement device. We're learning to build it based on the alien technology. It's housed in another section of Beowulf. You'll see it later."

"And all these diagrams and schematics?"

"Some are technical modules obtained from the three fragments. Each piece is made up of microscopic bubbles that resemble a honeycomb. We've been able to access and decode most using the quantum computer. The schematics reveal spacecraft specs. Apparatuses. Devices. Engineering designs. A few are still a mystery."

"All this came from the crash site?"

He nodded and I felt a rush knowing I was surrounded by images of artifacts that might have come from another planet, maybe even another galaxy. "This is in-fucking-credible."

Chaucer grinned forgivingly, as if my profanity still was not fervent enough to describe what I was looking at. It was the most animated smile I'd seen from either Kepner or Chaucer.

"Agent Decker, if you think this is in-fucking-credible, wait until you see what lies ahead."

CHAPTER 11 - NOT IN KANSAS
Beowulf Headquarters

I followed Chaucer across the hub to a heavy-looking metal door. He pressed his thumb onto the optical scanner of a biometric fingerprint lock. I heard a click signaling the release of the deadbolts.

Chaucer opened the door, and as he led me along a corridor, the deadbolts clanked behind us. A short distance farther, a set of doors blocked our way. A workstation and two overhead monitors stood nearby.

"What you're about to see, few others have. Even the staff is not allowed beyond this point—only me."

"Where are the real alien artifacts? Those back there were only scans or photos."

"Secure in a vault in Beowulf. The staff works with scaled models, photos, scans, or schematics, rarely the genuine artifact. Chemists researching and testing the chemical and molecular structure of some of the Roswell artifacts see more of the authentic items than others."

He typed in a command at the workstation and the doors slid open to reveal a cavern with striations the color of rust and straw, ochre and terra cotta, from which dozens of other passages spread out like spokes on a wheel. But that wasn't the most intriguing attribute. All about me were objects, both large and small, that appeared to be Egyptian, complete with hieroglyphics, as well as some possible Asian items. There were stone objects and those made from copper and gold and other metals. Urns, vases, tablets, drawings, and statues. Some items

I couldn't identify. The objects were everywhere, in abundance, like an eclectic museum. I was so completely blown away, all I could do was turn in circles and stare. It was like I had entered a fantasy world at a theme park. There was so much to behold. *Toto, I've got a feeling we're not in Kansas anymore.*

"Any idea what all this is?" he asked.

"A hoard of artifacts from ancient civilizations."

"In a way, you're correct. But when you think ancient civilizations, you probably have the wrong conception."

"Egypt, Mesopotamia, Crete, China?"

"Hang on to your seat, Agent Decker."

I was trying to knit together Roswell with Egypt and other civilizations, but nothing added up. What the hell was I looking at?

"Let me give you the background so you'll grasp why Beowulf is located here, what has recently happened, and why we need you."

At this point I was more than all ears.

"In 1908, an explorer named G.E. Weaver made a trip down the Colorado from Green River, Wyoming. He worked for the National Historical Foundation. It was near here that he noticed stains in the sediment of the east canyon wall. Curious, he stopped to explore. Weaver discovered the entrance to a cave eight hundred feet above the Colorado River on the side of a sheer rock wall. From the rim of the Canyon above, it's about fifteen hundred feet down to the cave entrance. He was a skilled rock climber, and when he managed to ascend to the entrance and explore the cave, he found dozens of rooms containing wall drawings resembling Egyptian hieroglyphics. There were also rooms filled with countless objects resembling those found in the famous tombs of the Egyptian pharaohs."

"Is that cave what I see here?"

"Yes. You're looking at that very cavern."

"And all the passageways are like spokes that lead to more rooms?"

"Exactly."

I moved closer to a vase and briefly studied the glyphs. It didn't take but a minute to come to a conclusion. "But these aren't Egyptian hieroglyphs."

"No, they are not."

"They're the same type of glyphs that were on those I-beams in the photographs."

"The same. Unlike the Roswell artifacts, these were discovered in 1908 and had apparently been here for a very long time. It is believed that the beings who crashed in Roswell had established a base of some sort here inside the walls of the Grand Canyon over a hundred years ago. Our job is to interpret the writing, schematics, and technology found here. So it just made good sense for us to house the Roswell artifacts and the quantum computer here, too."

I was beginning to understand why Kepner hadn't spilled all this information back in my cabin. I never would have believed him. Even with Chaucer's controlled, slow rollout, hell, I still had a rough time wrapping my head around it. "Okay, I *do* get it. Everything except how I fit in."

"Several days ago, we discovered that some of the most important artifacts—those pieces of what look like broken porcelain that you were unimpressed with—were missing. There is no ulterior motive for bringing you in on this other than what has already been divulged—you have the skills, solid character, and you're savvy. We—"

A sudden blaring of alarms deafened me. At the same time brilliant revolving strobe lights flashed.

Chaucer's face turned ashen.

"What?" I shouted. "What's happening?"

CHAPTER 12 - THE CAVERNS
Beowulf Headquarters

"We're under attack!" Chaucer called out as he ran back to the workstation. I watched him type in a command and pull up multiple security camera feeds onto the monitors.

On the screen, I could see an armed assault team barge through the entrance of the National Park Service building at ground level and head for the elevator. A moment later, I saw a huge explosion at the entrance to the labs. Even this far below the surface we still heard the boom.

Another camera showed some of the assault team exiting the elevator and rushing onto a different level. I guessed it to be the staff's living quarters, since the intruders were forcing sleepy-looking people at gunpoint out of rooms and assembling them in a hallway.

Chaucer typed in another command and the screens turned solid blue with a flashing red message: *Execute Wipe. Yes or no?* He typed in *Yes*, and the next screen popped up. *Wipe once started, cannot be undone. Continue Wipe? Yes or no?* Again he typed *Yes*, and a progress bar appeared, rapidly moving from left to right. The label above the bar displayed: *Expunging All Server Drives*.

Chaucer shot a glance toward the labs. "The security door won't hold them for long. They'll be coming through it any second." A succession of muffled explosions affirmed his prediction.

"Follow me." He grabbed a battery-powered lantern from a cabinet beneath the workstation and headed into the caverns with me right behind.

"Who are they?" I asked.

"I don't know, but one thing's for sure, they're not ours."

With all this security and secrecy, how could an enemy assault team penetrate Beowulf? And who was the enemy?

I assumed the security lock that required Chaucer's thumbprint was now breached.

"This way. It's an emergency escape route in case of attack. Weaver found this tunnel when exploring." He motioned to one of the tunnel spokes leading off to the right. A scattering of security lighting lit the way.

Chaucer moved briskly along an uneven dirt path that zigzagged around more of the strange Egyptian-like artifacts collection. The blaring of the alarm horns faded in the semi-darkness behind us, and soon only the crunch of our footfalls echoed off the sandstone walls. Finally, there were no more artifacts, and we came to the last of the security lights. The tunnel floor rose in a gradual incline, making it a harder go.

Chaucer paused and leaned against the cavern wall, out of breath. "Give me a minute." He was panting. "We won't be rescued. Nobody on staff knows about this old passage."

A loud bang roared through the tunnel, and Chaucer slumped to the ground holding his abdomen. Even through the faint lantern wash of light, I saw blood. One or more of the assault team must have followed and caught up. Chaucer staggered to his feet and I guided him around the side of an outcrop where we crouched.

"How bad?" I asked.

He groaned and pulled his hand away from the wound. "Hurts like a bitch."

Another shot ricocheted off the rock wall overhead, raining chips down on us.

I slipped my hand into my boot and pulled out the PPK. Keeping low, I eased around the outcrop and saw a silhouetted figure about thirty meters away. He hugged the wall and advanced carefully, his assault rifle at the ready. I figured he wore heavy armor, so I aimed low and fired.

I heard a painful yelp and saw him grab his thigh. He stumbled back around a curve in the path, but not before getting off three wild shots that struck the dark recesses of the cavern.

"Stay still," I said to Chaucer, and sprinted back along the path.

I found the man groaning as he lay gripping his leg. There was so much blood I realized I must have nicked his femoral artery. I kicked his assault rifle, an AK-12, out of the way and stood over him. I pulled his goggles and helmet sideways and aimed the Walther at the only unprotected part of him that promised a likely kill. Dead center forehead.

"Who are you?"

"Go to hell," he said with a thick East European accent, possibly Russian. His eyes revealed pain, and blood pooled beside his leg.

"Why the attack?"

He groaned again.

I stabbed my gun at his head. "Should I go ahead and put you out of your misery, or are you going to talk and pray your buddies get here in time to save you?"

I saw a flash of metal. A blade appeared in his right hand and he thrust it at me with the speed of a cobra. It bit into the side of my palm. In the same instant, I fired the Walther and the man went limp—his knife dropped at his side.

Glancing up, I checked the tunnel but saw no other soldiers. So I seized his assault rifle and ran back to Chaucer.

"Can you walk?" When he nodded, I said, "I bought us a little time. But we gotta go. Somebody had to have heard our gunfire."

With great effort, he stood. Draping his arm around my shoulder, I supported him as we wobbled along the ever-inclining path, now lit only by his lantern.

The cut on my hand stung but didn't seem serious. A bit of blood, but nothing like Chaucer's wound. I could feel him getting weaker with each step.

We paused a number of times along the way, Chaucer

saying little. Finally, "We're almost there."

"Where?"

"There's a gate at the end. Weaver installed it way back when exploring the cavern." His words came on labored breaths. Chaucer dropped the lantern and the light went out. As he collapsed to the ground, he grabbed my arm. "I can't make it."

CHAPTER 13 - THE GATE
The East Rim

"You've got to make it," I told Chaucer. "If you stay here you're certain to die. Get up, damn it. Get up!"

I wedged one arm under his shoulder and tugged until he stood.

"The gate is just ahead."

I noticed a slight glow coming from around a bend up ahead in the tunnel. Working our way forward, we rounded the turn and there it was.

An iron gate, similar to what you would expect to find in an Old West jail, protected the end of the path. As we came to stand before it, I sucked in my breath at what lay beyond. As far as I could see, the land seemed on fire in orange and red as the rising sun painted the great expanse of the Grand Canyon.

"Here," Chaucer said, taking a key from his pocket and then handing it to me.

I jammed the key in the lock and turned. Nothing happened. The lock was frozen. I removed the key and then inserted it again, wiggling it this time as I turned it. "Please, dear god, let this work." As I added a little more pressure the lock freed up. I pushed the gate open, and then peeked my head out and looked up and down. Above, I saw a narrow path, similar to a pack mule trail, winding up the side of the canyon. Gazing overhead, I realized we were close to the surface, about fifteen meters. I turned to him as he sat with his back against the cave wall.

"Looks like a steep climb from here, but not very far to the top. Think you can do it?"

"No." His voice was barely above a whisper. "Go on. Please." He gave a feeble wave for me to leave him. Tugging on the pocket of my jacket, he pulled me close and whispered, "Agent Decker, first—" He coughed. "First . . . first find the Monk's Tale."

"What?" *Is he delirious? Losing his mind from the pain?* But his voice seemed so sure. "I don't understand."

"You will." His grip slipped away as he said, "Trust no one."

I knelt beside him. His breathing was shallow, his eyes closed. Then his head fell forward and he tumbled onto his side. I felt his neck but found no pulse. *Damn.*

Glancing back the way we had come, I looked for signs we were being followed, but saw only darkness. Still, I had to move fast just in case. Before I stood, I checked his pockets for anything that might be useful, but found all were empty.

After slipping through the gate, I headed up the path to the canyon rim. Despite the chill of the morning air, I could already feel the warmth of the rising sun on my skin. It was almost impossible to keep my eyes on the narrow path without looking to the left at the spectacular panorama of the Grand Canyon.

Within five minutes, I stood on the rim of the plateau and took a last glimpse at the other-worldly view. It crossed my mind that perhaps the aliens were attracted to this place because it reminded them of home. Then I chuckled at the *alien* concept altogether. Just because Chaucer said it, didn't make it true. Still, Beowulf was an impressive place, and what I had seen there was astounding.

As I slung the AK-12 over my shoulder and headed south, my thoughts were of the assault team and their Russian rifles.

———

Colonel Nikolai Vyshinsky watched as one of his men searched the body. Finally, the soldier glanced up and shook his head. "All we have is his nametag. It says Chaucer."

"Toss the body over the side," the colonel ordered. He watched as two soldiers carried Chaucer beyond the gate and pushed it over. Six hundred meters down, it disappeared in a shelf of rocks and boulders, hidden from view by anyone traveling the Colorado River. "Let them wonder if Chaucer went with us. The more we can confuse and distract them, the better."

When the men were done, Vyshinsky said, "You two go back and join up with the others at the truck. Take your dead comrade with you. Leave nothing behind. Tell the others to take the Beowulf staff to the rendezvous point. I will meet you there."

The soldiers saluted and quickly disappeared down the tunnel. Once they were gone, Vyshinsky pulled out his cell phone. He was going to deliver bad news, and he didn't like delivering bad news. He hoped his commander would take into account all he had already accomplished.

Vyshinsky thought back to when he had painstakingly tracked down and retrieved another piece of the ceramic-like material—that one from a remote corner of Siberia near the site of the 1908 Tunguska explosion. The accidental destruction of the Tunguska artifact two years ago meant he had to find a replacement. He was given the assignment of arranging the extraction of the alien artifacts from the Beowulf facility. Despite the time span between the 1908 Tunguska event and the 1947 Roswell event, both sets of artifacts contained the same technology needed to complete the mission. The artifacts stolen from Beowulf were already on their way to the Middle East. Without those, the project would be forever lost.

Now he had to deliver less than excellent news about the second component of his assignment, but he was certain it was no more than a minor setback he could resolve.

Vyshinsky dialed his phone. When the line was answered, he said, "It was not on Chaucer and the computer servers have been wiped clean."

He listened to the response, and then said, "Yes, I know

who has it. I'll take care of it personally." The colonel pressed the end button. He checked his AK-12 to make sure he had a full clip. Slinging it over his shoulder, he headed for the gate.

CHAPTER 14 - THE PLATEAU
East of the Grand Canyon

The temperature rose fast as I made my way across the top of the plateau. After walking at a steady clip for over two hours I had worked up a sweat. I paused a moment and massaged my calves and then took my jacket off and tied the sleeves around my neck. I must have appeared quite yuppie except for the blood stains on my sweater and pants. And the assault rifle.

A couple of years into our marriage, Kenny and I vacationed in this area, driving up Highway 89 to Bitter Springs. I still remember the beauty of the Painted Desert stretching east from the road. So now I figured if I just kept moving in this direction, I should eventually run into the highway. I had already crossed over a well-worn dirt road. Probably park ranger patrol routes.

The way forward was uneven but walkable. I maintained a general easterly direction. The plateau up ahead leveled out for a few hundred meters, another dirt path cutting through. That's when I heard the motor.

I turned in the direction the sound of the engine was coming from. An SUV approached in the distance. As it got closer, I recognized the Ford Explorer painted National-Park-Service green. It slowed and came to a halt about fifteen meters away. The ranger must have spotted me while doing a simple routine check of the area, and I probably looked suspicious with the assault rifle. I watched him talk into his shoulder-attached radio, most likely reporting his location, maybe requesting backup, and asking for the sheriff to be notified.

I knew that as of 2010, firearms were allowed in National Parks, so I didn't worry that the rifle hanging over my shoulder was going to be a problem. He was simply being cautious.

But as he got out, shielded himself with his door, and pulled his pistol, I realized it was the blood stains that were causing him concern. He looked to be in his late twenties, with a round baby face, and blond hair.

"Place your weapon on the ground and put your hands on your head."

I've learned not to argue with people pointing guns at me— I have several bullet wounds that taught me that lesson. So I slipped the assault rifle off my shoulder and placed it at my feet.

"Drop to your knees and don't move."

"I'm OSI special agent Maxine Decker," I lied as I knelt. If I had inserted the word *retired* in the statement, it would have been closer to the truth.

The ranger walked forward, his gun aimed at my chest. Halting a few meters away, he said, "Whose blood is that?"

The left headlight of the Explorer exploded.

"What the—?" The ranger started to turn when a shot struck him in his upper right arm spinning him around and causing his gun to fly out of his hand. He hit the ground hard and cried out in pain.

I had no idea who was shooting at us, but we needed to get to the protection of the SUV fast.

I grabbed the Russian assault rifle then pulled the ranger to his feet, forcing him toward the car. A third shot struck him in the back of his thigh and again he howled with pain.

Jerking the passenger door open, I told the ranger to get inside. He couldn't manage on his own, so I shoved his body, cramming him in, and then slammed the door shut. I dashed around the back of the Explorer, ducking fire, and eased toward the still-open driver's door as I pulled back the bolt of the AK-12. Setting the rate at 3-round bursts, I took aim and used the mini scope to scan the horizon in the direction of the incoming.

As a fourth shot slammed into the fender of the SUV, I saw the sniper. Dressed in black, he lay flat on the ground about two hundred and fifty meters away. He had to be one of the assault team. I pulled the trigger, sending three rounds at my target. Through the scope I saw the puffs of dirt burst up around him. Two more pulls of the trigger sent him scrambling up and back toward an outcrop of rocks. That was my chance to jump behind the wheel. The engine was still running, so I shifted into drive, jammed the gas pedal to the floor, and made a skidding U-turn, throwing up a cloud of dust.

I heard a dull thud as another shot slammed into the back of the SUV. Glancing over at the ranger, I saw he was breathing heavily and obviously in a lot of pain. He opened his eyes and stared at me.

"Does your radio still work?" I asked.

He nodded.

I took the radio, pressed the call button and said, "Officer down."

CHAPTER 15 - ARREST
Coconino County, Arizona

In less than five minutes, I drove the SUV over the crest of a hill and saw in the distance a road I hoped was Highway 89. I also spotted a half-dozen emergency vehicles racing toward us on the dirt road. As we converged, I identified a couple of National Park Service SUVs, two county sheriff's cars, and an ambulance. Everyone came to a halt in a fog of dust and gravel.

A sheriff's deputy approached, his gun drawn, but at his side, while two EMTs went to the passenger's door. The ranger was bleeding badly as they pulled him out and laid him on the ground.

"Get out slowly," the deputy ordered. "Keep your hands where I can see them."

I realized that in addition to my blood and Chaucer's, I also had the ranger's stains on me. Admittedly, this didn't look good. I kept my hands raised while a second deputy came around and looked into the cab of the SUV. He reached in and pulled out the AK-12, holding it so the other officer could see it. He turned to me. "This yours?"

"No."

"Are there any more weapons?"

I bent to pull the PPK from inside my boot.

"Freeze." The first officer raised his gun. "Keep your hands up. Where is it?"

"In my boot."

The second deputy retrieved the automatic and showed it to

his partner. "What else?"

"As far as I know, that's it," I said. "If there are any other weapons in the vehicle, they probably belong to him." I glanced toward the EMTs, who already had the ranger on a gurney and were wheeling him toward the ambulance.

"Whose blood is that?" the second officer asked as he motioned to my sweater and jeans. Two park rangers had arrived and wandered over to watch.

"His." Again I motioned to the wounded man.

"What's your name?" the first deputy asked.

"Maxine Decker."

"Okay, Ms. Decker, let's take a ride."

CHAPTER 16 - INTERROGATION
Coconino County Sheriff's Substation

"I told you, my name is Maxine Decker," I responded to the investigator, Lieutenant Parker, who stood across the desk from me. He could keep on asking the same questions and he would keep getting the same answers from me. And if I told him the truth, he'd think I was crazy. I assumed there would be some cover story for what happened at the Beowulf facility, not to mention what kind of work went on there. So trying to explain about quantum computers, missing alien artifacts, and possibly a Russian commando assault would be laughable. All I'd told him was that I was a former OSI special agent. That would have to suffice. I felt like a soldier only giving up her name, rank, and serial number. Anything else would have to come down through channels way beyond my pay grade.

Parker smirked. "We've confirmed your identity and the fact that you're a retired federal agent. What I want to know is, what were you doing with this?"

He placed the Russian AK-12 on the desk in front of me next to my cell phone. When I didn't respond, he said, "These weapons are hard to come by, Agent Decker. Makes me curious as to how someone like you would get hold of the newest assault rifle in the Russian arsenal. Not even standard issue for the Russians yet. So again, what are you doing with it?"

I shrugged.

"You've got blood on you, more than what could have been produced from Ranger Clark's wounds. And I'm told by the emergency room doctors that the caliber of rounds taken out of Clark match the ones used in this." He pointed to the AK-12. "You also appear to have been hiking through some rough terrain. What were you doing? Or better yet, considering the blood, what did you do?"

"I told you, I don't remember."

"Right, I almost forgot."

Another insolent smirk.

"This isn't going to fly, Decker. If there's nothing to hide, why all this crap about not remembering anything? From your records, I see that at one time you were suspected of aiding some smugglers in Iraq. Even shot your partner."

"If not mistaken, it also states that I was innocent."

Why was this guy being such a dick? But I knew the answer. I'd been thoroughly indoctrinated during my OSI training, which had to be similar to his training. Red tape. Procedures. Protocol. However, with operations like Beowulf, none of those things really mattered because to the outside world, Beowulf simply didn't exist.

This guy had no idea what he was dealing with here. And he didn't know shit about me or what I'd been through, today or in the past. And even if he was just doing his job, he was still an asshole.

Be patient, I thought. Hopefully, the President had somehow been notified of the attack on Beowulf and by now must have gotten word of my predicament. All I had to do was keep my mouth shut—which wasn't one of my strengths. I wouldn't divulge information, but pressed, I might mouth off.

"Maybe you can at least tell us where you came from before you encountered Ranger Clark. And if you didn't shoot him, who did?"

I shook my head, then locked my eyes on his and stared him down. The opening of the door saved him. He turned to face the noise. I wanted to smile. I'd have outlasted him and would have savored the victory.

"Good afternoon," Peter Kepner said to Lieutenant Parker.

I felt a gush of thankfulness fill my body. Kepner had told

me he would be away from the Beowulf facility while Chaucer gave me the tour. I supposed he and I were the only ones left alive. Thank god the President had sent him for me.

"Excuse me," Parker said. "Who gave you permission—?

Before he finished, Kepner flashed an ID. The agent stared at it and worked his jaw.

It was a pleasure to see him irritated.

"Agent Decker," Kepner acknowledged.

I stood and shook his hand.

"Lieutenant Parker," Kepner said, "as a matter of national security, I'll handle this from here. You'll release Agent Decker into my custody. This questioning is over."

I grabbed my cell phone. "I want my Walther back."

"Sorry," Parker said. "It's still in ballistics."

Terrific. That meant I would probably never see it again. I motioned to the AK-12 on the table. "Keep it as a memento of our time together."

CHAPTER 17 - ALTOIDS
Coconino National Forest

"I thought you said you don't carry any ID." I sat in the passenger's side of Kepner's Jeep Wrangler as we sped along a rural road. After the endless barren landscape of the Grand Canyon, it was a nice change to see trees. We had left the sheriff's substation a few miles behind and entered the National Forest.

"I have several sets of identification to use for the appropriate occasion. What I showed the investigator was my NSA credentials."

"Well, whatever you used, it worked." I watched the oaks and aspen roll by, not unlike the forest surrounding my cabin. "I don't know how much longer I could have kept my mouth shut. Not about Beowulf. I wouldn't have mentioned that. But explaining away the blood stains and what happened to that ranger was going to be hard. And it wouldn't have taken much more for me to get rude and bad-mannered."

Kepner nodded as he turned the Jeep onto a secondary county road. "Then I arrived just in time."

I glanced at him. "I had to leave my Walther with them. Think you can help arrange for me to get another firearm? I feel naked without one."

"You mean the one I told you not to bring?"

I nodded guiltily.

"I'll see what I can do."

"And thanks for coming to the rescue. Without being able to say anything specific to them, it wasn't looking so good for me."

"You did fine. And no thanks needed." He laughed and glanced my way. "Gotta justify my job."

So the man did have a sense of humor. As we traveled along, the forest became thicker. My memory flashed back to the attack on Beowulf and Chaucer's quick response to wipe the computers clean. As if reliving it inside my head, I heard the blare of the alarms and the pounding of our feet as we ran through the caverns. And then the thunderous bang of the shot hitting Chaucer in his side, watching his back arching, then his stumbling. The blood.

I felt a chill as I shook the memory out of my head and touched my bandaged hand. I was lucky. Chaucer was not. I had done all I could to get him out of the cavern to safety. But it wasn't enough.

I returned my attention to the passing landscape. "Where are we headed?"

"To a safe, secluded location out of harm's way. The President wishes you to continue on with the mission. I informed him of everything you have been through and how you seem to have handled it. He was impressed."

"Where does he want me to go from here? Chaucer had the computers wiped clean, so there is no data. The scientists working on the project are probably dead. There's nothing but a big black void."

"Don't be so sure. Think positive. There are clues."

"Like what?"

"Let's talk about that later."

"When we get to that secluded location, I presume?" It looked to me like we had achieved the goal of seclusion already. But I figured he wasn't going to disclose much, anyway.

"By the way, Decker, did Chaucer tell you anything or give you anything before he died? An object, notebook, information? Anything at all?"

I laughed at the question. "We were running for our lives, being chased and shot at. There wasn't any time for chitchat."

Then I remembered what Chaucer had whispered to me. "There was one thing he said before he died. He pulled me close. He was so weak. It didn't make sense. By then he was most likely delirious."

"Really?" Kepner said, curiosity riding on his voice. "What did he say?"

"He could barely talk. It sounded like 'Find the Monk's Tale.'"

"The Monk's Tale is part of *Canterbury Tales*. Ever read it?"

"A long time ago."

"Me, too. From what I recall, during the spring, people from all over England gathered at an inn on their way to Canterbury to receive the blessings of St. Thomas à Becket. The host at the inn challenged everyone to tell a story. When it came time for the monk to tell his story, everyone expected a jolly tale, but instead he related a series of tragedies. There were lots of other guests who also shared their tales. Canterbury Tales is a collection of their stories. That's about it for my recall of English 101. I'm surprised I remember that much."

"Better than me," I said. "I wonder if as he was dying he actually thought he was Chaucer in the flesh."

"Maybe."

My mouth was dry. Out of habit, I reached into my coat pocket for my mini tin of Altoids, only to remember that I hadn't been allowed to bring anything with me. But my fingers did find a small object hiding there. I plucked it from my pocket. Chaucer must have dropped it in when he pulled me down to him.

A flash drive.

CHAPTER 18 - THE CABAL
Katrina Hunting Lodge, Eastern Anatolia

Moghaddam was nervous, more so than he thought he would be. Even after being personally assured by the liaison to the Iranian Supreme Leader that this meeting was in everyone's best interest, he still felt moisture forming under his arms at the thought of sitting in the same room with three of the most powerful men in the Russian Republic.

"Gentlemen," the young man in the black suit announced as he walked into the private library, "may I present Dr. Mostafa Moghaddam, Director of Uranium Enrichment for the Islamic Republic of Iran. Dr. Moghaddam, these are your hosts, General Yuri Lushev, Chief of the General Staff of the Russian Army; Boris Ivankov, Chairman and CEO of the Russian Central Bank; and Vladimir Butorin, President of Red Star Media Group."

"Thank you, Lieutenant," Lushev said. "That will be all." As the young man left, closing the door behind him, the general came forward and shook Moghaddam's hand. "It is a pleasure to meet you." He motioned the scientist to one of the wingback leather chairs. "Would you like something to drink— tea, coffee, or stronger after your trip?"

"I'm fine, thank you." He glanced around the ornate, wood-paneled library, part of the recently refurbished hunting lodge originally built in 1902 for the last Russian emperor, Nicholas II. He looked back at Lushev. The general appeared quite physically fit, even for his age. The casual, open-collared shirt hid little of his muscular build, no doubt from years of setting an example as a leader of the Russian Army.

"How was your flight?" asked Ivankov. Unlike the general, the Russian banker was portly and balding, and bore the veined, red nose of a heavy drinker. He, too, was dressed casually.

"Uneventful."

Vladimir Butorin, the billionaire industrialist and media oligarch, said nothing. Instead he stared at the scientist as an undertaker would a corpse. Butorin was lanky with hollow cheeks and shadowy, sunken eyes. Moghaddam assumed that if Butorin smiled, his face would break.

"Doctor, have you had a chance to examine the Roswell artifacts?" General Lushev asked.

"They arrived from Amsterdam two days ago."

"And your evaluation?" Ivankov asked.

"The three pieces actually make up slightly more mass than the original Tunguska sample. We will have enough to create displacement."

Lushev swirled the vodka in his glass. "No mistakes this time. We want no questions. Almost every developed nation has satellite surveillance of the entire world. Can you imagine the thoughts of those who were actually monitoring the Sudan with their satellite intelligence feeds at the precise moment when the previous Sudanese facility vanished in front of their eyes? I am certain they could not believe it. Those archives must have been reviewed and analyzed countless times and inevitably always the same conclusion was reached. There was no explanation. A repeat would be disastrous. There would be investigation followed by investigation. But worse, and I don't have to remind you, Doctor, if we do have another disaster, there are no more artifacts. The Roswell pieces are all that are left."

"I can assure you, General Lushev, that I am acutely aware of the unfortunate mistakes of the past. All precautions are being taken at the new facility. Safeguards are in place that did not exist before. The final touches are being made as we speak."

"Have you determined what happened to the desert facility? I mean, where exactly did it *go*?" Lushev asked.

"We don't have definite confirmation, but we believe, based upon our monitoring of seismic anomalies and an unusual atmospheric disturbance occurring within a microsecond of the event, that it displaced to a remote region of the Amazon jungle near the Brazil-Peru border."

"Any chance it will be found?"

"Only by monkeys and snakes, and the indigenous natives."

"Could the Tunguska artifact have survived?"

"I have no idea, sir."

General Lushev pressed further. "And the Beowulf staff? Are they cooperating?"

"They were resistant at first. We determined the least critical of the group and executed him in front of the others. Now they are hard at work helping to complete the project."

Dr. Moghaddam knew there was only one thing left hanging in the air. It was no secret back at the new underground Sudanese facility that the last piece of the puzzle, the critical piece, was still missing. He had hoped one of the three members of the Russian cabal would offer a status report. But after an awkward moment of silence, he cleared his throat. "And what of the thumb drive?"

General Lushev said, "Well, there's been a slight delay in acquiring it. During the raid on Beowulf, the director, a man named Chaucer, was critically wounded. He was searched and the drive was not found on him. Before he died, we believe he passed it to a woman visiting the facility. The woman, a retired federal agent, escaped. Both Colonel Vyshinsky, the leader of our assault team and a second man, our Beowulf contact, are in the process of recovering it. We should be no more than a few days getting it to you."

"The project is useless without the data on the thumb drive, General, and the drive is useless without the password."

Lushev leaned forward in his chair, his face growing stern. "Tell us something we don't know, Dr. Moghaddam."

"My apologies, General. I am only speaking out because of

my passion to make displacement a reality."

"We will get you your key, and we have methods of breaking passwords." The general appeared to relax back into his chair. "Your job is to make it work."

"Understood, sir." Again the scientist cleared his throat. "I was wondering if we should give the displacement device a name."

"You have a suggestion?" Boris Ivankov asked.

"Actually, I do. Since its function is to stand between us and our enemies, I suggest we call it the Shield."

Vladimir Butorin finally spoke. "Perfect."

CHAPTER 19 - FLASH DRIVE
Coconino National Forest

I stared at the 1 TB flash drive with the Beowulf logo on it and then at Kepner. "I've got something."

He glanced at me, and then down at my hand. "Where'd you get that?" He looked energized.

"It was in my pocket. Must be Chaucer's. He wasn't using my jacket to pull me closer—he was dropping this in the pocket."

"Grab my laptop." Kepner pulled over to the side of the road. "It's in the backseat."

Releasing my seatbelt, I twisted around so I could reach the computer. "Okay." I opened the laptop and turned it on. While waiting for it to boot, I took a glimpse out the windshield. The forest was dense and thick with underbrush pierced by jagged rock formations. When Kepner had said *secluded*, he wasn't kidding.

The computer chimed and came to life. I inserted the drive and waited, then double-clicked on the icon when it showed up on the screen. The Beowulf logo came up with a box that asked for the password. "Do you know the password?"

Kepner shook his head. "Chaucer had to have said something to you. Some idea to what the password might be."

"Nothing that I haven't already told you. Passwords can be cracked. I know somebody who—"

"He wouldn't have handed the drive over without at least giving you a clue how to open it. Put in monk's tale or *The Monk's Tale*." Kepner's jaw worked back and forth

I typed in both of his suggestions with and without caps and the apostrophe, but had no success. Then a message flashed that too many attempts had been made. The Beowulf icon disappeared, as did the icon for the drive. "It's shut us out."

Kepner slammed his palms against the steering wheel. "Give me the drive."

His gruff words sounded like an order rather than a request, and caught me off guard. A fresh tension rolled through the fibers of my muscles as I removed the thumb drive and gave it to him.

He stared at the drive and then made a call on his cell. "I've got it, but not the password." He listened then said, "Yeah, everything is under control."

Kepner shoved the drive in his pocket before pulling the car back onto the road. His face was pallid and his eyes narrowed. I saw his nostrils flare a few times with some deep breaths.

"You really shouldn't be so upset," I said, feeling the need to calm him. "Chill out. I told you, I know someone who might be able to crack the password."

Kepner didn't respond. Didn't even blink, as if his thoughts were miles away.

Ten minutes later he swung the Wrangler onto a dirt road that resembled nothing more than a hunter's track.

"Doesn't look like this road has been cleared in a long time," I said. "I assume we're still headed to the safe spot." *Secluded* was no longer a good descriptor. *Isolated* seemed a better fit.

After about two kilometers, Kepner stopped.

The tension I had tried to disregard a moment earlier now coiled inside my gut.

He sucked on his teeth making a disagreeable sound. "So Decker, what am I going to do with you?"

Do with me?

Kepner leaned over and opened the glove box.

I reached for the door handle.

CHAPTER 20 - PONDEROSA
Coconino National Forest

Kepner pulled a handgun from the glove box and pointed it at me before I had a chance to open the door. He shifted the car into drive and steered with his free hand. "A little farther and we'll be able to take care of business. Enjoy the view, Agent Decker. It's going to be your last."

If I tried to wrestle the gun away from him, there was a good chance he could pull the trigger before I got it. Shooting me in the Jeep or in the woods probably didn't matter much to him. I had to think of an alternative escape plan.

We'd been on the dirt road for about five minutes when the sky darkened. Gun-metal gray thunderheads quickly moved over us. The ride became rough and the vehicle joggled left. Kepner jerked the wheel right. If it started raining, the Wrangler would have a tough time maintaining traction.

It grew darker as the rain started. Lightning ripped the clouds and a loud thunderclap followed. Another flash and boom. Now we faced a downpour as the rain fell in sheets, saturating the road.

Kepner corrected the Jeep again and it slid sideways in the mud and skidded. He squinted and put both hands on the wheel gaining better control. He still held the gun, just not pointing it directly at me.

I leaned toward him.

"Don't try it, Decker. I'll shoot you right now if I have to."

I angled back into the seat but never took my eyes off the gun.

As the Jeep continued bouncing along, the rain pelted the windshield and the lightning flared all around us. Like bombs, earsplitting thunder shook the ground and the car. The road became slicker and nearly impassable. Kepner was having a difficult time keeping it under control.

While rubbing my bandaged hand and listening to the thunder and the slosh of the tires, I knew I had to do something, even if it was risky. I was going to die anyway, so what the hell.

I strained to see through the rain-drenched windshield, looking for any type of clearing in the thick forest. I spotted one a few meters up ahead and waited for the perfect moment. When we were beside it, I grabbed the wheel and forced it left, wrenching it from Kepner's grip.

The Wrangler swerved and slid off the road. I prayed it wouldn't roll and kill us both.

Through the slurry of mud and rain on the windshield I glimpsed a tree ahead. We were headed straight for it. I braced and leaned back, my hands against the dash.

The impact sent us both shooting forward. Kepner's forehead slammed into the windshield, leaving a spider web of fractures in the glass. Then whiplash pitched our heads backward.

As the vehicle came to rest, I was relieved to feel shook up but okay. I looked at Kepner. He was unconscious, with bloody trails flowing down from his forehead. He also had a gash in his right upper arm that pulsed blood. He must have reached out just before we hit and his arm had gone through the windshield. The broken glass must have gouged out the flesh when he pulled his arm back.

His gun! It lay on the floor near the accelerator. I needed to get to it before Kepner. I fought at my seatbelt, but it had jammed in the crash.

Kepner groaned. Confusion filled his eyes, but in a moment he seemed coherent and went for his seatbelt and then the gun.

As he bent for the pistol, my seat restraint disengaged, and I dove out of the car into the drenching rain and dashed into the woods.

I heard Kepner's grunts of pain as he tried to get out. He was coming after me.

I figured his injury would slow him down so I could get away. I ran through the underbrush for about thirty meters when my foot caught on a rock and I tumbled face down, my ankle twisted and burning. Lying there, I was a perfect target. But with the pain in my left ankle, outrunning him was no longer an option. I had to do something to keep out of sight. The undergrowth here was too sparse to hide me.

I spotted a Ponderosa pine with low branches. Crawling toward it, I choked back my moans from the pain. Beneath the tree I rose on one foot, grabbed the pine for balance, and then hoisted myself up. I climbed the ladder of limbs, using my good leg and dragging my throbbing foot behind me until I was about three meters off the ground. The tree trunk supported my back. I waited for Kepner, like a hunter in a duck blind. The only difference was he was the one with the gun.

The downpour turned to drizzle, and a few moments later I heard the stir of underbrush. Kepner came into sight and paused, propping himself against a tree a few meters away. He wiped away the blood running down his face and then nursed his blood-soaked arm.

If he returned to the Jeep and drove away I was screwed. I needed the vehicle to get away from anyone else who might be searching for me.

I plucked a large, cone from the pine and threw it to the ground beneath my tree.

Kepner's head snapped toward the sound. I wanted him to think I was close enough that he could track me through the forest. He pulled up straight and headed in my direction.

Huddled in the tree, I hushed my breathing and remained still.

Kepner staggered several steps. He was weak, but appeared to have a firm grip on the handgun. He stopped.

My thoughts were loud and clear. He couldn't give up and

go back to the car. *And god, don't let him look up.*

Blood soaked his shirt from his scalp wounds. He bent over as if getting blood to his head might keep him from passing out.

A moment later, he straightened and stumbled forward, a sign he was not giving up. He must have resigned himself to finding me or die trying.

The tension in my muscles triggered a cramp in my uninjured leg. I didn't dare move, but the spasm was unbearable. I flexed my foot in the boot, trying to stretch my leg and relieve the pain. The movement cracked off a branch.

Kepner moved to stand directly beneath me. He leaned back and looked up.

CHAPTER 21 - VICTORIA'S SECRET
Coconino National Forest

I shoved off and leapt from the tree, landing squarely on top of Kepner with an impact that knocked the breath out of me and sent a pain roaring up my leg from my ankle. Stunned, Kepner's breath gushed out. His arm was outstretched, his fingers gripping the gun handle. I rolled off him and went for the weapon.

I freed the gun from his hand without much effort. The loss of blood had robbed him of his strength.

I sat beside him and stuck the gun through my waistband. The gash in Kepner's arm still pumped blood. I pulled my arms through my sweater sleeves, unhooked my bra, took it off, and then threaded my arms back through the sleeves.

"I don't know why I'm doing this," I said, tying my bra around Kepner's arm just above the wound.

His lips moved with a whisper, "You don't realize what you've done, Decker."

"Eat shit." I attached a stick to my bra and twisted the makeshift tourniquet. He didn't move, not even a flinch or blink. I realized my Good Samaritan move was too late. He was dead.

I fumbled through his pockets and found his cell phone.

The rain roared in again, soaking me—if it were possible to be wetter than before. I held out my arms and lifted my face to rinse some of his blood away, then glanced back at Kepner. *What a waste of a fifty-dollar Victoria's Secret bra.*

I stood, putting as little weight on my foot as I could, and dragged him into a clump of brush. The bastard was heavy. I hoped the buzzards would pick him clean before his body was found.

I was glad I didn't have to shoot him. I would have, if it had come to that. I'd done it before when I had to, and the memory still hung in a dark place in my mind.

I climbed in the still-running Jeep and hoped I could back it up onto the road. Shifting in reverse, I checked the rearview mirror and glanced out the back window. The rain was still coming down, but my view was fairly clear. I stepped lightly on the gas, afraid the tires would spin. The Wrangler groaned as it fought to gain traction.

I carefully gave it more gas, and the tires finally grabbed. I backed onto the road.

The road to where? I wondered.

And what was on Chaucer's flash drive?

There was one way to find out.

CHAPTER 22 - NO ONE TO TRUST
Coconino National Forest

It was my left ankle that I'd hurt, so I had no problem operating the Jeep, which thankfully had an automatic transmission.

My boot was uncomfortably tight—I knew the ankle was swelling. I thought about removing the boot, but changed my mind. The compression would keep down the swelling and the boot would give support to my ankle. And if I got it off, I might not be able to get it back on. Then I unwrapped the bandage from my hand and checked the knife wound. Manageable and the least of my problems.

I drove down the soaked road, wondering if I should have turned around and gone back. I could be heading to Kepner's safe spot only to find an accomplice waiting. But if I returned to the main road, someone could already be looking for his car and tag number. Had we gone off the radar yet and triggered a search? Kepner said he took orders from the President, but was he lying? He had lied about everything else. Was he just a maverick who'd gone sour? Or was this a conspiracy that went to the highest levels? I had no answers. At this point I didn't know who to trust.

I saw another dirt road and decided to change direction. I did that several more times, hoping it would make finding me more difficult—no logical trail to predict.

I heard the whir of a helicopter in the distance. Was it coming for me? To help me or kill me?

My brain surrendered to my gut and I gunned the engine,

pulling off the road into the thick forest. I turned off the car's ignition. The sound of the rotors grew louder. I cracked open the door and peered up through the trees toward the sound. The forest was not thick enough here for me to hide. If they were searching for me, the Jeep would be easy to spot.

If I abandoned the vehicle, there may be no getting it back. I got out and started gathering tree limbs and fallen branches, then heaped them on the hood and roof. The cover was skimpy, but it would provide some camouflage. Better than nothing.

The sound of the helicopter echoed through the forest. Time for me to run or stay put—I had to decide now.

Just as I was about to hobble deeper into the woods, the noise of the helo decreased, as if it had turned. The sound weakened until I couldn't hear it anymore. Either they hadn't spotted the car or they weren't even searching for anyone.

I waited, listening intently for about ten minutes, but the chopper didn't return. Then I got in, cranked the Wrangler and backed onto the road, taking a sapling or two out in the process.

Hoping to glean some news about what had occurred at the Beowulf facility, I fiddled with the radio, hunting for a station. All I got was static.

The road evolved into nothing more than a path of patchy dirt and brush. Since it was getting close to sundown, I needed to pick a place to park for the night.

After another twenty minutes of thumping along searching for a place with enough cover to pull into, I spotted a structure up ahead—a log cabin.

Maybe I was going to get lucky. Knowing my ankle wouldn't allow me to walk too far, I took a risk and drove closer before turning off the engine and getting out. If someone was inside, they could have already seen me. Hopefully, no one was home. My ankle hurt like hell. I grabbed a sturdy fallen branch and used it as a walking stick. That helped with the ankle but irritated my palm.

Finally, I crouched and approached a side window of the

cabin. Rising, I peered through the dirty glass.

CHAPTER 23 - HUNT CAMP
Coconino National Forest

I limped back to the Jeep, turned the key to the on position and powered up the navigation system. I sorted through the menu until I found the GPS with my latitude and longitude coordinates and entered them in *notes* on my smartphone. Then I switched off the ignition and took the key.

After stuffing the gun and a few other items I found in the Jeep into my jacket pockets, I grabbed Kepner's laptop and thumb drive, and headed back to the cabin.

Through the window I had seen a room with a fireplace, an empty gun rack, a rustic, sagging and tattered sofa, and rough-hewn coffee table made with two-by-fours. In the same room was a kitchen area with a wood-burning stove.

A hunt camp. Better yet, an apparently unoccupied hunt camp.

I shambled up the single step to the small uncovered porch, grimacing as I put pressure on my ankle.

Even though there was no evidence of occupation—no vehicle or horse tracks—I still rapped on the door. I guess it was my upbringing and also one last assurance that no one was inside.

I noticed a paper wedged between the planks of the porch. I removed it carefully so it didn't tear. It was a laminated piece of what felt like card stock with a hole punched at the top.

Angling myself so the fading sun shed light on the words, I read the handwritten note.

Dear visitor,

Welcome to my cabin. If you are in need of shelter, please find the door unlocked. I would prefer you open it as intended rather than bust it down in which case it would be a pain and an expense for me to repair when I return for maintenance before the hunting season. Please note that inside there is nothing of value to steal. I would appreciate it if you would leave my getaway as you have found it.

And best of luck on the safe and successful completion of whatever adventure you are on.

Beside the door was a brass hook. Probably where the note had hung. Wind had most likely set it free. I put the note on the hook and turned the doorknob, and as the note promised, the door opened with just a whine of the hinges. I was glad I hadn't needed to bust out a window.

The place was tidy, but with nothing of value in it. If somebody came all the way out here to steal, it would be a long haul for nothing but a sagging old couch. It was a remote hunt camp after all, not the Marriott.

A rectangular wooden table, surrounded by a mix-match of metal and wood chairs, took center stage in the kitchen area. I sat, propped my injured foot up on another chair, and emptied Kepner's stuff from my pockets onto the table. Nothing of particular interest.

Once more I opened the laptop and inserted the flash drive, yielding the same results—Beowulf logo and request for a password. Apparently, the attempt counter resets after a time period. I couldn't think of any new words or phrases to try.

I picked up a ballpoint and a gas receipt I'd salvaged from the glove compartment. Opening my notes on my phone I scribbled down the GPS coordinates. *God bless satellites.* Then I closed the notes and checked my reception. It wasn't strong, but at least I had it. I dialed Kenny.

"Hey, Max, what's my ex-bride up to?"

I went straight to the point. "Kenny, listen, I'm in deep-shit trouble."

I gave him a quick sketch of what had happened and told him I'd fill him in with the details later. I was unnerved, but worked hard to remain calm. I told Kenny my GPA coordinates and asked if he could get the next flight out of D.C. and meet me here. "I need you. You've got to take a shot at cracking this password so I can find out what is on the drive. Whatever it is, people have been killed for it, and I'm most likely next on their to-kill list."

"All right, Max. I'm on my way. I'm not in D.C. I'm in L.A. at a conference, so it won't take me long to get there. I'll bail out of here ASAP and be there in the morning. You're probably safe for now, but keep Kepner's gun on you and stay alert. Good thinking with all the zigzagging. It's a big forest, and for all they know, whoever they are, you headed back home."

"I hope you're right."

"Do this immediately after hanging up. Check your settings on your phone and see if location is turned on. If so, switch it off. Then turn your phone off and take the battery and the SIM card out. Stay put. You might need a little help getting the battery out. Look for a small screwdriver or a razor blade. Do this right away. I mean fast. Do you understand?"

"Yes. What about the navigation system in the car? Can it be tracked?"

"No. Nothing to worry about there. It works off satellites, not network cell towers. Think good thoughts. See you soon."

I pushed the end button. I hurriedly rummaged through drawers and luckily found a small set of screwdrivers for repairing glasses, but I had to use my fingernail to pop open the phone case. After disabling my phone, I sat for a moment as if catching my breath from a 10K race.

The sun had only a few more moments before completely sinking below the horizon as I stared down at the pile on the table. Suddenly, it hit me. *Jesus, Kepner's phone.* I needed to disable it as well. But before I could even pick it up, it rang.

CHAPTER 24 - DEEP WOODS
Coconino National Forest

I stared at the caller ID as the air turned icy. The display read *Tennyson.* Chaucer's last words burst into my head. *Trust no one.* The President, if it really was him, was calling Peter Kepner. Did he know Kepner was a traitor? Or was he deceived just like me?

I pushed *talk* but said nothing.

"Peter?"

"No, Mr. President. It's Maxine Decker."

"Is Peter there?"

"How about I call you right back."

There was a pause. "Of course. You know the number?"

"Yes, sir."

I pressed end. Just as I did back in my Colorado cabin, I dialed the White House main switchboard. When the operator answered, I said, "I'd like to speak to Tennyson."

I was placed on hold for only a few seconds.

"What's going on there, Agent Decker?" I heard no trace of concern in his voice, more of curiosity.

"I'm afraid I have some bad news."

"Which is?"

"Peter Kepner is dead."

"What? How?"

"I killed him."

The President said nothing for at least ten seconds. When he spoke, I noted a slight change in his normally smooth Boston baritone voice. "Now it's my turn to call you back."

"I'll be waiting."

The line went dead.

———

I wanted to pace, to burn off the edginess, but my damn ankle kept me seated. Every creak of the cabin made me flinch. I checked the clip in the gun, then checked it again.

When Kepner's cell finally rang, the caller ID simply read *unknown*. The President explained that he had changed his location and was now calling on a heavily encrypted line. He told me he had not heard from Kepner and the time allotted for the Beowulf security chief's daily report had passed. That's why he called.

I bit down on my bottom lip, unsure of just how much I should reveal. Was there information I should hold back? I concluded that I would spill it all.

My hesitation made him say my name, as if he wondered if I was still on the line.

"Yes. I was just thinking of where to start." It took me a few minutes to tell him what had happened from the moment I was awakened at my home until I shot Kepner and found the hunt camp hiding place. When I finished, I heard him give a long drawn-out sigh.

Finally, he said, "Beowulf was as fortified a stronghold as can be designed. A value can't even be put on what has been lost. And I am not speaking in monetary terms."

"Yes, sir."

"Where is Chaucer's flash drive now?"

I looked at the small USB drive on the table. "I have it."

"I don't want to alarm you, Agent Decker, but you hold a very important key that unlocks what could be the most advanced piece of technology known to man. Under no circumstances can it fall into the wrong hands."

"Who do you consider the wrong hands?"

He sighed again. "At this point, everyone. I'm launching a Special Forces rapid response team to secure the facility until forensics can enter and assess the situation. I'll be sending someone to take you into protective custody and recover the thumb drive. Once that's done, we'll take it from there. Your work is finished."

"I don't understand."

"What part?"

"With all due respect, sir, I was brought into this at *your* request. So far, I've been shot at multiple times, witnessed the murder of the Beowulf director and the kidnapping of the staff. On top of that, I was arrested, and in self-defense, was forced to shoot and kill your trusted man, who happened to be a traitor. I think I deserve a little slack here."

"I admit you have a valid point, but this is way beyond your pay grade."

"Then give me a raise."

"The fewer who know the true nature of Beowulf, the better."

It was obvious he wasn't going to give up any more details. That meant I was on my own until Kenny arrived.

"I want you to sit tight until help gets there. You'll just have to trust me on this, Agent Decker." He hung up.

Trust no one.

CHAPTER 25 - FLEE
Coconino National Forest

It was scary to wonder if I could even trust the President of the United States. Chaucer's words about trust clanged in my mind like off-key church bells. Who was who? The only person I could believe in was Kenny.

I performed the same procedure on Kepner's phone as I had on my own.

Maybe that helicopter I'd seen earlier *had* been searching for me. But maybe they hadn't yet locked on my cell or Kepner's. Otherwise, certainly they would have found me.

Everybody including Kenny and the President wanted me to stay put. That was no longer an option. If the President was part of this, that team he was sending might be unhealthy for me. *I need to get out of here—now.*

The only problem was I had no way to let Kenny know. The best I could do was to leave him a note. And since anyone who arrived ahead of him would also read it, I couldn't be specific.

I pulled a paper towel off a roll by the sink and scratched out a note saying circumstances had changed and I had to leave. I'd get in touch as soon as I could.

If I could get to a small town I'd be able to pick up a disposable phone. But that would probably be after Kenny had deplaned and was at the hunt camp. Timing wasn't on my side.

I planted the note on the table and weighted it with a saltshaker.

After stuffing Kepner's gun in my waistband, I threw

everything back in my jacket pockets, shoved the laptop under my arm again, and headed out to the Jeep. I tossed my coat and the laptop on the passenger seat, but not Kepner's gun, which I positioned under my thigh with the grip sticking out the side for an easy reach. I wanted it ready.

I flexed my cut hand, loosening it up, and was surprised at the lack of pain. Sure there was a little discomfort, but no more than a kitchen nick when cutting a tomato. It was my ankle that was still giving me a fit.

Glancing up at the sky, I saw the stars glittering like they did in the heavens above my mountain cabin. *Damn, Max, how do you manage to get caught up in crap like this?*

I started the engine and turned on the navigation system. I scrolled through the menu and found a Travel Aid for Coconino National Forest. It looked like I wasn't close to much of anything. I did see a route that led in the direction of Flagstaff. I settled on giving it a shot. At least it might get me out of the forest.

Damn, my ankle hurt. And exhaustion was starting to take over. My whole body wanted to surrender to sleep, but the adrenaline kept me awake and jittery. All I needed was a good night's rest, with no worries, back in my Colorado cabin, like I had planned for my retirement. *But, no, Max, you get screwed up in all kinds of shit like you have no sense at all.*

At least the rain had stopped, but the road was muddy, and now I didn't have daylight to aid me. The feel of the road was like trying to stay aboard a slippery eel. As much as I wanted to put the pedal to the floor, I knew better.

The humidity fogged the window so that I had to turn on the windshield wipers and the defogger. For a moment I could see nothing as the fan blew on the windshield. I slowed and waited for the condensation to clear.

It wasn't much help, but I at least had a wispy view of the road.

I glanced at the GPS screen. I had quite a ways to go.

The engine sputtered.

Then it died.

CHAPTER 26 - TOO QUIET
Coconino National Forest

Dawn came fast as Kenny Gates steered the Toyota Cruiser off the blacktop and onto what was probably once a logging road. Based on Maxine's coordinates, his iPhone mapped him along these back roads to the hunt camp where she was hiding.

Earlier, as soon as he hung up from her call, he checked out of his conference hotel, took a taxi to LAX, jumped on a regional commuter for the one-hour fifteen-minute flight to Flagstaff, rented the four by four, and headed out of the city to the national forest in a record five and a half hours.

Several times Kenny pushed the button to spray and wipe the windshield to wash away the splattered mud. He tried to keep the paint of the rental from being scraped off by the overgrowth of tree limbs as he thought back on his long relationship with Max, their marriage and divorce.

They met right after she joined the OSI, fresh out of college with a degree in archaeology and just getting started. Kenny, on the other hand, was an experienced agent, ten years her senior. Few stepped up to help the rookie female agent, so Kenny made time to guide her through the ins and outs of her new job. He acted as mentor, even though their fields of expertise were different. He was an OSI Computer Crimes Investigator specializing in computer forensics and encryption, while Max covered the black market in stolen antiquities. If Air Force military personnel committed a crime, OSI agents were usually called.

After a decade of marriage came their divorce. Max had

become obsessed in her drive to succeed, wanting to spend more time working on her career and less time working on their marriage and starting a family. And Kenny wanted a family, something that always seemed to take a backseat as she rose through the ranks at OSI. It hurt him. But too much time had passed to start digging up those bones.

Then the incident in Iraq—five years after their divorce. Maxine was on a joint OSI-Iraqi sting operation when she was forced to shoot a fellow agent and became critically wounded in the process. The long physical rehab and subsequent Department of Justice investigation that came just short of accusing her of being an accomplice in the smuggling operation nearly destroyed Max.

At that time, Kenny was still confused and hurt about the divorce. Because of the bitterness of the breakup, he didn't go out of his way to defend her during the drawn-out investigation. What she interpreted as his betrayal must have felt like a knife in her back. In the time between the divorce and the Iraqi shooting, they had essentially deserted one another. Still, even with all the pain, Kenny knew that none of it had been because they didn't love each other. He was certain of that. The shooting brought her twenty-year career to an end as she chose retirement and sought solace at her Colorado mountain cabin.

They had really botched their marriage, he thought. What a frigging shame.

He checked the navigation map again. There was still some distance to the hunt camp. Time wasn't moving fast enough. He needed to be there already.

In the early light, through the smeared windshield, Kenny caught a glimpse of a vehicle ahead. As he cautiously approached, the headlights brought a Jeep Wrangler into view. In the next moment he realized the Jeep wasn't moving. He slipped his hand in his carryon on the seat beside him and gripped his SIG Sauer. Fortunately, as a Title 10 federal agent, he was allowed to board a commercial flight with a sidearm. Often, he would hand the flight attendant his United States Air

Force Office of Special Investigations business card and ask that she give it to the captain. On the back he would write, *I am armed.* And just as often, the pilot would make a special trip down the aisle to thank him for being there and for his service.

Kenny made a slow scan of the forest surroundings. There was no movement, not a breath of wind, no birds singing. Nothing.

Too quiet.

Had someone gotten to Max ahead of him? Why was the Jeep just sitting in the roadway? His insides bound into a tight knot at the thought of finding her dead body inside the vehicle.

He pulled to a stop and was about to reach for the door handle when he saw a dark figure standing thirty meters to his left beside a thick tree trunk. At first, the details were hidden in shadow. Then he realized the figure was holding a pistol with both hands, aiming it directly at him.

Kenny pushed the button to lower his window. Then he stuck his head out and called, "If you ever wanted to shoot me, now's your chance."

CHAPTER 27 - SUITS
Coconino National Forest

"If I wanted to shoot you, I'd have done it long before now." I lowered Kepner's gun. "Am I glad to see you." I flashed him a big smile, my relief palpable.

Kenny got out. "You okay?"

"Just banged up a bit and in need of some sleep." I limped toward him. Before I could stop the wave of emotion from rolling over me, I was hugging him and crying into his shoulder. *Safe.* He held me for a minute, and then I pulled back, wiping my nose. "Sorry."

Kenny pulled me close again and smoothed my hair down the back of my head. "It's okay, Max."

We stood there quietly a few more minutes. Finally, I said, "We better get going."

Kenny put my arm around his neck and shoulders and helped me to his SUV.

"Let me look at your ankle." He lifted my leg.

"It's not broken. Just sprained. The boot is stabilizing it. You can fuss over me later when we have more time."

"Want anything out of the Jeep?"

"Grab my jacket and Kepner's laptop in the front seat. We're going to need it."

Kenny helped me slide all the way in the passenger seat. "I'll get it." He closed the door.

When he returned he had my jacket and the computer, along with the portable Garmin. He maneuvered the Toyota around and headed back the way he had come. "What's this all about?"

"Ever hear of Beowulf?"

"Sure. Couldn't get out of high school without reading it."

"No, I mean a secret Air Force black operation—a blacker-than-black op."

Kenny glanced at me then back at the road. "Never."

"You ready for a long story?"

"We've got a long ride."

I began with the middle of the night arrival of Kepner at my cabin, and then told the rest of what had transpired up until Kenny found me.

"Then the President could be deep in the middle of this?"

"I have no idea. At this point, you're the only one I trust. He told me he was sending someone to get me out. They could be at the hunt camp already and know I'm on the run. *Or we could run into them on this road.*"

Kenny stopped the SUV and opened his iPhone GPS navigation app. Then he opened Google Earth.

"What are you doing?"

"Finding the scenic route. Not too many choices, but whoever is coming for you will be on this road for sure."

"I didn't see anyone all night. Nobody until you this morning."

"Takes longer for them to get from DC. If this Beowulf organization is as covert as you say, the President, whether he is on the level or not, has to handpick someone for the job. Lucky they haven't found you already. Could be they are on the way to the camp right now."

Kenny pushed the accelerator. "There's a turn off up ahead. We'll take that."

Suddenly, Kenny's face blanched as we rounded a curve. "Shit. Get down! Throw the jacket over you."

Kenny put his SIG in his lap while I did as he ordered. I pushed the button for the seat to slide way back and I crouched on the floorboard with my head and torso on the seat under the jacket. "What's wrong?" I clutched Kepner's gun close.

"Car coming." He squirmed in the seat.

He put the laptop on top of me, followed by his carry-on from the back seat.

"Close?" I asked.

"In a minute."

Kenny's shirt dropped down beside me. What the hell was he doing taking it off?

"Just stay quiet and don't move."

I heard a click and country music flowed from the radio.

In a moment I could tell the Toyota was slowing and then it came to a stop. I heard the whir of the window going down.

"Hey there," Kenny called. "You need some help?"

A stranger's voice said, "We're looking around for some property. Looks like good area for elk."

"That it is," Kenny said. "Spent the last couple of days fixing up my place so it'll be ready. Probably gonna have to make another trip. Generator took a crap and I've got to get it working so we can use the fridge."

"Know of any places around here for sale? Or ones we can look at?"

"Nothing for sale that I know of, but I can ask around. Got a number or email?"

"Wouldn't want to put you through all the trouble. We're just roaming around the area at this point."

"All righty then. You guys have a good day. Don't get yourselves lost. It's easy to get turned all around up in these parts."

"Thanks. Hey, let me ask. We were going to meet a buddy out here but haven't caught up with him yet. Seen anybody on the road?"

"Not a soul. There's an abandoned car down the road a piece. A Jeep. I stopped, thought maybe somebody had car trouble. But nobody was there. Hope that wasn't your friend's. Good luck."

The vehicle edged forward and I heard Kenny's window go up. "Don't move, yet. They were checking us out. They'll be watching in the rearview."

I kept my scrunched position until Kenny finally told me it was okay to get up.

I sat back up on the seat and looked at his bare chest.

"What are you staring at? You've seen me without a shirt before."

"I think I like your country boy, big game hunter look."

"I had to play the part. Saved your ass, so show some respect for my pecs and abs—I've been working on them."

"Thanks." I twined my fingers in his chest hair. "Looks a little grayer than I remember."

He touched the silver hair at his temples. "Yeah, it's working its way down."

"What made you stop? Think they were the guys looking for me?"

"The driver waved me down. I would've looked suspicious if I'd kept going. And yes, I'm pretty sure they were looking for you. The driver really strained to see what was on the passenger side. And the questions about having seen anyone on the road . . ."

"Maybe they really were elk hunters looking for a place to build a camp."

"Dressed in suits?"

CHAPTER 28 - DISPLACEMENT
Underground desert facility, north of Khartoum, Sudan

Dr. Mostafa Moghaddam stood on the glass-enclosed observation deck and watched the activity below. The Beowulf staff, along with their Iranian counterparts, went about their duties of finishing the construction of the displacement device—a gleaming chrome and glass enclosure big enough to hold two or three standing individuals. It was surrounded by a series of upright, transparent, multi-colored rings. They reminded him of the ones surrounding the planet Saturn, except these stood on end.

As he watched with arms folded, he saw an occasional glance up at him from the Americans, their expressions filled with contempt and fear. From Arizona, they had been smuggled into Mexico, then put on a twenty-hour military transport flight to the Middle East, which had taken its toll. They all looked exhausted from jetlag. Good—they were likely too worn down to fight. But he was taking no chances. Heavily armed Revolutionary Guards were posted around the launch chamber, their eyes constantly taking in every movement of the American scientists.

Mohgaddam checked his watch for the tenth time. Soon, the presidential party would arrive. The newly elected Iranian president, on the job for only two weeks, had already raised the concerns of the West even more so than his predecessor. The constant call for caliphate and cleansing the world of Zionists and Western infidels had ratcheted up the tension to its highest levels in years. Mohgaddam was about to meet the president for the first time, and had no idea what to expect.

As Mohgaddam checked the time again, the doors to the control room swung open and four soldiers armed with assault rifles swept in. They spread out around the room and were followed by a number of imams and administrative assistants. Then the president entered. He was small, Mohgaddam observed, barely breaking one and a half meters. He wore a black suit with an unbuttoned white, point-collar shirt. A pen of the Islamic Republic of Iran graced his lapel. Like the abundance of photos Mohgaddam had seen of the man, he bore his perpetual smile. Only his dark eyes revealed a hidden force that the scientist knew was to be feared.

"Dr. Mohgaddam," the president said as he came to stand beside the scientist in front of the observation window. "I have been looking forward to this moment."

"It is an honor, Mr. President, to have you here to bless our humble facility."

"Although I have only yet been briefed in general terms, I understand that what you are trying to accomplish is anything but humble."

"Thank you," Mohgaddam said with a slight bow.

"How did your meeting go with the Russians?"

"They are anxious to proceed."

"I am sure they are. Almost as anxious to continue sending us their shipments of gold bullion to keep us steadily moving ahead. If they insist in digging up the decomposing corpse of communism, who am I to argue?" He turned back to the window. "So explain to me how your device works. Especially why the first one you built failed. I have little time, so give me the abridged version."

"Mr. President, the first device failed because we did not have control over the size of the displacement, and tried to launch too soon. It was a mistake—"

"Displacement?"

"This may take longer than a few minutes, sir."

"Proceed." The president waved his hand in a gesture to get on with it.

Mohgaddam took in a deep breath. "One of the most profound questions the human race has ever asked is if we are alone in the universe."

"And you can give me the answer?"

Mohgaddam nodded. "We are not alone, sir. That I know beyond a doubt."

"And how can you be so sure?"

"Because the device you see before you is based on technology not of this earth." Mohgaddam paused for a response. When none came, he said, "One of the major problems with believing we have been visited by beings from some other world is the question of how they could travel such vast distances."

"And why they would want to come to this remote rock in the first place."

"Unfortunately, that is something we may never know. But the fact that they did is without question."

"So how?" The president's interest seemed to grow.

"When it comes to technology, we tend to think in terms of mankind's accomplishments in tens of thousands of years; for instance, going from the invention of fire to creating nuclear fusion. The technology you see before you today could easily have come from a civilization hundreds of thousands or even millions of years ahead of us."

"You still haven't told me what displacement is."

Clearing his throat, Mohgaddam said, "Displacement is how the aliens traveled light years in a reasonable amount of time, perhaps months or weeks—maybe even less." Again he waited, but the president never took his eyes off the device being assembled below. "Let me give you an example. When someone draws a bath, once the bather sits down in the tub, the water is displaced by the mass of the bather's body. In this case, the bather is an alien craft launched into the bath of space. The space is displaced as the craft moves through it."

"But space is a vacuum," the president said. "There is nothing in space, certainly not anything like water in a bathtub."

"That is true, to an extent. Space is filled with two things we know little about—dark matter and dark energy. We can see neither, but we know of their existence by how they affect other objects. It is theorized that dark matter fills the universe and is the glue that holds everything together. The alien technology is able to displace dark matter while utilizing dark energy to propel an object quickly across great distances."

"But the distances do not change. It still takes time to make the journey, does it not?"

"As the object or spacecraft moves along the displacement path from its launch coordinates to its target coordinates, it compresses time before it and then expands the time back to normal once it has passed. Keep in mind that the passage of a displacement event is faster than we can imagine. Because of the compression and expansion of time, the object can exceed the speed of light by thousands if not tens of millions of times. Our rules of physics flew out the window when we discovered what these aliens could accomplish."

"I thought one could not defy the laws of physics, especially exceeding the speed of light."

"That is true of the laws as we know them, sir. But there are physics principals we have not yet discovered. Consider this— the planet Gliese 436 is coated in burning ice. Then there is a blue planet only sixty-three light-years from here that gets its color from the constant raining down of molten glass. Not exactly what we would call conforming to our laws of physics."

The president pointed at the device. "It looks like you could not fit more than three people in that thing. Am I to believe an entire spaceship could fit?"

"We are building it to the specifications the Russians supplied us."

"So they want to utilize this displacement device to do what?"

"We know that displacement can propel an object across vast distances—millions of light years—in reasonable amounts of time. Now consider what it could do over short distances— say thousands or hundreds of miles."

The president stared at Mohgaddam. "It would be . . ."

"Instantaneous. We can measure the duration of the displacement in nanoseconds, sir, but in reality, for any distance here on Earth, it would be instant."

"So you put something in that device, hit go, and a couple of nanoseconds later, it shows up someplace else?"

"Yes, sir, with accuracy down to ten thousand microns."

The president rubbed his chin. "And what types of items could you place inside the device."

"If it fits through the portal and the interior dimensions of the enclosure, pretty much anything."

The man with the perpetual smile moved to within inches of Mohgaddam. In almost a whisper, he said, "A weapon?"

The scientist nodded.

The president turned to face his entourage. "Clear the room."

CHAPTER 29 - BLOODHOUND
Flagstaff, Arizona

We sat in the parking lot of the Jack in the Box off Milton Road as I scarfed down a Jumbo Jack and fries. I hadn't eaten since before leaving my Colorado mountain cabin, and was famished.

"Slow down," Kenny said as he watched me.

"I swear this tastes better than a filet from Ruth's Chris."

"That notion will pass quickly."

Prior to stopping at the fast food restaurant, we went to Walmart so Kenny could buy me some bloodstain-free clothes, sneakers, an Ace bandage, pills for pain and to reduce swelling, ice, baggies, and a giant container of wet wipes. After taking a moist towelette "bath" in the backseat of the Toyota SUV, I changed into the fresh jeans and shirt. Next, I took off my boot, wrapped my ankle, and iced it.

"What would motivate a guy like Kepner to turn traitor?" Kenny asked as I finished my burger. "You'd think before they put him in charge of security at a secret facility like Beowulf, he'd have been vetted down to his most recent colonoscopy."

"Good question, especially with his direct ties to the President. Could be money—or maybe he's sympathetic to some cause. Or, let's face it, there are things in everyone's past that can be used to tighten the screws. Whoever wanted the alien relics must have dug up a doozy."

"You got that right. And there are also things people can bury about themselves as long as they have the right connections."

As we talked, I watched a mom struggle to get an infant in a car seat out of the back of an older model Ford. It was a major production that included a big bag of baby stuff. "Chaucer said the artifacts had been missing for two days. I arrived at Beowulf on Thursday, so Kepner must have smuggled them out on Monday night or Tuesday."

"You figure he used the tunnel system?"

"I don't think so, or he'd have anticipated Chaucer's escape route. For all we know, he could have walked out the front door."

"So Chaucer discovers the theft and alerts the President. By Wednesday night, Kepner's on his way to Colorado to bring you to Beowulf. Do you think involving you was part of the plan?"

I shook my head. "I think that came from the President or someone around him, and it probably took Kepner by surprise. The President told me he wanted someone off the radar, and that was me. The problem for Kepner was he had to cover his ass and make sure I didn't get too close to discovering the truth."

"Kepner was likely aware that Chaucer always carried the latest updated info on a flash drive. So he calls in the guys in black with the snazzy Russian assault rifles to get it."

"What also worries me is how those guys were able to move around unrestricted. They shoot up the place and snatch the Beowulf staff, and no one on the outside seems to notice."

"You said yourself that the facility was blacker than black. Why should anyone react to an emergency at a place they don't know exists?"

"In some ways, Beowulf's stealth contributed to their downfall."

My eyes diverted from Kenny as two teenage boys came out of the Jack in the Box and got into a new red Camaro. The big V8 roared as they burned rubber out of the parking lot. More money than brains.

"How Kepner got the artifacts out doesn't matter," I said as the smell of the tires reached our car. "We need to find out where he took the pieces and who he gave them to."

"No telling where the handoff took place. We need a bloodhound."

"We've got Kepner's GPS, don't we? Don't those things have memory?" I reached for Kepner's Garmin, which Kenny had grabbed from the Jeep, and plugged it into the car's 12-volt socket. "Let's see where he's been."

Once it powered on, I chose *previous destinations*. The most recent was from Monday night. When I selected it, a map of Flagstaff appeared, and an electronic voice said, *When you can safely do so, please make a U-turn.*

I turned to Kenny. "How about a digital bloodhound?"

CHAPTER 30 - THE HANDOFF
Flagstaff, Arizona

Kenny and I stood at the registration desk of the single-story Butler Avenue Sunset Motel. A woman in her mid-twenties emerged from a back office.

"Can I help you?" she asked.

Kenny pulled his OSI Department of Defense ID from his jacket and held it for her to see. "I'm Special Agent Kenneth Gates. This is Special Agent Maxine Decker. We need to ask you a few questions, if you don't mind."

The smile faded as the girl stared at Kenny's badge and photo ID. "Sure, I guess. What kind of questions?" She glanced around as if seeking out a manager or coworker.

Kenny put his ID away. "We're looking for information on someone who may have been a guest here last Monday night."

"Sorry, but I'm not allowed to give out information about our guests. You'll have to talk to my manager tomorrow."

Kenny hardened his expression. "We're investigating a matter of national security involving a federal employee. If you would rather, I'll be happy to arrange for a United States Marshal to serve a federal search warrant. I can have him here within thirty minutes." He motioned to a couch. "We can wait over there."

Even I was impressed with Kenny's authoritative tone. I knew he lived to talk tough like that.

The girl seemed unable to make a decision. I pointed to her computer screen. "The name of the man we're looking for is Peter Kepner."

I could see her start to crumble as we both pressured.

"You could save us a great deal of time if you checked your records to see if he stayed here last Monday night."

I gave her a motherly smile. "Your full cooperation will be noted in our report to the regional office of the FBI."

"I definitely want the report to say I cooperated." Turning to her keyboard, the girl typed in some parameters and waited for the results. "This is kind of a quiet time of year for us. Should be easy to see if . . ." Leaning in toward the screen, she shook her head. "No Peter Kepner registered here Sunday, Monday, or Tuesday."

"Any men traveling alone book a room during those three days?" I asked.

She continued typing. "Four regulars. Mostly long-haul truckers."

"That's all?" Kenny asked.

"No, there were a couple of families passing through—tourists."

"No one else?" Looked like we'd hit a dead end.

"Just a woman."

"She a regular, too?" I tried to get a better angle to see the monitor but wasn't successful.

"No. Actually, she was Canadian. I remember because I was on duty and checked her in myself. Her picture ID was a Canadian passport. She was really pretty."

"Did you make a copy?" I asked, wondering if Kepner could have handed off the alien artifacts to a woman. I was guilty of profiling—I'd been picturing a man.

"Yes, we retain a copy of all photo IDs. Hang on and I'll go get it." She went to the office and returned a half-minute later. "Here you go."

Kenny and I stared at the picture. Patricia Barney from Calgary, with light-colored hair that fell to her shoulders, wearing a turtleneck under a blazer and a string of small pearls. The best passport photo I'd ever seen.

"Do you have surveillance video of the parking lot that might show this guest and whether she had any visitors on

Monday night?" I folded the copy of the passport and slipped it into my pocket.

"I hope I don't get into trouble—"

"You won't," Kenny said.

She swiveled the monitor around. "I can call up the recording disk from here. Just give me a sec."

Kenny and I glanced hopefully at each other.

"This is the camera that would show any visitors to the Canadian woman's room."

I remembered the GPS device showed 8:30 PM as the time Kepner programmed the route request. "Can you forward to eight PM?"

The girl nodded. A moment later the timestamp displayed 8:03.

"Go ahead and fast forward," Kenny said.

At 8:52, a Jeep pulled up in front of the woman's room. "That's him," I said as we watched Kepner get out and knock on the door to the motel room. A few seconds later, it opened and he went inside.

"Want me to fast forward again?"

"Please," Kenny said.

At 9:05, Kepner emerged. He went quickly to his Jeep, backed out, and drove out of the frame.

"When did Patricia Barney check out?" I asked.

The clerk went back to the previous screen. "Six the next morning. Paid with a credit card."

"We'll need a copy of the bill and card number," Kenny said.

The girl shrugged as if she was already in this so deep, why refuse now. A moment later, she handed over a copy of the bill and card info.

"You've been extremely helpful," I said. "You've assisted in the possible apprehension of a criminal. We thank you."

She looked pleased with herself as we turned and left the lobby, heading for Kenny's rental.

Once inside the car, Kenny said, "The woman could be anywhere by now."

"True, but if she left the country using that passport, there'll be a record with TSA."

"Let me make some calls and see what I can come up with."

I reached to the back seat and pulled Kepner's laptop from Kenny's bag. Booting it up, I removed Chaucer's thumb drive from my pocket and plugged it in a USB port. As before, the Beowulf logo appeared and in an entry box, the cursor blinked, waiting for a password.

"Whatever's on this drive was worth a great deal to Kepner. Any ideas to try for a password?"

"None. And I've got a feeling that even if I had access to a Cray supercomputer, that drive is so encrypted that it would take decades to crack, if at all."

"There's no way you could break in?"

"About the only thing that could do it within a reasonable amount of time would be a quantum computer. And no one's been able to build one of those, yet."

I turned and stared at my ex-husband.

"What?" he said.

I reached and patted his thigh. "Today might be your lucky day."

CHAPTER 31 - MOON SHADOW
The East Rim

"How will you know where to turn off the highway?" Kenny asked as we drove north on 89. "Even with a bright, full moon, everything looks the same to me."

"I'll know." I watched the dusty gray of the moonlit landscape roll by. It appeared alien and foreboding. But I knew we had to try to get back to the Beowulf facility. The answer to what resided on Chaucer's thumb drive could only be unlocked by a quantum computer. We had to find out what was really going on before more people died.

We had lain low during the day, resting at a remote campground outside of Flagstaff. I was able to catch up on my sleep and later fill Kenny in on the events of the last few days, including why both the Roswell artifacts and the quantum computer were housed in the same location. I could tell by his constant grinning that he was itching to get his hands on the most powerful computer in the world. He loved anything technological, and that's what made him so good at his job.

"Pull over here and kill the lights," I said as we passed a cluster of old mobile homes and shacks on the west side of the road. It was the first landmark I remember right after I was arrested. I recalled thinking the abandoned trailers might have belonged to the Navajo.

For five minutes we sat on the shoulder with few cars passing in either direction. When there were no headlights for miles, I said, "Let's go. The turnoff should be right up on the left." It only took a second to spot it.

"How close do you think we can get to the facility?" he asked. "The place could still be crawling with bad guys. Or the good guys have it locked down. Either way, they won't welcome visitors."

"Even if someone is there, we might be able to get in undetected through Chaucer's escape route. No one else seemed to know about it. We can take the car to the point where I ran into the ranger. After that, the rest will be on foot."

"How's your ankle. Will it hold out?"

I wiggled it and was surprised that it did feel better. The swelling was gone. "No choice, unless you want to carry me."

He grunted.

"I'll re-wrap it tight and put my boots back on. It really isn't that painful any more. Ice and ibuprofen are good things."

"I don't know if you are tough or stubborn." Kenny turned on the radio. The old song "Where or When" came on and softened my tension. The lyrics reminded me of the two of us.

Kenny followed my directions. Though the road was unpaved and rough, it was travel-worthy. Frequent use by the Forestry Service probably helped maintain the grade. We drove over the hill and Kenny hummed to the music. I rested my head against the window. I'd missed his confidence and his strength. This was the safest I'd felt since escaping Beowulf.

The panorama was the opposite of the Coconino Forest— this was nearly barren landscape of flat earth, sagebrush, and plateaus stretching as far as I could see. I hoped I had picked the right place.

After a couple of minutes, Kenny asked, "You sure this is the road?"

"Trust me." We moved on to a spot where another dirt road intersected. "This is it."

Kenny pulled the car over and turned it off. I got out, and in the light from the headlamps I pointed to the splashes of dirt where the bullets had pummeled the ground. A handful of spent casings reflected back at me. "The ranger was shot here." A dark spot contrasted with the desert sand. "We're definitely heading in the right direction."

"How far to the rim?"

"Two hours, give or take."

"Then it's a go. We'll take it slow and rest your ankle now and again."

He grabbed a flashlight from the back of the SUV, turned off the headlights, and locked the car.

"Don't use the light unless we need it," I said. "Someone could spot it for miles. Besides, the moon and stars are amazingly bright way out here."

No flashlight made the going a little more treacherous. A noise diverted my attention. "Listen. Hear that?"

Kenny froze and cocked his head. We stood quiet for a few moments. "What did you hear?"

"Could have been a helicopter, but I didn't see any lights." I prayed we hadn't been found. I was on edge and my senses on overdrive. "Probably just the wind."

After about thirty minutes, I was limping. The uneven ground didn't help. As time passed, I needed to stop more often and give the ankle a break. I hated the time lost, but I wouldn't be able to make it all the way without the stops.

"It shouldn't be far now," I said, estimating how long we had traveled. I leaned on Kenny for support. By the time my ankle had about given out, we arrived at the rim. In case anyone might be guarding the entrance to the tunnel, we spent time in the shadows of a large rock formation, watching for movement and listening—and resting my ankle. Satisfied we were clear, we decided to take our shot.

"The path down to the gate is somewhere near here," I said. "We're close."

The full moon provided enough light to make out objects and shadows. No need for Kenny's flashlight.

It didn't take long for me to locate the path. "Here it is," I said, and we started down, Kenny one step behind me.

Finally, the gate appeared and I opened it. The old hinges gave out a tepid squeak.

Like the dark patch of the ranger's blood in the desert, a

similar dark patch appeared on the rock floor, unmistakable in the splashes of moonlight.

"The tunnel's no secret anymore."

"Why?" he asked.

"Someone took Chaucer's body."

CHAPTER 32 - BACK TO THE FUTURE
The East Rim

I had barely known Chaucer, but pausing at the location of his death made my belly tighten with sadness and fright.

"If they know about this tunnel and nobody has stopped us, that means the facility is probably empty," Kenny said. "Most likely the guards are posted at the main entrance and its immediate perimeter."

"Maybe. Keep alert."

The moonlight through the gate faded, and the air chilled as we took the first bend in the tunnel and moved farther along the passage. Kenny switched on the flashlight.

My ankle throbbing, I kept one hand on his shoulder as he led the way. My toe stubbed into a pile of rubble rock, and a few pebbles skittered away, echoing off the stone. My heart pummeled.

He killed the light and we froze, listening and watching for a sign that someone had heard the noise. After a few moments, we continued on the winding and gradually descending path.

In the distance I saw a dim glow flagging the end of the tunnel where it emptied into the first of the caverns filled with the Egyptian-style hieroglyphics and carvings. *Does that mean the electricity is still on inside?* I blinked, thinking I saw a shadow—a man's silhouette—briefly in the pale glow.

I squeezed Kenny's shoulder. "Did you see that?" I whispered.

"Shh."

He positioned me against the wall and then stood beside me. We waited. I thought I heard a faint scraping of soles on stone and sand. Then silence.

"Guess I'm a little jumpy," I whispered. "There's only scattered emergency lighting." We finally started forward again.

During our trek across the moonlit plateau, I had described the Egyptian-looking artifacts to Kenny. But as we entered the first of the caverns holding the strange ancient relics, he blurted, "My god." He shined the light around, his mouth agape. "Max, you didn't do this place justice."

"Wish we had time for a tour."

Kenny reluctantly turned away from viewing the massive collection of artifacts and led the way through the connecting chambers until a set of metal doors came into view. They stood partially open. Passing through the gap, we entered the Beowulf facility. A corridor led to another door, one that had required Chaucer's thumbprint to open. Now it was partially ajar, the biometric fingerprint lock replaced with a black, jagged hole.

"This is the stuff they collected from the Roswell crash site." Even in the faint glow of the emergency battery lights, I could tell all the chrome and glass dazzled Kenny.

"It's more than I can take in at one time," he said, shining his light around the room. "We gotta come back here for a closer look."

"If we don't unlock that thumb drive, we might not live to see it again." I pointed ahead. "The quantum computer is on the lower level."

"Lead the way, boss."

We descended the steps and arrived at the glass enclosure housing the computer terminal and operator's position. I opened a door on the side of the enclosure and Kenny entered. He sat and glared at the unpretentious, almost simplistic keyboard and monitor array. It was then that I noticed what lay beyond the smoked glass wall behind the computer terminal. Three black mainframes, each about the size of a refrigerator, stood like monoliths. It occurred to me that there may not be any electricity to power up. I held my breath as Kenny reached for a switch on the front of the terminal.

"Know what you're doing?"

He gave me an evil look. Then he flipped the switch.

Nothing happened.

"Impressive."

"You wanna drive?" Kenny leaned back with his hands behind his head, his standard posture for deep thought. "Up until now, I had no idea one of these actually existed. And you expect me to know how to turn it on? Cut me some slack."

That's when I felt a distant hum that seemed to enter my body through the floor and flow up my legs. At the same time, the sleeping mainframes started coming to life. Rather than LEDs or other processing indicators, the front of each began to radiate from different areas of the surface. The glowing became brighter as the hum increased in strength. Then the monitor array also flashed on and a multitude of virtual boxes appeared, each offering areas in which to input information.

Kenny watched intently as the glow of the mainframes and monitors washed over him. I had seen that look of wonder on his face many times before. He had just entered a different world from the one the rest of us occupy. I knew better than to interrupt what was like a technology drug to my ex-husband.

"How about I leave you to play with your new toy while I take a look around." I grabbed the flashlight. "And good luck finding a USB slot on that monster. If there is one."

Never taking his eyes off the light show, he said, "What are you going to look for?"

"The Monk's Tale."

CHAPTER 33 - THE MONK'S TALE
Beowulf Headquarters

I couldn't help but be mesmerized once again by all the artifacts, displays, and schematics, and the wealth of knowledge stored there. As I stood rooted, surveying all the incredible clues to the past and future that surrounded me, I wondered why most of the depository remained unscathed. If Beowulf was lost, it could compare to the loss of the Imperial Library of Constantinople or the ancient Library of Alexandria. Beowulf wasn't filled with papyrus scrolls and codices, but the riches of its content were just as impressive.

The facility had not been ransacked. The strike on Beowulf was surgical.

And where were the bodies? I'd seen security guards go down during the attack. All bodies, including Chaucer's, were gone. Who removed them—the attackers or the government?

Other questions tumbled through my mind on the way into Chaucer's office, but I had no answers to any of them. It would have been so much easier to hand over the flash drive to the President—if we were certain he wasn't involved. The situation was much too convoluted at this point.

Chaucer's office surprised me. It *had* been ransacked. The raiders must have been searching for the thumb drive. As chief of security, Kepner must have been aware of the drive and had informed the assault team.

The desk drawers were emptied onto the floor and the bookshelves swept clean. Chaucer's executive chair was overturned.

A noise behind me made me turn. The scene was eerie in the illumination of only the emergency lighting. Shadows played haunting tricks, and I felt like a child again, in bed at night scared of the ominous dark dancing silhouettes of my window curtains on the wall. I shone the flashlight in all directions but there were no ghosts, no monsters under the bed. And no terrorists.

Turning the desk chair upright, I saw that the cushion had been slashed open and the foam torn out. Shining the beam on the books, I gathered and stacked a few of them on the desk and checked the titles. The genres ran the full gamut from classical fiction to advanced theoretical physics. Many of the older volumes appeared to be first editions. After going through a dozen books I lifted the next and checked its spine. *The Canterbury Tales.*

I shoved the others to the side and sat. The cover of the The Canterbury Tales had the image of a robed man riding a prancing white steed and a passage in elaborate script written in Middle English. That wasn't a good sign. If it was the original version I was going to have a difficult time reading it.

I opened the cover and flipped through the front matter. Keeping my beam trained on the title page I discovered a handwritten note.

To Jeff, Congratulations upon your graduation. I am so proud of your achievements.

Below that, also handwritten, was a quote.

What a heavy burden is a name that has become too famous. — Voltaire

May your success be so great that you must carry such a burden.

Love,

Aunt Lillian

In the Voltaire quote the word *name* was highlighted with a yellow marker. A clue? Had his aunt done the highlighting or had Chaucer? I reread the Voltaire quote again and thought there was much truth in its advice, but also in Aunt Lillian's wish. I turned the page and began flipping through the book. I'd been right. There was neither a modern translation nor any sidebars for assistance.

When I came to The Monk's Tale, I stopped and read, or made my best attempt at sifting through what, to me, was mostly gibberish. I did however get somewhat of a notion of what each story was about. Instead of a single poetic tale, there were multiple, each with a famous person as the title. I struggled through, sometimes speaking the words aloud in hopes that it would make better sense.

I scanned the tale several times. Each individual story told by the Monk was about a fall from grace—people of high rank descending to misery or death. But nothing came to me or stood out as a clue to the password. Where was the clue that the dying Chaucer wanted me to find? Or had he been rambling nonsense? I slammed the book closed. The only interesting thing in the whole book was the dedication to Jeff from Aunt Lillian. I wondered if Chaucer was his real surname—Jeffrey Chaucer, like Geoffrey Chaucer? Was that why *name* was underlined? Or for some other reason?

I propped my elbows on the desk and rested my forehead in my hands, pressing the heels to my eyes. *What, what, what?*

After a few minutes, I decided to give it another shot and opened the book to the Voltaire quote with the highlight. I wrote down the quote with no spaces between the words. Plenty of letters, but even computers with a basic hacker program could quickly pull out the letters in chunks that made words. No, that couldn't be it. And what did that have to do with The Monk's Tale?

I opened to The Monk's Tale. What about page numbers? No, they would be in order, which would be another easy decipher.

Starting at the beginning of the collection, I let the pages bristle past my thumb while examining them for other highlights. Nothing.

There were no clues other than Chaucer's whispering to me as he was dying, and the highlighted word, *name*.

Why single out the word *name* in the entire Voltaire quote? Still, the quote wasn't in The Monk's Tale. It was just a part of a dedication. If Aunt Lillian had done it, then there was no connection, but suppose Chaucer had marked it with the yellow marker? Then that would mean something. But what?

Name. I turned to The Monk's Tale again and thumbed through it. As I did, something clicked. Each tale was titled with the name of the character who suffered the tragedy. Was that it? But then if it was the combination of the names, a computer—hell most people—could figure that out. I found a piece of paper and rummaged through the mess on the desk until I recovered a pen. Then I wrote a list of the names—all 17 of them. What could make them random, so random that there would be no pattern, no encryption for a computer to unscramble?

I thought back to the escape from Beowulf and Chaucer's last words. Trust no one. That made sense. He was lucid, not out of his mind. So, when he said I needed to find The Monk's Tale, he was definitely giving me a clue. He wasn't delirious. I concentrated, trying to hear his voice again. Had I missed anything? *First find The Monk's Tale.* Well, I had done that, so what next? I stretched back in the chair, rubbing my temples, listening in my mind again to Chaucer's faint whispering. *Agent Decker, first—"* Then he had coughed, kind of a gurgling cough. *First, first find the Monk's Tale. Nothing is as it seems.*

He'd said *first* three times, stumbling over his words. Then an idea popped into mind. What if he wasn't stumbling?

I rested the flashlight on the desk and grabbed the paper and pen.

CHAPTER 34 - THE COLONEL
Beowulf facility

I traced my way back through the darkened halls past the expanse of glass-partitioned workstations around the central hub. The ibuprofen Kenny had bought in town was keeping my discomfort in check and I was walking with no more than a slight limp. I was about to turn a corner when I heard voices.

Kenny was saying, "It's empty. I swear there's nothing there."

A man's voice, thick with a Russian accent said, "You are lying."

I peered around the corner and saw a tall man dressed in black combat gear holding a gun on my ex.

"See for yourself." Kenny motioned to a screen on the monitor array. "The password opened the thumb drive, but there's nothing on it."

The low hum of the quantum computer mainframes suddenly faded, as did the lights on the front of the three colossal machines. The monitor array grew faint and went black.

"What have you done?"

Kenny held up his hands. "Nothing. The emergency backup power for the mainframes must have run out."

"Turn the computer back on." The Russian punctuated his demand by bringing the automatic pistol closer to Kenny's face.

"It is on, Colonel. I'm telling you the power has run down."

Whoever the colonel was, I heard him breathe out a heavy

sigh. "Get the thumb drive. Let us go find your wife."

"We're divorced."

"Then she is a smart woman. Now retrieve the drive."

I slipped Kepner's handgun from my waistband and backed into a dark corner. I waited until Kenny and the colonel passed beside me. As they did, I rammed the barrel of the gun against the Russian's skull. "Freeze!"

"I guess we found her," Kenny said.

"Place your weapon and cell phone on the floor and back away with your hands up," I said.

The Russian complied.

"Kenny, you okay?"

Kenny picked up the gun and pointed it at the Russian. "I'm fine. I never saw this guy coming. He surprised me from behind while I was engrossed in the computer."

"Well, now we've given him a little surprise." I took the gun away from his head but still kept a bead on him. "You won't need this anymore." I stomped on the Russian's cell and crushed it under my heel. "And who are you?"

"I have already introduced myself to your husband."

"Ex," I corrected. "But I'd like my own special introduction. So go ahead, please."

"Colonel Nikolai Vyshinsky of the new Soviet Army."

I hesitated for a moment trying to understand what I had just heard. "The new *Soviet* Army?"

"That is correct, Agent Decker."

He knew my name.

"Colonel Vyshinsky," I said, "either you haven't been keeping up with the world events or you're living in a fantasy world."

"How is that?"

"The U.S.S.R ceased to exist in 1991."

"I was referring to the *New* Soviet Union. The one that is about to become a reality."

"Here's what's really about to become a reality," I said. "You're going to get us out of here or you're going to die trying."

"You have an impressive power of persuasion, Agent Decker." He motioned back in the direction of the tunnels. "After you."

"Not likely," I said, and waved the gun for him to go first.

"Why not go out the front?" Kenny asked.

I knew he was fishing for info.

"There is no electricity for the elevator, Agent Gates. And the front entrance is under guard by your military."

That answered our question about security around the facility. And how Vyshinsky had gotten in.

"How do you know about the tunnel but the military guarding this place doesn't?" I asked.

"Perhaps you would like to go ask them?" Vyshinsky smiled but it wasn't friendly.

I wondered if he had discovered the tunnel during the attack and followed me out. He could be the one who shot the ranger and tried to take me out. At this point, it didn't matter.

"Then the tunnels it is," I said. "Don't try to be a hero."

"I am already a Hero of the Soviet Union, awarded in 1990 for bravery in the First Afghan War. Being a hero again would be redundant."

"Congratulations on your medal. Now move," I said.

Colonel Vyshinsky shined his flashlight as he led us back through the artifacts room and into the caverns. The emergency lighting was down to nothing—the only thing we had was our collective flashlights.

"So was that your man I shot and killed somewhere around here?" I asked as we inched our way along the gradual incline of the tunnel.

"Yes," Vyshinsky said. "He should have anticipated you being armed. He disappointed me."

"What's this all about?" Kenny asked. "Why attack Beowulf? Kill Chaucer?"

"So many questions," Vyshinsky said. "Why not accept the fact that what is done is done and move on?"

"How did you turn Kepner?" I asked.

"Peter Kepner was a CIA counter-intelligence officer. On

his first assignment as a case officer, he was stationed in Turkey, where his job was to target Soviet intelligence officers for recruitment. We saw through his cover."

"And? How did you get to him?"

"He had financial problems in his personal life—alcohol abuse and high-stakes gambling debts. Kepner began spying for us in 1985, when he walked into the Soviet Embassy in Washington and offered to reveal secrets for money. It was easy to see his potential."

"And the attack on Beowulf?" I asked.

Vyshinsky stopped, then turned to face us. "Agent Decker, I assume you were fascinated with all the things Chaucer showed you, were you not?"

I nodded.

"Multiply that fascination to the tenth power. What my comrades and I are about to do with that alien technology will advance mankind by hundreds of thousands if not a million years."

We all stood in silence for a full thirty seconds.

"Bullshit," I said. "Keep walking."

Vyshinsky shrugged, turned around, and continued up the tunnel.

Kenny and I glanced at each other, doubt and uncertainty in our eyes. I would have branded the colonel a nutcase except for what Chaucer had revealed to me. But a million years? Please.

We walked on in silence until we came to the gate, then made our way up the side of the cliff to the plateau.

I took the bottle of ibuprofen from my pocket and dumped four tablets into my palm. I tossed the meds in the back of my mouth and choked them down. It wasn't easy without using water as a chaser, but I managed to swallow them. Between those and Kenny's help, I hoped I'd be able to tolerate the hike.

I shoved Vyshinsky in the direction of where we had left the rental. "It's a two-hour walk, Colonel," I said. "You look fit. Let's go."

Our flashlights only lit a short distance, so we relied mostly on the moon to light the way for us, but a few high-altitude clouds had diffused its brilliance. I wanted us to be back at the car before dawn. We still needed the darkness on our side. Careful not to stumble, we moved on across the other-worldly landscape.

"So what exactly are you going to do with the alien technology?" Kenny asked.

"I have no intention of revealing the details. I'm not even sure you could grasp the concept."

"Try me," I said.

"Are you familiar with Albert Einstein's famous equation, E equals MC squared?"

"Of course."

"He got it wrong."

CHAPTER 35 - END OF THE LINE
East of the Grand Canyon

The horizon was turning from black to dark gray when we arrived at Kenny's rental.

"End of the line, Colonel," I said. "I hope you've enjoyed our moonlit desert hike."

He seemed to take the news in stride as I said, "A couple of days ago, a sniper tried to kill me and a park ranger right here on this spot. You wouldn't know anything about that, would you?"

"If I had wanted you dead, Agent Decker, you would not be standing here right now."

"Or you're a bad shot," Kenny said.

The colonel chuckled.

"What's to stop me from putting a bullet in you and leaving your body for the vultures?" I asked.

Vyshinsky smiled. "Nothing." He shrugged. "You do have a reputation of shooting people—your former partner, your twin sister, and a terrorist intent on blowing up Las Vegas. So if you did pull the trigger right now, I would not be shocked."

The thought of accidentally killing Francine in that horrible incident in Cuba made me burn with anger. "No, you'd have no time to be shocked. You'd be dead, because I am an excellent shot. However, I don't kill for sport. That's not my nature. Now give Agent Gates your flashlight."

As Vyshinsky handed it over, I continued, "Colonel Nikolai Vyshinsky of the new Soviet Army, how did you get to Beowulf, anyway?"

"Why should I tell you, Agent Decker of the OSI?"

"Because in your heart, you want me to know how clever you are. You've been waiting for me to ask that question. We didn't pass any other vehicles along our trek."

"Ha! You got me," Vyshinsky said and laughed. "Women are like cats—so curious. Perhaps sometimes to a fault. Now, your ex-spouse, he does not care how I got here. To him it does not matter. To you, it is a worm burrowing in your brain, an itch you need to scratch."

"Never mind," I said. "You're enjoying this too much. I'd rather you were miserable."

"Let's go, Max," Kenny said. "Don't waste any more time on him. We should just shoot the bastard."

"By helicopter," Vyshinsky said. "My comrades dropped me off. They will be back soon. You should stick around and meet them."

"We'll pass," I said.

There were a few trees spotting the area. Kenny shoved the colonel over to one a few meters away. He slipped the colonel's belt out of the waistband loops. "Turn around." He pulled Vyshinsky's arms behind him around the tree and strapped the Russian's wrists together. Before threading the buckle's prong through a hole in the belt, Kenny gave it one last strong tug. Vyshinsky groaned.

"That should keep you. I'll make an anonymous call to the local sheriff and give your location. Make up whatever story you want. I think they'll get to you before the coyotes."

"We'll meet again, Agent Gates."

"Looking forward to it."

Kenny and I headed for the SUV.

I watched Vyshinsky fade into the night in the side mirror. Then I turned to Kenny. "Are you telling me that after all the shit that's happened, Chaucer's thumb drive is empty?"

In the faint illumination of the dashboard lights, I saw Kenny smile. "There's a boatload of data on it."

"So why didn't it display? The drive appeared blank."

"There's a hidden partition that doesn't show up until you

have a separate password to open it. I checked the volume properties just before Vyshinsky showed up. The drive appears empty, but the invisible partition is taking up about eighty percent of the space."

"That's great news."

"Actually, it's not."

"Why?"

"It'll take another quantum computer to break the encryption."

I glanced at the copy of The Canterbury Tales in my lap. "I was sure I had broken the drive's password."

"What did you come up with?"

"The first letter of each name title in The Monk's Tale." I explained how I had come up with that conclusion and read him the letters from the paper I had stuffed in my pocket.

"You nailed it," he said. "Except for one minor detail."

"Are you saying I have the same deductive powers as a quantum computer?"

"Not exactly. A quantum computer computes at ridiculous speeds, but science hasn't been able to recreate the brain and all it can do. You had Chaucer's words, his clues, and access to the source. You got the password almost right, only the correct one is backwards from yours."

"Maybe it's the same for the hidden partition."

"I tried that. No luck."

"Since we no longer have a quantum computer, I guess there's only one thing left to do."

"Which is?"

"Exactly what I was hired to do. Find the alien artifacts."

CHAPTER 36 - FAVORS
Flagstaff, Arizona

"You know what I don't understand?" I stared out the windshield at the thin orange horizon of breaking dawn. "Why did Chaucer give me *The Monk's Tale* clue if that wouldn't help me decipher the second password? Does that make sense?"

"Maybe he trusted that you were smart enough to realize there was something more than a blank drive. He reasoned you would then get it to a tech guy who would check the properties and see there was data stored in a hidden partition."

"But why didn't he give me that passcode?"

"Who knows? Maybe it's too long and you'd never have been able to remember it."

My brain was fried from thinking. "There's something else. Could be when he told me 'Nothing is as it seems' meant the code I would discover was really backward? Or maybe he meant it would seem like the drive was empty. Who knows what the man was trying to say."

"We probably won't ever get answers to that, Max, so let it go and concentrate on what we do know."

Kenny was right. Getting riled up wasn't moving us forward.

I twisted so I could see in the rear of the SUV. "We've got Kepner's stuff from his car—his laptop, GPS, and the contents of his pockets and glove box. And we have Patricia Barney's ID, the copy of *The Canterbury Tales*, and various items."

"What's our next move?"

I studied the clutter then turned back around. "I vote we

find Barney. If Kepner did hand off the artifacts to her, then she's our only lead. Instead of follow the money, this would be a follow-the-artifacts approach."

Kenny laughed. "Or it could be a follow-the-money deal if Patsy girl turns out to be a prostitute and Kep boy was lonely."

"I like your choice of words. *Lonely*. Yeah, right."

"Or she could have just been a fuck buddy."

"Or she's got the artifacts."

"I'm going with that one, too," Kenny said. "That settles it. RadioShack, here we come."

———

After purchasing several burner phones, Kenny parked the rental in a crowded supermarket parking lot in case the colonel came searching. He stuffed all of Kepner's articles into a backpack he'd purchased earlier at Walmart, and strapped it on. We walked a couple of blocks to a diner for breakfast.

"I've got to call DC3," he said once we settled into a booth. "Request some time off. I haven't taken a vacation in two years. I think they'll work with me."

After we ordered, Kenny used one of the cell phones.

"Hey, Major. This is Kenny Gates. Yes, the conference was great, but it kept me on the go from six AM to midnight every day. I'm beat. I need a little time off. R and R. I'd like to use up some of that vacation time. Think that's workable?"

He paused, listening.

"Yes, that would be perfect. Sure you don't need me? Nothing pressing at the moment?"

He listened again and then laughed. "Yes, I know, OSI can run without me. I appreciate it. Thanks, Major."

Kenny ended the call. "I've got one more favor to call in."

Our breakfast was served and we ate with hardly a word in between bites. Finished, Kenny paid in cash.

When we got back to the rental, he looked over the copies we had of Patricia Barney's ID.

"Got anything cooking in that head of yours?" I asked.

"Not yet."

"What's the other favor you were going to call in?"

He picked up the cell and dialed, then held up one hand to silence me.

"Hey, Bo. This is Kenny. I need a favor."

I gave Kenny a curious look. He waved me off.

"I need you to run a background check." He spelled Patricia Barney's name and read off her credit card number. "And run her passport through TSA to find out recent travel destinations and dates."

As he gave out the information I wondered if that was really her name and if we were going on a wild-goose chase for a one-night-stand tryst.

"Right, I'll wait for your call." Kenny gave him the cell number. "Are you sure you can do it within the hour?"

My ex winked as he spoke to his friend. That was a good sign.

"All right, guy. You're the best. One more thing. Let's keep this between the two of us for now, okay? Perfect." Kenny ended the call.

"Well?" I said.

"My contact will have what we need before the hour is up."

"That fast?"

"It's all about connections, favors, and technology. He just has to be careful not to attract attention."

Thirty minutes later the phone rang. Kenny answered and listened. "Great. Thanks. I owe you."

"Good news?" I asked as he put the phone on the seat.

"Hope so."

He started the engine. "Got your passport, Max?"

CHAPTER 37 - LETHAL DOSE
American Consulate, Amsterdam, The Netherlands

"Patricia Barney is not her real name," said CIA Station Chief Mark Terry. "But you probably already figured that out." Terry sat across from the two of us in a conference room at the American Consulate. He appeared to be in his mid-fifties, balding, with thick-rimmed glasses and a gray goatee. Behind him, an expansive window framed the Van Gogh Museum across the street.

Kenny and I had racked up some serious frequent flyer miles after leaving Flagstaff and flying on to Phoenix, Chicago, and finally Amsterdam. The jetlag was killing me, and all I wanted to do was check into our hotel and sleep. Kenny, on the other hand, had consumed enough coffee along the way to keep awake for a month.

Kenny's contact had called while we were driving back to Flagstaff. TSA confirmed that Barney had flown from JFK to Schiphol Airport in Amsterdam six days ago. That's where we decided to head first.

"She checked into the Amsterdam Marriot before taking a taxi to the RAI Center," Terry was saying. "Her attendee card barcode was scanned when she entered the international electronics tradeshow."

"Do we know if she visited any exhibits or booths while she was there?" I asked, trying not to yawn.

Terry shook his head. "We've asked for access to the surveillance footage, but the tradeshow management is slow to respond. We've got the local *politie* putting pressure on them."

"But you're sure the body in the morgue is her?" Kenny asked.

"No doubt. The fingerprints match what's on file with Interpol. Patricia Barney goes under a number of aliases, but her real name is Lela Goldman. She was born in Tel Aviv thirty-eight years ago, joined the Israeli army as a teen, and became one of the most decorated snipers on record. When she left the military, she got a job with a German private security firm and disappeared. Last verified info was she had become an expensive—understatement, incredibly expensive—courier and assassin. It's never been proven, but she is thought to be responsible for at least a dozen political assassinations. Her beauty was equaled only by her ruthlessness."

"So who killed her, and how did they do it?" I asked.

"Toxicology showed a lethal dose of Ketamine in her system. It's a horse tranquilizer, and there was enough to, well, kill a horse. She was also asphyxiated." Terry shifted back in his chair. "As to who, she had plenty of folks wanting her dead." He poured water from a pitcher into a glass and handed it to me. "You need to get some sleep, Agent Decker."

"Sorry. It's been a while since I traveled this far, this long."

"Understandable." He poured a glass for Kenny. "Now that I've shared my intel with you guys, tell me what this is all about. Why is the OSI involved?"

I sipped the water, then cleared my throat. "Barney—I mean Goldman—is suspected of stealing some valuable historical artifacts from a government project, one that falls under the supervision of the Air Force."

"What kind of project?" Terry asked.

"Blacker than black," Kenny said.

"Of course," Terry said with a chuckle. "Aren't they all? So where are you going from here?"

"Not sure yet," I said.

The station chief's cell phone rang. "Excuse me." He listened for a moment then said, "Excellent."

Ending the call, he smiled at us. "We got the surveillance

footage from the RAI Center. We know who she met with."

CHAPTER 38 - THE BIG THREE
American Consulate, Amsterdam, The Netherlands

Kenny, station chief Terry, and I stared at the video monitor on the wall of the conference room as the surveillance footage from the RAI Center streamed in. I saw Patricia Barney approach an exhibitor's booth—a company called Red Star Innovations, a division of Red Star Media Group, Moscow—and be greeted by one of the exhibitors.

Terry pointed. "That man is—"

"Colonel Nikolai Vyshinsky of the new Soviet Army," I said.

"You know Vyshinsky?"

"Know him? A couple of days ago he tried to kill me."

"Last time we saw him," Kenny said, "he was strapped to a tree, in Arizona."

This seemed to set off mental fireworks in Terry's brain as he stared at us.

"The person you encountered is the point man for a group of Russians who want to go back in time to the good old days of the Cold War. These guys are rich, radical, and dangerous. We know little about their plan, other than it consists of destroying the government of the Russian Republic and creating a vacuum so large that only they can fill it."

"How's that possible?" I continued to focus on the frozen image of Vyshinsky on the monitor.

"The three principals of the Russian cabal are General Yuri Lushev, Chief of the General Staff of the Russian Army; Boris Ivankov, Chairman and CEO of the Russian Central Bank; and

Vladimir Butorin, President of Red Star Media Group."

"Same name as the exhibitor," Kenny said.

"Correct. These three men control the military, the country's finances, and all communications networks."

"But realistically, isn't Russia way beyond ever going back to Communism and the Cold War?" I asked.

"The problem in Russia right now," Terry said, "is that the gap between the haves and the have-nots has grown so wide that extreme poverty and out-of-control opulence are the new norms. You'd be amazed how many Russians look back to the old days and wonder if it wasn't so bad. Everyone had a job, everyone was guaranteed retirement. No one got rich, but then no one had to work too hard. Life was manageable. Now a whole lot of people are fed up. They want their old comrade status back. The cabal knows this and plans to make their move by taking advantage of the unrest."

"How would the U.S. and our allies react?" Kenny asked.

"I'm not sure there's much we could do," Terry said. "This is an internal Russian problem. The last thing we'd want to do is step into a possible civil war. The American voters would revolt at the thought of another war. Plus the U.S. managed to exist alongside the Soviets for over forty years. From a military standpoint, their armed forces are in shambles. The main point of contention with this takeover would be political."

"So how do they plan on pulling it off?" I asked.

"That's the big question. The only clue we have is a recent meeting between the big three and a Dr. Mostafa Moghaddam, who heads up uranium enrichment in Iran."

"That sounds ominous," I said.

"I agree," Terry said, "but so far, there's no solid proof his visit has anything to do with the plans of the big three." Terry used a remote to turn off the monitor. "Why did Vyshinsky want to kill you?"

"I've got something he wants."

"And you still have it?"

I nodded.

"Then I'd predict you'll be seeing him again soon."

Kenny's cell rang. He checked the caller ID, but seemed to draw a blank. "This is Gates." He paused. "Who's calling?" He handed the phone to me. "It's Tennyson."

CHAPTER 39 - BAIT
Amsterdam, The Netherlands

"This is Agent Decker."

"I'm glad you're safe." It was the President. "Both you and Agent Gates."

"Thank you, sir."

"Still in Amsterdam?"

"Correct. We're at the consulate with Station Chief Terry?"

"During your meeting with him, did you refer to the Beowulf facility?"

All I could recollect was that we had called it a blacker-than-black op. "No, not by name."

"And you're still in possession of Chaucer's flash drive?"

"Yes."

"Good. And of course you will not give any indication to Terry that you are talking to me. If he asks, I'm simply an OSI friend from your old days checking up on you."

"No problem."

"I must apologize. You've been put in harm's way without intention. At the time we recruited you, we unfortunately didn't foresee the events that took place at Beowulf."

"I came close to being killed a number of times by a psychotic madman."

"You're referring to the Russian, Colonel Vyshinsky? We have no doubt he led the assault on Beowulf. He and his mercenaries are extremely dangerous, as is the Russian cabal he works for. We are following their activities closely. So is the Russian government. The leaders of the New Soviet movement are powerful men, but not powerful enough to bring down the Republic. They are no longer a concern to you and Agent Gates."

Am I just supposed to take his word for that? Vyshinsky was pretty sure of himself and his comrades.

I stood and looked at Terry. "Excuse me for a moment. I need to step away."

He nodded while Kenny gave me a concerned stare. Once outside in the hall with no one else around, I spoke softly, "How can Vyshinsky and his men move in and out of the country at will, sir? How can they kidnap the Beowulf staff and smuggle them out?"

"The same way we do it, Agent Decker. Just like our operatives, they are highly trained in the art of deception. Although we haven't confirmed that the Beowulf staff has been taken outside our borders, they may have been."

"I've been told that I'm in possession of world-changing technology. What am I supposed to do, knowing that people want to kill me for what's in my pocket?"

"I understand your concern."

"How about I hand it over to Terry and walk away?"

"I'm afraid I need you to hang onto it a little longer."

"You realize that paints a big target on my back."

"Unfortunately, yes."

I waited until two men walked by and were out of earshot. "I don't get it."

"I am asking you to continue your original mission of finding the stolen artifacts. And do it while in possession of the thumb drive."

It hit me. "You want me to be the bait that brings out the guys who stole the alien stuff. I assume they can't make whatever they're working on without the info on the drive."

"It would be impossible for them to acquire it while it's under guard at the consulate without a full-blown assault. An international incident would occur, since the Dutch are responsible for the safety of our diplomats. Getting it from you would be much easier and would bring them out into the open.

All we need is to get our hands on one or more of their members, preferably Colonel Vyshinsky, and our special team of interrogators will convince him to reveal what they intend to do with the artifacts."

"That's your plan, sir?"

"I'm asking you to trust me. We believe that more is at stake here than anyone can imagine. Agent Decker, I need you to do this for your country. We'll do everything in our power to protect you."

I should have never answered the door when Kepner came to my cabin. I could be watching the sun come up over the mountains and reflect off the glass-flat surface of Big Bear Lake. I had sworn I wasn't going to be a target again. And yet, here I was with a huge bull's-eye on my back. Not to mention putting Kenny in danger. He never agreed to get this involved. So how do I respond to the President when he asks me to do it for my country?

"All right, Mr. President. If you see no other way out of this, and if the stakes are really that high, I'll accept. But for the record, it's with reluctance."

"Thank you, Agent Decker. You're a true patriot. And believe me, the stakes are sky high—literally. Keep me abreast of any developments."

"How will you know I'm not speaking under duress?"

There was a pause. "I'm sure you'll think of something."

I ended the call and reentered Terry's office.

"Everything okay?" Kenny asked, obviously trying to hide his concern.

"Just an old buddy from OSI. You remember Tennyson."

"What did he want?"

"A favor." I turned to Terry. "We appreciate your time. If we come up with anything new, we'll be in touch." We shook hands. "And I'd appreciate it if you did the same."

"You bet," Terry said.

A few moments later, standing on the sidewalk outside, Kenny said, "What kind of favor?"

"He wants us to go fishing."

CHAPTER 40 - THE HOSTEL
Amsterdam, The Netherlands

"Stayokay Hostel Amsterdam Vondelpark," Kenny said as we climbed into the taxi.

"Hostel? Like a dormitory? I don't think so."

"We'll get a room for two. Bunk beds. You'll be more comfortable that way. And I doubt anyone looking for us would think *hostel*."

He was right on two counts. If someone was tracking us down, the assumption would likely be that we would stay in a high-profile, high-priced hotel. And sleeping together wouldn't be a good idea right now. I needed a clear head, not one muddled with personal emotions. So bunk beds were perfect.

Speaking softly so the driver couldn't hear, I filled Kenny in on what the President had said on the phone. "I'm not going to be bait for anybody. I'm going to turn the tables somehow. If the President wants me on stage, then it's my show. This business of just hanging out waiting to be killed is bullshit. Maxine Decker doesn't play that game."

Kenny laughed. "No, you don't, babe."

"No *babing* me, okay? We're working partners, not marital." Even as I spoke I knew I sort of liked him calling me babe.

"At least your neck isn't blotching, so I don't think calling you babe made you too mad."

I turned and looked at him. "Damn you, Kenny Gates. You know me too well. I rested my head on his shoulder as we passed long stretches of Renaissance architecture, stepped gable roofs, canals, and endless rows of bicycles. We rode that

143

way in silence for a few blessed moments. I was finally catching my breath and comfortably crashing, even if only for a short time.

"I'm whipped," I said. "This jetlag is killing me. I need a drink. A big-ass drink. And then a week's sleep."

Kenny patted my knee. "Johnnie Walker Black sounds about right."

I liked Kenny's pat. Old times were good times. "Blue Label," I said, dusting away the thoughts of Kenny and me in yesteryear. Johnnie Walker Blue Label. The stuff that dreams are made of. "If only I could afford the Blue. Red will work, and it's easier on the wallet."

"We don't have the luxury of popping into a pub to casually sip Scotch and shoot the shit."

"No, we don't."

Kenny tapped the driver's seat and had him pull over in front of a stretch of storefronts. "*Wachten*," he told the driver, then to me he said, "I'll be right back."

In a few minutes he returned with a bottle of The Silver Grouse whisky and a bag of toiletries.

"Thanks." I looked through his purchases of deodorant, toothpaste, shampoo, bar soap, and lotion. "Good job . . . for a guy." I laughed and so did Kenny.

He motioned for the driver to proceed on to the hostel.

It only took us another few minutes to arrive at our destination. Inside, the lobby was much different from what I anticipated. It was modern with modular furniture. Bright solid colors, tile floors, a computer station, big screen TV on the wall. Lots of natural light. Quite European-looking. After we checked in, we were directed to our room.

Ikea-ish was about the only way I could think to describe the sparse but clean room. It was as bright and airy as the lobby.

We settled in and sat on the bottom bunk. "I'm not sure what our next step should be," I said. "I need to think."

Kenny opened the bottle of Scotch whisky and took a swig, then passed it to me. I followed his example, but couldn't hold back a sputtering cough after swallowing.

"First, we know Vyshinsky wants the thumb drive. He needs the information on it," Kenny said.

"Right. He led the assault on Beowulf and obviously knew what was going on there. His team ravaged Chaucer's office." I wiped my lips with my wrist and returned the bottle to Kenny. He took a quick sip then held it out to me.

"I'm done," I said. "My mind is already muddied enough."

Kenny screwed the top on the bottle. "Max, I have to ask again. Why don't you just turn the damn thing over to the President?"

"I can't trust anybody. You didn't see Chaucer's face when he told me that."

"Maybe he was warning you about Kepner. Maybe he knew about him."

"When Chaucer said no one, he meant no one. The only person on the face of the Earth I trust is you."

"Then let's go over this until we have a strategy."

"We could go to Russia, maybe draw the colonel out, but then what? Hold him at gunpoint and ask him why he wants the thumb drive so bad? What's on it? What are they going to do with the alien artifacts?"

"How ironic," Kenny said. "We had him, left him, and now we need to find him."

A thought bombarded my mind. I stood and slapped my forehead. "Jesus, are we stupid? We're going to Russia, all right. But Vyshinsky's not the reason."

CHAPTER 41 - THREE COMPUTERS
Amsterdam, The Netherlands

"We're not going to try to find Vyshinsky?" Kenny said.

"If the colonel needs that thumb drive, he has to believe he or someone on his side can open it with the correct password."

"But he doesn't have the password."

"He might not have it yet, but he must know he can get it if he has the drive."

Kenny palmed his jaw. "That means he knows where there's another quantum computer."

"You got it."

Kenny took another burner cell from the backpack.

"Who are you calling?"

"My connection."

A moment later he spoke into the phone. "Hey, it's me again. I need another favor. See if you can find out if there is intel on the Russians building a quantum computer or maybe even possessing one already." Kenny listened a few seconds then thanked his source.

He looked at me and shrugged. "We wait."

———

Kenny and I decided to allow ourselves a night's sleep, fitful as it was for me. Being so tired, I thought I would quickly fall asleep, but that wasn't happening. I kept staring at the bunk above me thinking how comforting it would be to be wrapped in Kenny's strong arms. I wondered if he was thinking the same thoughts. Then I heard snoring and abandoned that idea.

I wanted to make sense of this whole Beowulf mess, but so much of it didn't add up. Chaucer had convinced me that what I witnessed in the facility was from some other world. I knew the quantum computer was real. So was the bloody trail I'd left in my path. But what was this Russian cabal Terry called the big three doing? From what I gathered, the missing artifacts dealt with propulsion. Were the Russians building a new type of aircraft? Maybe a faster submarine? Whatever they needed, lives had already been lost. Chaucer said to trust no one. He also said all this could change the course of history. The President wanted me to be the candle to draw the moth—a deadly moth. If I'd ever been jerked around more than this in my life, I couldn't remember when.

I finally felt sleep approaching, that wonderful sensation of an ocean wave taking me under. My thoughts melted into dreams.

———

I awoke with a start at the sound of Kenny's cell phone ringing. Darkness surrounded me as I tried to remember where I was. Kenny hopped down from the upper bunk and fumbled around until he found his phone. The glow from it as he answered the call lit his face.

"Gates here." He listened for a moment. "Really? Hey, let me put you on speaker." He came and sat on my bed. "Okay."

"Who's there with you?" a male voice asked.

"Maxine," Kenny replied.

"Ah, yes, your better half then and now."

"You're right," Kenny said. "Now, repeat what you just told me."

"Despite popular belief, quantum computers do exist. There are a whole bunch under development around the world at research centers and universities. But none are reported to be fully functional. Almost none, that is. There are actually three believed to have performed high-speed calculations in ongoing tests. One is somewhere in the U.S.—location unknown, but it's rumored to belong to a secret government research organization."

Kenny and I looked at each other. Beowulf.

"Then there's one reported to be in Russia, which my inside contact confirmed is operational."

"Where?" I asked.

"Moscow, at the Institute of Physics and Technology. Head of the project is Dr. Mikhail Drozdov. Not common knowledge. Even the Institute is probably unaware, or word of it would be on the street, not buried in classified, top-secret docs."

"How easy is it to get to him?" Kenny asked.

"No idea. But he is on the faculty. Why do you want to find him, anyway?"

"His life might be in danger, for starters," Kenny said.

"You mentioned three computers," I asked. "Where's the third?"

"Now that's the craziest thing of all," the contact said. "Several years ago we had info that there was one in Sudan, but that facility blew up or self-destructed. Our recon just had it vanish. Very bizarre documentation. Maybe it's too classified for my eyes. However, there's new evidence that a quantum computer exists somewhere else in Sudan."

"Sudan?" I almost laughed, but what was going on here was no laughing matter. I looked at Kenny. "If you'd have given me a million guesses, I never would have picked that."

CHAPTER 42 - DROZDOV

Moscow, the Russian Republic

While we waited for our checked bag—the one containing our weapons—in the baggage claim area of Sheremetyevo International Airport, Kenny called the Institute and requested a meeting. He used fake names, and told Drozdov's assistant we were freelance journalists writing a piece on quantum physics. The assistant took Kenny's number and, by the time we were getting into a taxi, the professor called back, agreeing to meet us that evening.

"What if Drozdov is part of this whole operation? There *is* a Russian connection. Do you think we're taking a big chance meeting with him?" I said.

"He's our only link to a quantum computer, Max. I don't know any other way. We'll be armed and vigilant."

"He might not cooperate."

"No, he might not. But it's our only shot at finding out what's on the drive and what is really going on."

Kenny was right. "Just checking," I said and grinned at him.

Our ride through Moscow took us past the Kremlin. I saw the five gold domes of Assumption Cathedral rising up from inside the walls. I pointed to them. "That's where the American TV journalist saved the life of the Russian president a few years back."

"I remember that. What was her name again?" Kenny asked.

"Stone, Cotten Stone. I've always wanted to meet her."

"Maybe you will someday."

Twenty minutes later, our taxi pulled up in front of the modest two-story brick home concealed on a slight rise by thick evergreens.

When Professor Drozdov opened the door, he was nothing like I had imagined. I had pictured an elderly, gray-haired scholar in a tweed jacket smoking a hand-carved briarwood pipe. In reality, he was tall, slim, and fit-looking, with dark hair. He looked to be in his early fifties, and wore sweatpants and a black T-shirt with the Star Wars logo on the front.

"Dr. Ledbetter, come in," he said to Kenny.

"Professor, this is my colleague, Fiona Chase. We can't thank you enough for seeing us on such short notice."

"No problem. I love the chance of seeing my name in print. I save the articles in an album for the grandchildren to read when they are old enough to appreciate their *дедушка*. Grandfather," Drozdov interpreted and then shrugged. "One of the few perks of this lonely life of science."

He waved us into a living room furnished with a large leather sectional, marble coffee table, big-screen TV, and a wall of books that would make my Colorado community library jealous. There was a total lack of a feminine touch. I could already guess that the professor was married to his work. I didn't believe many Russian people lived so comfortably.

"May I offer you something to drink? Coffee, tea . . ."

"Water would be wonderful," I said.

Kenny agreed. "Thanks, I'll have some, too."

Drozdov fetched us each a cold bottle of water and then settled into a matching leather easy chair. "So what publication do you work for again?"

I cringed, worried he wanted to check us out. But Kenny was a step ahead of Drozdov.

"We're freelance," Kenny said. "We come up with an idea, get a few editors interested, then do the piece on spec and shop it around."

"Sounds a bit risky, but I guess you know your business better than I."

"You speak excellent English, professor," I said. "That

must be from your studies in England and the U.S."

He nodded. "I've spent a good deal of time lecturing at Cambridge and MIT. And I researched alongside some of the greats, including the brilliant Seth Lloyd." He cleared his throat. "What exactly is your article about?"

"Quantum computers," I said.

I detected an inkling of amusement in his expression. "Of course." He chuckled. "That seems to be the only thing on everyone's mind these days. Does one exist? Did you build it? How fast is it? Can it break governmental security codes? The same litany of questions from every journalist. I was hoping you would have something more original to talk about. Why don't you come back when you have a topic that actually stimulates my imagination?" He started to rise.

"You mean like advanced propulsion technology recovered from an alien spacecraft?"

Drozdov's expression went to stone as he locked his eyes on mine and settled back into his chair. After a moment of obvious mental churning, he said, "Much better, Ms. Chase. That sounds interesting. Please go on."

"First, let me ask one of those common questions you get so often—have you built an operational quantum computer?"

Again, he hesitated as if considering options. "Perhaps. Perhaps not."

It sounded like a confirmation to me.

"What is it that you really want?" Drozdov said, not sounding quite as amused.

"Professor, we need your help," Kenny said. "We have a flash drive that is under heavy encryption and we need the use of a quantum computer to access the information it contains."

"Where did this data come from?"

"We're not at liberty to say," I said.

"And you need to break the password?"

"Passwords," Kenny said. "One to open the drive and the other to mount a hidden partition containing the data."

"I'm sorry, I can't help you."

"Please reconsider?" I said. "This is a matter of great

importance to my country and yours, I believe."

"Doesn't your government have a quantum computer? It is well-rumored that you do. Why do you come to me?"

How were we going to get this man to cooperate? And why should he?

"The rumor is true," Kenny said. "But unfortunate circumstances have rendered it unavailable."

"Please," I said again, hating the way I sounded, like a child begging for a piece of candy.

Drozdov shifted in the chair, tipping his head to the side as he stared at us for a moment.

I loosened my jacket for better access and nudged my weapon that was tucked in my waistband. I needed to be ready.

"All right, *freelance journalists*." Drozdov hesitated, shook his head and grumbled something to himself.

When he looked at us again, I saw anger in his face. My heart picked up speed and my right hand gravitated to my side under my jacket.

Drozdov scowled. "I do all the work and get no credit." His voice had deepened and resonated with resentment. "They take my creations from me—rob me of my accomplishments. I am done with them. Bah, I don't care anymore. Yes, I built a working quantum computer, but it was disassembled a week ago. Crated up and shipped to someplace in Africa."

"Sudan?"

"I assume so, since that is where they sent the first one."

"You built two?" Kenny said.

"The first was to be used to access the data in the bubble memory of the artifact collected from Tunguska."

Kenny and I looked at each other.

Drozdov must have sensed our confusion. "Artifacts were collected at both Tunguska and Roswell."

"What are they going to do with this technology?" I said.

"No idea." Drozdov twitched his lips. "I think I have said too much."

"Who took the computers?" Kenny asked.

Drozdov laughed out loud. "This is Russia, Dr. Ledbetter

or whoever you really are. Questions like that are never asked."

The doorbell rang and Drozdov looked up. "Excuse me for a moment." He rose from the chair and walked to the front door.

As he opened it, I heard what sounded like a greeting in Russian. I turned to see Colonel Vyshinsky framed in the doorway. He pulled an automatic pistol from beneath his coat and walked toward me.

"Agent Decker, so good to see you again."

CHAPTER 43 - COCKROACH
Moscow, the Russian Republic

I stonily looked at Vyshinsky. "We do have a way of being in the same place at the same time. This is the third, I believe."

"The third as far as you know, Agent Decker."

That statement made my stomach feel unsettled.

"I have brought along a comrade I would like you both to meet." Vyshinsky leaned on the doorjamb and another man filled the opening. "May I introduce General Yuri Lushev, Chief of the General Staff of the Russian Army."

The name registered. He was one of station chief Terry's big three.

Drozdov backed away ushering in the colonel and the general.

"No need for the gun," Kenny said.

Vyshinsky waggled the weapon as if to taunt us, aiming first at me and then at Kenny.

As he lowered the weapon, my taut muscles loosened.

"Sit down, my friend," General Lushev said to Drozdov.

The professor followed orders and planted himself in the leather chair. "Like everyone else, they want to know about the quantum computer. But they know too much. They are not journalists."

Lushev's eyes narrowed. "You think you tell me something I do not know? I believe it best you say nothing. Understood?"

Drozdov responded with a sheepish, "*Da*."

Vyshinsky said, "First, your weapons. Please remove them and place them on the floor. Slowly. Then kick them toward me."

I removed Peter Kepner's automatic while Kenny pulled out Vyshinsky's pistol from our encounter at Beowulf and kicked them away.

"Ah, my SIG," the colonel said. "I hoped you would keep it safe."

The general angled his head toward us. "Sit."

With no other choice, we obeyed. I doubted we would come out of this alive, but it was a mystery why Vyshinsky hadn't already blown me away. He knew I had the thumb drive—he could just shoot me and take it.

"I think we can conduct business as civilized men and woman," the general said, seeming to go out of his way to make sure I was given equal respect. He moved to a rolling office chair where all of us were in his line of sight. He looked at Kenny. "Agent Gates, I understand you are familiar with the workings of quantum computers."

"Somewhat."

"You were able to operate the one at Beowulf with success. Is that not so?"

Kenny nodded.

Vyshinsky moved to stand beside Kenny,

This line of thinking made me wonder if they wanted to get rid of Kenny as much as me but for different reasons. They had Drozdov, so Kenny was expendable. It wasn't making a lot of sense. Why didn't they just shoot us and get it over with?

The general looked at me. "And Agent Decker, I believe you have something I want?"

Here we go. Adiós, Maxine.

"It will be so much simpler if you hand it over and we can be done with all the drama. This is getting tedious for me, and it must be for you, too. You do not even trust your own government."

He was right about that. I couldn't tell the white hats from the black.

"Will you cooperate?" the general asked me. A nasty smile leached into his expression. He motioned to the colonel.

Vyshinsky pressed the gun barrel to Kenny's temple.

Think Maxine, think. There's got to be a way out of this.

The general leaned forward. "Give it to me."

"I don't have it," I said. "I stowed it somewhere safe."

"Really?"

"If you kill Agent Gates, I'll never tell you. What do I have to lose? Once I hand the drive over to you, I'm of no further use."

General Lushev laughed. "Come now. You think I am a fool? Unless you hid it in the backseat of the taxi from the airport, you have it with you. I could search your travel bag and your dead body if you prefer. But for the same reason Colonel Vyshinsky did not kill you in the desert, we do not want to chance damaging the drive." He tapped the center of his forehead with a finger. "Of course a single bullet here at close range would not harm the drive."

I saw no mercy in Lushev's expression. He would have Vyshinsky kill Kenny with no more conscience than stepping on a cockroach. He was going to get rid of us both, but if I turned over the thumb drive, at least I would be spared seeing Kenny die first.

"May I stand?" I asked.

Lushev nodded.

I reached in my pocket and removed the drive. "Here."

Lushev got up and approached me. His eyes told me that Kenny and I were nothing more that cockroaches to him.

The general held out his palm. The bastard was literally making me *give* it to him. It was a mind game—an attempt to emotionally defeat me.

"Take it," I said, staring him down.

Finally, he snatched the drive from my hand and dropped it in his pocket. He then reached down, picked up Kepner's gun from where I'd kicked it, and took aim.

The deafening blast filled the room.

CHAPTER 44 - FUGITIVES
Moscow, the Russian Republic

Drozdov never saw it coming. Blood spattered his leather chair as he slumped forward and crumbled to the floor.

Kenny shot up from the couch. I started to take a step toward Drozdov just as Lushev aimed the automatic at me.

"Leave him," the general said. "He is of no further use to us."

Us? Who is us? It sounded like he was including Kenny and me.

"The professor had loose lips. Unacceptable." The general motioned with the pistol. "Now, both of you, sit back down."

As I eased back onto the couch, my thoughts spun like the helicopter blades that took me from my cabin. I felt as if someone had turned out the lights, leaving me with no idea where I was or why. I had just witnessed a cold and callous murder. *For what?*

Kenny seemed to be in the same state of confusion.

The general adjusted his uniform.

"How did you know we'd be here?" Kenny asked.

"Drozdov's assistant at the Moscow Institute," Lushev answered. "You spoke to a temporary who reports to us. As far as the world is concerned, the real assistant is on extended hiatus somewhere in Tibet. In reality, he met with an untimely demise two years ago while helping with the original Shield project at a desert facility in Sudan. He was to precede the arrival of Drozdov and execute the preparatory work. From what I understand, Drozdov's assistant and the facility itself are scattered across the rainforest of Brazil. They really should have waited for the professor, but you know how greed for fame and fortune goes." Lushev frowned. "Fucked up our timeline and set us back. I have no tolerance for such egos."

I continued to eye the dead body, wondering if that was a prelude to our future. "You've got the thumb drive. You don't need us anymore. Just let us go and you can get on with your *Shield* thing." I doubted he would agree on any level, especially after this. His reaction to my request was what I anticipated.

The general laughed as he leaned back. "You could not be more wrong, Agent Decker. As a matter of fact, you are in this right up to your eyeballs."

"What makes you think we want to be a part of it?"

"Because you have no choice. By tomorrow morning, you both will be charged with the murder of Dr. Mikhail Drozdov. To cover up the ruthless killing, you doused his body with petrol and set this house on fire. But his *assistant* will tell the authorities that you had a meeting with Drozdov just before the house caught fire. They will be able to connect the fatal bullet to Peter Kepner's pistol, the one you brought into this country in your checked bag—the one with your fingerprints on it."

It felt like a vacuum opened in my stomach and cold, deadly air rushed into the cavity.

Lushev placed the gun back on the floor. It was then that I noticed he wore flesh-colored gloves.

He would never get away with this outlandish plot against us. "That's ridiculous." I started to stand but thought better of it. "There's no way you can blame us for his murder." Again the general smiled which was starting to annoy the hell out of me.

"Agent Decker, the charge of murder is the least of your problems."

"Okay, let's scrape the crust away and get to the bottom of your plan. What do you want?"

"You and Agent Gates will come to work for us."

"You think so?" Kenny said.

"Do not be too hasty, my sarcastic friend. You have not heard all the details, yet."

"What's in it for us?" I asked, trying to find out if there was even a slight chance we could buy some time? Sweat formed a veil on my cold palms and beaded up on my back. I felt a trickle work its way down my spine.

"You have all the resources you need," Kenny said. "What can we possibly add?"

"You both have unique skills that we can utilize. Agent Decker, what is in it for you is your life. And the same for Agent Gates. The alternative to not joining our cause is less than desirable."

"You mean a bullet like you gave your associate?" I asked.

"Oh, no, Agent Decker. Much worse than that. We have put into place a trail of accusations that will leave you no alternative but to do as we say."

"What accusations?" Kenny asked.

"Evidence is about to be forwarded to Interpol, the FBI, and other global law enforcement agencies that make you both the prime suspects in the planning and assault on a classified United States government facility, the kidnapping of government employees, the deaths of Chaucer, Peter Kepner, and Patricia Barney, the shooting of a National Park Ranger, and the theft of valuable government property. You are about to become international fugitives and two of the most wanted individuals on the planet. You will be despised and hunted down like rabid dogs. Every day of your existence will be filled with dread and fear. You will live a life of torment and anguish that won't even end when they catch you—unless you are executed as a traitor."

I felt sick, like I might vomit. I hoped I would—I'd puke all over his shitty shiny shoes. My chest tightened, making my breathing shallow. This was way more than I could take. A bullet might be better—at least it would be quicker. What the hell could they possibly want from us that would warrant such a setup? Kenny glanced at me with an expression mirroring my shock.

"All circumstantial evidence," Kenny said.

"You are right, Agent Gates," the general said, "A *mountain* of circumstantial evidence."

For now I figured it was best for us to hear him out and give Lushev an academy-award-winning act that would convince him we had caved in. With a voice echoing complete acquiescence I said, "Tell us what you want us to do."

"Much better attitude." Lushev turned to Kenny. "Let us start with you, Agent Gates. Now that Chaucer and Drozdov walk with the angels, you are the expert we need to access the thumb drive and decode the contents."

"You must have countless computer experts far more experienced in the operation of a complex quantum computer."

"We need someone we can trust. And when I say trust, I mean someone who not only has the skill but is also, let us say, strongly motivated. Our deceased comrade, Drozdov, seemed to have lost such enthusiasm." Lushev faced me. "And Agent Decker, we need you for just as important a reason—your direct contact with the President of the United States. He has confidence in you. You have his ear. We must be able to communicate with him directly. You can do that." He added, "And because you trust no one at this point, that makes you even more valuable."

How the hell does he know all that? I started to get my thoughts back together and shake off my initial visceral reactions. More rational, I realized we would at least get to walk out of here alive. That was more than I could say for Drozdov. Second, the charges piled against us were so outrageous that there was the possibility we would never be convicted. But proving it could take years. Initially, the hunt for Kenny and me would be intensive. We had to avoid it or spend the rest of our lives in prison fighting legal battles. Doing what General Lushev wanted would give us some time to figure out how to put together a plan of action.

Vyshinsky left the room a moment and returned with two large cans of gasoline. He poured the contents of one of them over the dead body.

Watching him intently, I asked, "How will this arrangement work?"

"First," the colonel said, "you will renounce your American citizenship. Then you will declare that you want to seek political asylum."

When he mentioned renouncing my American citizenship, the vertebrae in my spine seemed to shudder.

"Political asylum?" I said. "In Russia?"

"Heavens no," General Lushev said. "In Iran."

CHAPTER 45 - LECLAIRE
Oval Office, The White House, Washington, DC

President Guy LeClaire gazed at the pictures of his family on the table behind his desk—three beautiful children, two boys, one girl, and his wife. He missed her. His eyes lifted to look out the window onto the playground where the two boys romped. His thoughts drifted back to a time when he had watched his wife, pregnant with their daughter, push the boys on the swing. It was a better time, then. In every way.

He heard the others entering the Oval Office for the briefing, but he continued to gaze out the window. The office of the presidency was burdensome. There were some things a president could not share. Today he understood he would not be able to reveal everything, and certainly nothing about Beowulf, which was going to make this meeting even more difficult. Finally filing his memories away, he greeted his select guests—Vice President Waite, Secretary of State Butler, and National Security Advisor Scarborough.

The President gestured toward the gold and white brocade couches, an invitation to sit. After they were seated, LeClaire opted for one of the striped chairs. He checked his watch. It was two minutes after 9:00 AM. CIA Director Singer was late, as usual. The President liked to start his meetings on time, and Singer's habitual lack of promptness irked him. "Good morning, gentlemen," the President said. "Director Singer has not managed to arrive on time, but I suggest we proceed."

LeClaire aimed to be personable and amicable in public and on the campaign trail, but during meetings he was blunt and direct. "I don't believe any of us have time to waste. Is that agreeable?"

After confirmative nods, the President spoke again. "I have put several issues on our agenda. I hope you have blocked out time in your schedule so we can discuss the matters at length if need be. Hopefully, extended time won't be necessary."

When the CIA Director Singer entered, the President and vice President turned to him. The National Security Advisor and Secretary of Defense shuffled papers, obviously grasping the awkward moment.

"Sorry," Director Singer said, huffing and finger-combing his disheveled hair. "The traffic was brutal." He sat beside Butler and put his briefcase on his lap.

During Singer's entrance, President LeClaire's kept his annoyance in check and said nothing. He picked up where he left off without making any effort to make Singer less uncomfortable.

"I'll start with a question for you, Director. What is the status of the two fugitives, OSI Agents Decker and Gates?"

Singer clearly scrambled to get his notes from his briefcase and put them into order. The President wondered how much more the Director would do to irritate him. LeClaire waited, tapping his fingers together.

Finally, Singer stacked his papers into a neat pile and looked up. "The last we know is they went through customs at Sheremetyevo International Airport."

"Tracking Vyshinsky, I presume."

"Most likely," Singer said.

"And now?"

"Not sure. Neither of them has been in touch."

LeClaire crossed his legs. "That's your job. You need to stay on it and see to it that your department sets Decker and Gates as priorities."

Singer stretched his neck to the side as if working out a kink. "With all due respect, I'm not sure I understand the gravity. Can you be more specific as to their importance? We have a lot of hot spots around the world. Why are—?"

"They've already demonstrated a public display against the United States in a television broadcast. Did you miss that?" One of LeClaire's eyebrows arched.

"No, sir. The news media is all over it. But it's not like they've given away any secrets or even have much to offer, so I don't get it. So they've switched out, but I don't see how they can be proclaimed traitors. The definition of trai—"

"I know damn well what a traitor is, Singer. Just do what I say. Prioritize them." LeClaire's belly churned. No way could he inform the director about the artifacts or Beowulf.

"Guy," Vice President Waite said, "What do you think about treating this as if it is insignificant? Downplay the Decker and Gates thing, at least to the public. You know what the people and the media will start saying—that it's a distraction to take the focus off our failure to get Iran and Israel to the table."

"I agree," said the Secretary of Defense, taking an apple from the tray of fruit on the cocktail table.

LeClaire sat silent for a moment, tapping his index fingers on the ends of the chair arms. "Just do what I say, Director Singer."

Waite shifted his position on the sofa. Secretary Butler took a bite of the apple.

LeClaire changed the subject. "What's happening with the Russian cabal and their mission? Any progress?"

Singer's cell rang. He peered at the screen, then at LeClaire. "Excuse me a moment, Mr. President. I should take this."

Singer crossed the room, stepping past the seal on the rug and coming to stand as a silhouette in the window.

President LeClaire rubbed his forehead in annoyance.

Everyone paused. When Butler bit into the apple again, it sounded as if a bullwhip had been cracked.

Singer took his phone from his ear and returned to the group. "Mr. President, I have just received confirmation that Agents Decker and Gates have crossed into Iran and appealed for political asylum."

CHAPTER 46 - WILD CAMELS
North Africa, the Republic of Sudan

It was late afternoon as the Nubian Desert drifted six hundred meters below. I watched from the window of the eight-seat Hawker Beechcraft. It carried Kenny and me to an undisclosed location somewhere in the mountains west of Port Sudan on the Red Sea. They explained that it was the site of a secret underground Iranian facility, much like Beowulf and with the same purpose.

Now some pieces of the puzzle had already assembled in my head. We hadn't been killed because they needed us. The Russians wanted to bring back the Soviet Union in all its glory and they were conspiring with the Iranians to do it."

Some of the facts or theories of mine were coalescing, but I was still missing something. What were they working on that would achieve their goals? More to think about on this plane ride.

A narrow aisle ran down the middle of the plane. Colonel Vyshinsky sat in the seat in front of Kenny, a Russian soldier occupied the one in front of me. Behind us, the rest of the seats were empty. Up front, the Iranian pilot and copilot busied themselves.

A private jet had carried us from Tehran to the Sudanese port where we were transferred to the twin-prop Beechcraft. This was after a week of non-stop chaos as the Iranian government paraded us in front of the world media. We were instructed to say nothing other than how fed up we were with the cruel and oppressive policies of the U.S. government in imposing economic sanctions against Iran for trying to pursue a non-threatening, legitimate nuclear power program. How the cruel restrictions had hurt the Iranian people. We publically denounced our country and our citizenships, and sought political asylum in the Islamic Republic of Iran. The press accused us of trying to escape capture for our crimes of conspiracy and murder. International arrest warrants were issued in the event we ever stepped foot outside of Iran. Our secret flight to Sudan was known only by the highest-ranking officials of the Iranian government and the Russian cabal.

After an hour of flight with little said, Vyshinsky looked over his shoulder at me. "Have you ever been to the Sudan?"

"I was in charge of an OSI recovery operation about ten years ago. I was in Khartoum for a couple of days."

Looking down on the desert, I noticed a scattering of stone ruins. The Nubian civilizations once thrived in this region 2000 years ago. I could make out a handful of wild camels dotting the monotonous desert sands. A grouping of tents and a few vehicles came into view, and a dozen men emerged from them as we approached.

"What about you, Agent Gates?" Vyshinsky asked.

"I'm not a field agent, Colonel. Most of my work is done back in DC in the forensics lab. I've never been—"

A loud thump caused us all to jump. It sounded as if someone hit the side of the plane with a hammer. It was followed by two more. Vyshinsky's man yelped and slumped over into the aisle. He grabbed his side as blood colored his jacket.

"They're shooting at us!" one of the pilots yelled.

Phantom icy fingers gripped my gut. If the pilots were hit, we were done.

"Who?" Kenny said.

"Rebels. Probably al-Qaeda." Vyshinsky reached to assist the soldier. "Their training camps are scattered throughout this area."

The plane took another hit and dove. I thought my stomach would lurch up into my throat. I unbuckled my belt and knelt to help the wounded Russian. "Why are they firing at us?"

The plane shuddered as more bullets slammed into it. A quick glance out the windows revealed flames pouring from the left-side engine. Black smoke streamed behind as the prop stopped spinning. We were going to die.

"We have no markings," Vyshinsky yelled. "They shoot at anything they suspect might be government surveillance."

A window shattered. Because of our low altitude, there was only the deafening scream of the wind across the opening—no crippling pressure drop.

The nose dipped as the cabin filled with smoke and the choking odors of electrical fire and burning fuel. A flash of orange from the opposite windows told me the other engine was on fire.

Panic set in as the plane violently vibrated. *Going down! Going down!*

Like riding a rodeo bull, we were thrown about. I wound up by a window and saw a trail of smoke shoot up from the desert camp, rushing at us like a roman candle.

Seconds later, the back of the plane burst into flames as the shoulder-fired rocket tore off the tail section just behind the empty seats.

I was going to burn alive even before we hit the ground!

Kenny grabbed my hand.

The plane flipped.

I thought of wild camels running in fear.

CHAPTER 47 - VODKA
Moscow, the Russian Republic

Boris Ivankov knocked back his Vodka and poured himself another, straight up. He sat on the couch opposite Vladamir Butorin and General Yuri Lushev. The coffee table between them had a plate of black bread and cheese, several bottles of vodka, and three tumblers. After Ivankov swallowed, he spoke. "Now that we have the thumb drive, what is the use of keeping the woman agent alive?"

"Maybe none," Vladimir Butorin said. "But we must think ahead. If the other OSI agent does not cooperate, she could be our leverage."

Ivankov took a swig from his freshly poured drink. His nose and cheeks had already flushed from the three drinks he'd downed since the group had assembled less than thirty minutes ago. "What do you think, General?"

"I believe we keep her—both of them—alive. Think about it. We have no current quarrel with the Americans. Why should we provoke one? The U.S. disapproves of our relationship with Iran, but they take no action against us. They huff and puff at Iran, but the Iranians do not take the Americans seriously even though they should. As long as we play both sides, we win. Our only fight will be with our people. But we will win them over. They live for the old days. And that is precisely what we will deliver. The New Soviet Republic will be a global dominating force to be feared and respected."

Ivankov rested his empty glass on the end table. "Where are the two American agents now?"

General Lushev answered, "On their way to the Sudan facility. Vyshinsky is escorting them. He will let me know when they arrive."

Ivankov lifted the nearly empty bottle of vodka. "Yuri?"

"No." The General placed his hand over the top of his glass. "Boris, you need to stay clear-minded. You drink too much."

"Ahh, you worry too much." Ivankov tipped the bottle, topping off his drink. "I will tell you how clear-headed I am. We have all the control we could want. I take care of the finances, Vladimir has the media under his thumb, and you, General, are putting together a fine Russian military. Our problem is not the American agents or our people. There is only one thing that burrows deep in my brain that causes me some tribulation."

Vladimir Butorin rolled his sunken eyes. "And what might that be? The Vodka gremlin?" He laughed and General Lushev joined in.

"You scoff," Ivankov said. "But I am serious. It is our backs we need to watch. I do not trust the Iranians."

Lushev reached for the vodka. "You are out of your mind."

Ivankov's face blossomed with red veins. "You say I am fucking crazy?"

"Calm down," Butorin said.

"I am telling you, something smells," Ivankov said. "I am not talking about you, Lushev, even though I think you smell like dog shit. I cannot explain it, but something prods me to be suspicious of them. We chose our mission to extrapolate all the information we can about the alien artifacts and what it could mean for us. Both times we agreed to carry it out in Sudan so as not to bring attention to the New Soviet Republic. But I think we make a big mistake if we trust the Iranians. Iran's most supreme desire is to destroy the Great Satan—the United States. I believe they plan to use us to do it."

CHAPTER 48 - CRASH
North Africa, the Republic of Sudan

I couldn't breathe or see. Was I dead? The heat burned my face. *Am I in Hell?*

I coughed, sputtering out a mouthful of searing sand while turning to my side. *God, it hurts. My ribs. What happened?*

My mind began to clear as I spit a little more sand, my mouth still gritty and dry. Finally flopping on my back, I brushed my eyes and face to try to see. Squinting, I glimpsed the last of the setting sun. The desert. The crash.

Pushing up to sit, I saw the upside-down, smoking fuselage embedded in the orange sand at the bottom of a long incline. We had crashed on the side of a hill and slid to the bottom. I was probably still alive because the angle of the hill had softened the impact. I realized my seat lay on its side near me.

The damn sand was killing my eyes and making them tear. I blinked, afraid to rub them and sandpaper my eyeballs. I allowed the tears to flow and blotted them away carefully with my jacket sleeve.

"Kenny?"

I heard a groan. "Max?"

He was alive. Tears streamed down my face. *Thank, God!* Relief flooded through me. My vision was slowly returning. I managed to get to my knees, then crawled to the aircraft. Through a torn-open section, I saw him hanging upside down, still strapped in his seat.

"Are you hurt?" I said, sobbing at the sight of him. I cried from the joy that Kenny was alive and from the fear that he was injured. I crawled closer.

"I don't think so. Get me out of this, quick"

I smelled fuel and what had to be smoldering electrical wiring. *Shit. Need to act fast.* I pushed on his seatbelt's release button, but it was jammed. "Hold on." I frantically searched for something I could use to cut the belt. A ripped fragment of metal lay close by. I grabbed it and hurried back to Kenny, then took off my jacket and wrapped it around my hand.

"Hurry, Max. It's gonna blow."

I pressed the metal's sharp edge against the seatbelt and slashed through the material.

Kenny thumped down from his seat.

"Let's go," he said, reorienting himself.

"What about the others?"

"I don't know. Didn't hear anyone."

"We've got to check." I pulled my jacket back on.

"Max, we need to get clear before this thing goes up."

He pushed me forward, and I crawled out into the open with him following.

"We can't just leave them."

"For god's sake, Maxine. The goddamn plane might explode any minute. Move!"

I hobbled toward the front of the plane and peered through the shattered cockpit window. "Shit." The pilot and co-pilot were obviously dead. One side of the pilot's head was so crushed it had no features. The co-pilot's eyes were open and so was his neck—a jagged wound—he had already bled out.

"Where's Vyshinsky?" Sweat dripped into my eyes, burning them.

"It doesn't matter. Go."

"He has the thumb drive. We've got to find him."

I scrambled back inside the plane. The fuel and smoke odors were overwhelming. I tasted blood. The pain from my earlier ankle injury flared up. My hands were cold and clammy while the rest of my body felt like it was roasting.

Everything was upside down—it was hard to make sense of the mangled mess. I pushed cushions and other debris away, clearing a path. "Vyshinsky?"

There was no answer.

I came upon the dead Russian soldier's body. When I felt someone touch my arm, I jumped. "Vyshinsky?"

"*Da. Da.*"

The Russian was pinned under the soldier and buried beneath debris—I only saw his hand on me.

"Kenny, help me. I've found him."

Kenny shoved the dead soldier off the colonel and peeled away chunks of electronic gear, parts of the plane, and some kind of material that looked like insulation, until we finally got to the Russian. From the corner of my eye I saw sparks from the direction of the cockpit.

"Twist him so you can grab his arms," I said.

Kenny turned the colonel, confiscated his automatic pistol, and dragged him out of the wreckage—not an easy task while on his hands and knees. I followed.

Once clear of the wreckage, I searched Vyshinsky's jacket until I located the thumb drive. I slipped it into my bra before helping Kenny haul him a safe distance from the smoking aircraft. Then we collapsed.

"We could have left him by the plane and let him go up in smoke," Kenny said.

"We could have." My heart beat so fast it was like a bomb ticking in my chest. Winded, I turned on my back and stared at the sky, now filled with the first stars of the desert night. That's when I heard a screaming whoosh. Kenny rolled on top of me.

The desert lit up orange.

CHAPTER 49 - DEATH FROM ABOVE
North Africa, the Republic of Sudan

"Rebels," Kenny said. "They came over the hill and used a shoulder-fired rocket on the Beechcraft."

That was what had caused the explosion. I watched out from beneath Kenny as the last debris rained down around the impact zone. The flames popped and crackled with smaller explosions that rattled the wreckage.

"Maybe they didn't see us," Kenny whispered as he rolled off me.

The explosion had lit up the area for only a few seconds. I heard a moan. We both looked over at Colonel Vyshinsky. He brought his hands to his face. "What happened?" he managed to ask.

"The rebels shot us down," Kenny whispered.

"Animals." Vyshinsky sat up and spit out sand. "They fire at anything that moves."

"Quiet," I said. "They're still up there." I motioned to the top of the hill. Against the starry backdrop, the black silhouettes moved along the ridge.

"How did I get here?" Vyshinsky asked, this time just above a whisper.

"Against my better judgment, Max decided to save your sorry ass."

"I was only concerned with saving the thumb drive," I said, not revealing that I had retrieved it before we dragged the colonel away from the burning plane.

He reached inside his jacket searching for the USB device.

His expression told me he realized I had it.

Vyshinsky stretched out his arm. "Now, give it back."

"You're real piece of work," Kenny said, pulling the automatic pistol from beneath his jacket. He pointed it at Vyshinsky. "I hate to use this so soon after dragging you all the way out here so you didn't vaporize."

"I'll hang on to the drive for now," I said.

"Don't think about destroying it, Agent Decker."

"If I'd wanted to destroy it, Colonel, I would have left it in your pocket and let it burn up along with you."

Kenny glanced up at the ridgeline. "We've got to get out of here before those guys come down to check out their work."

That's when another whoosh screamed through the night—this one much louder.

CHAPTER 50 - GPS
North Africa, the Republic of Sudan

"What the hell just happened?" There were no more men standing on the crest of the hill. In fact, a gaping hole took their place. The sounds of the explosions faded, replaced with the glow of fires.

"Listen." Vyshinsky pointed skyward.

I heard a faint buzzing sound like a distant bee, but I could see nothing in the blackness.

The colonel waved to the heavens. "Smile. I'm sure we're all on camera."

"But whose drone is it?" Kenny asked.

"Whoever it belongs to knows we're here," I said. "We need to move out fast before friends of those rebels come looking."

The colonel got to his feet, a bit wobbly as he tried to find his balance. Kenny and I did the same.

"Anybody got any ideas?" Kenny brushed the sand from his clothes.

"Give me my cell phone, Colonel."

"We agreed you would call your president only after we arrived at our destination. Besides, you'll get no service out here in the middle of nowhere."

"I have no intention of calling anyone," I said. "We need to find out where we are and which direction to move."

Vyshinsky seemed to hesitate for a moment before pulling my phone from his pocket. Even then, it took him a moment before he stretched out his arm and handed it to me.

I powered on my iPhone and checked the connection status. "No Service" appeared at the top. Not surprised. Then I scrolled to a special GPS app, one that I often used while hiking in the mountains around my cabin, and let it connect to the most accessible satellite. A moment later, a map and our coordinates appeared—a small blinking red dot in the middle of a light brown background. There were no roads or landmarks.

I placed my thumb and finger together over the surface of the phone and spread them apart to zoom in on the surrounding area. A few unidentified landmarks came into view. I handed it to Vyshinsky. "Here's where we are. Tell us where we need to go."

He studied the display for a few moments, readjusting the screen to increase the view and scrolling the map in various directions. Finally, he said, "We are about sixty kilometers from our destination. It is west-north-west from here."

"Any ideas on how we can get there?" Kenny asked as I took the phone back from the colonel.

"Unless you can catch a few of those camels," Vyshinsky said, "we walk."

"Maybe not." I could still hear the distant buzz of the drone as I stared in the direction of what used to be the rebel encampment.

CHAPTER 51 - SURVIVORS
Oval Office, The White House, Washington, DC

"Mr. President," CIA Director Douglas Singer said as he entered the President's office.

LeClaire checked his watch, stood, and came around his desk. "Thank you for coming, Doug."

"At our last meeting you said to place Agents Decker and Gates as a priority. The agency complied."

The President took a seat on one of the striped chairs in front of his desk and gestured for Singer to sit in the matching one.

"I'm still not clear why you felt so strongly about that, but I did as you asked. There is something going on, but without much more information, I'm not certain what we should be looking for."

LeClaire ignored his probing. "What have you got?"

Singer smacked his lips, obviously irritated that the President wasn't as forthcoming as he would like. "In order to be more watchful of Decker and Gates, it has spread the agency a little thin, in my opinion. AFRICOM is still demanding more aid in intel-gathering in Africa. That area is about to blow. The threats are on the rise. It's the newest safe house for terrorists. And Russia is a political bubbling pot about to boil over with this cabal threat. Hell, there are dozens of places and groups where we need to concentrate our efforts. I just—"

LeClaire dropped the first name basis in his interruption. "Director, I get briefings every morning. You really don't need to tell me about the state of the world. Do you have info on the two OSI agents or not?"

The fair skin of Singer's face flushed. His eyes sparked with a harshness the President couldn't miss. "I do, sir."

"Good. Then get to it."

"After arriving by private jet from Tehran, the targets boarded a small two-engine prop plane in the coastal city of Port Sudan and flew four hundred miles inland before suddenly crashing in the desert."

LeClaire stood. This was not a good turn of events. He felt a burst of adrenalin streak down his arms. "How?"

"All indications are they were shot down. Anti-government rebels, al-Qaeda—we can't be sure. No one is claiming responsibility. And why would they? This sort of thing happens all the time in that region. There are dozens of factions at odds with each other."

LeClaire looked at the ceiling and breathed a loud sigh. "Survivors?"

"We believe there were."

The President glared at Singer. "Were?"

"Three to be exact. But they were under fire on the ground until we hit the rebels and their encampment with Hellfire missiles from a Predator drone."

"So you can't identify who the three survivors are?"

"Not positively, but our analysis suggests one is a woman."

CHAPTER 52 - DESERT WALK
North Africa, the Republic of Sudan

From the distance, I had spotted an old Nissan pickup that had survived the Hellfire missile attack on the rebel compound. We checked it out and were in luck—the owner had left the keys in the ignition. Kenny looked through the glove box. "Not much. Paperwork, screwdriver, flashlight."

The three of us loaded up. The colonel turned the key and it cranked. "Not much gas, but it will get us part way." He stepped on the accelerator and the truck rattled along what was hardly a road, more like two parallel grooves in the sand. He drove while I was squeezed in between him and Kenny. Because of the overcast sky and no moon, the blackness of the desert pushed in on us, even seeming to dilute our headlights down to the weakness of flashlights.

"Ever get the feeling of déjà vu?" Kenny asked.

I laughed. "Same threesome, different desert."

Vyshinsky grunted.

"Problem, Colonel?" I said.

"I recall that you abandoned me the last time."

"And I recall you tried to kill me in that same spot."

"I already assured you that if I intended to kill you, Agent Gates would be placing flowers on your grave right now."

"Wow, I feel so much better knowing that." Turning away, I tried to make out any details surrounding us. How could I feel claustrophobic in a place as wide open as this? "You know, Colonel, maybe we should just leave you out here and have one less thing to worry about."

179

"You will not do that."

"How can you be so sure?"

"Why would you go to the trouble of saving my life, Agent Decker, only to leave me to die out here? Which makes me wonder, why *did* you pull me from the plane?"

"Come on, Colonel, you're not stupid. But in case you've had a thump on your head that has impaired your memory and logic, I'll list my reasons. Number one, you had the thumb drive. Number two, I'm not a hunter and I don't kill for sport. It doesn't give me a high or an adrenaline rush. And maybe I believe there's already been too much death with this whole fiasco."

"How do you know it is a fiasco, Agent Decker?"

"The United States will never stand by and let you destroy the Russian Republic and bring back the fear and lunacy of the Cold War."

"They will have no choice." The dashboard lights gave Vyshinsky's face a green tint like the Wicked Witch of Oz.

"We're the most powerful country on Earth. We'll stand by the legitimate Russian government and make sure this takeover never happens."

"You are basing your predictions on current military strength and technology. You envision the need for warfare, battles, weapons, great armies fighting each other. What is about to happen will be nothing of the sort. There will be no great conflicts, no bloody battlefields, not even a bullet fired. The transition from the current Russian Republic to the New Soviet Republic will take place in the blink of an eye. And there will be nothing anyone can do about it."

"You'll be part of the new Soviet military?" Kenny asked.

"Perhaps. I am but a humble soldier, Agent Gates. I do as I am ordered. For a price, of course. I work for the winner. If the cabal wins, I win and continue to draw a salary. Otherwise, I move on to the next well-funded, potential winner. I am always on the side of those who win."

"I think they call that a mercenary." Kenny said.

"I prefer to think of myself as a professional warrior who

offers a significant return on investment."

"Like I said, mercenary."

"So you don't owe your allegiance to General Lushev?" Kenny asked.

Vyshinsky adopted a bemused expression. "He pays me for my expertise."

I challenged his smug attitude. "You know, Colonel, for a guy with so much expertise, you let a woman take you prisoner, not once but twice."

His eyes probed mine for an instant. I'm sure the intent was to make me uneasy. "Do not count on it happening again, Agent Decker."

The truck's engine sputtered. I glanced at the gas gauge. The needle rested below empty. Damn! A few meters further, the motor coughed and died. The colonel tried the ignition but there was no response.

I clasped my hands on the top of my head in frustration. "Looks like we walk from here."

"Check your cell's GPS," Kenny said.

"Good idea." I pulled out my phone. As the display lit up, I noticed that one bar appeared in the upper left corner. I had cell service. Not much but enough to possibly make a call. How could that be, out here in the middle of nowhere? Then it occurred to me that we must be close to our destination—the secret Iranian facility. That would require some sort of cell service and they must have installed it themselves.

"Here's our location." I showed Vyshinsky the display, making sure my finger covered the upper corner so he would not know my discovery.

He studied the map for a moment as I held the phone. "We are about a kilometer, maybe two, from our destination."

"Then let's get moving." Kenny took the flashlight from the glove box and opened the passenger's door. As he lit the way, Vyshinsky and I got out, joined him, and started walking along the desert road.

After ten minutes or so, I thought I made out a rock formation off to the right of our path, perhaps a hundred meters away. But it was hard to tell. "I have to take a potty break. I'm going over there behind those rocks. You two try not to get into trouble while I'm gone." With that said, I headed off into the darkness.

When I was safely behind one of the outcrops, I glanced back to make sure Kenny and Vyshinsky were staying put. I could see Kenny's flashlight beam in the distance.

I turned on the phone and checked the signal again, breathing a sigh of relief at the sight of the cell service still holding on one bar. Then I tapped the phone icon and made the call. The signal was weak and filled with static, but when I heard the voice on the other end answer, I said, "I need to speak with Tennyson."

This time there was no recorded message or callback. "Are you all right?"

"Yes, Mr.—" I caught myself before I said President. "I'm alive, so are Agent Gates and Colonel Vyshinsky. Minor cuts and bruises from the plane crash, but nothing serious. The pilot, copilot, and a Russian soldier are dead."

"Do you still have the thumb drive?"

"Yes. Was it your drone—?"

"Let's not discuss that."

"Are we not on a secure line?"

"Yes, we are. What's your destination?"

LeClaire was as evasive as Kepner.

"Vyshinsky says we're about a kilometer from a secret Iranian underground facility in Sudan. We're on foot headed there now."

There was a moment's pause as I heard other voices in the background with the President. "We have your location confirmed and also have pinpointed what we believe is the facility near a remote set of ancient ruins."

"What happens now?"

"You're done."

"I'm sorry?"

"Your mission is over. When we last spoke, I said I needed you to continue on with your mission until you draw out the men who stole the alien artifacts. You have obviously done so. You met with them in Moscow. We now know where the artifacts are being kept—at the facility in the Sudan desert. It's time for you and Agent Gates to come home."

"And just how are we supposed to do that?"

"A Navy SEAL team will be launched from a CIA base in South Sudan. The new government there is cooperating with us to supply a staging area for a possible assault on the facility."

"How soon will they be here?"

"Six hours."

"And until then?"

"Hide. Stay out of sight. Wait for the rescue team to pick you up."

"What should I do with the thumb drive?"

"Keep it safe. We can't allow the Russian cabal to carry out their plans to destroy their government. That includes not allowing them to unlock the thumb drive once it's at the desert facility. You must do whatever it takes to keep that from happening."

"What about Vyshinsky?"

"Take him along. Leave him. Shoot him. I don't care. Do whatever it takes to ensure that you and Gates aren't captured and the drive taken from you."

I stared at the phone. This was madness. Where were we going to hide in the desert? And what about our fugitive status? Was the President planning to rescue us?

Or capture us?

"You still there, Agent Decker?"

"Yes."

"Good luck."

The call ended.

I turned off my cell to conserve the battery power. Then I looked to see if Kenny and Vyshinsky were still where I left them.

That's when I felt the gun barrel press against the back of my skull.

CHAPTER 53 - THE CAVALRY
North Africa, the Republic of Sudan

An angry male voice barked behind me in Arabic. When I didn't respond, he jabbed the gun barrel into my back.

"Hands on head!"

I quickly tucked my cell phone into my pocket and did as he ordered while I tried to see Kenny and the colonel in the distance. But Kenny's flashlight beam was gone.

"Walk!" Once again the man jabbed me.

As we moved across the sand, I could smell him. It wasn't pleasant. I should have picked up on that a moment earlier. He was definitely good at sneaking up on people. I never heard a thing until I felt the gun.

"What do you want?" I tried not to trip on one of the rocks that littered the area and cause him to accidently shoot me.

He responded with another jab.

Then I spotted Kenny and Vyshinsky, their hands raised as a second man held them at gunpoint. The distinctive banana clip of his weapon told me it was an AK-47 pointed at their backs.

"You okay?" Kenny said as we approached.

"Just ducky."

"Halt." When I did so, my captor spun me around as he searched my coat and pants pockets for weapons. He confiscated my phone. I started to worry that he'd find the flash drive, but realized that being Muslim, he'd never touch my breasts or search my bra. Besides, he was looking for weapons, not a small thumb drive.

Most likely these guys were some of the same rebels we had left cooking back at the encampment.

"Hands behind back."

I felt a coarse rope being tied around my wrists. Then a rough cloth bag was pulled over my head. It scratched my face and my heart pounded, and even in the chill of the desert night, I broke out in a sweat. Is this the end? What a shitty place to die.

"You will not need this," I heard the captor say. He must have found the pistol tucked behind Kenny's back.

"You are making a big mistake." Vyshinsky's voice was muffled. He probably had a sack over his head, too. "I am Colonel Nikolai Vyshinsky of the Russian Army. Let me go and no action will be taken against you. But if you—"

Vyshinsky gave out a loud grunt. Scraping sounds and a gasping for air told me the Russian was probably lying on the ground in pain. One of the men must have used the butt of the rifle on the colonel's kidney.

"Get up, Russian colonel!"

I heard Vyshinsky struggling to stand. A moment later, the three of us stood beside each other.

"Start walking."

With a convincing shove from the two captors, we began blindly trudging along the desert road.

"Are you all right, Colonel?"

"Pricks," he said just above a whisper.

"Silence!"

I realized that being forced to walk blindfolded and bound meant we were being taken prisoner, not about to be executed. This was a good sign. At least that was my theory.

About ten minutes into our trek, I heard a thump. I imagined a baseball bat striking a side of beef. It was followed by a thud as if a large sack of potatoes dropped to the ground. An instant later, a second bat against beef and potato drop occurred. Kenny? Vyshinsky?

Then I realized the repetitious shuffle of two pairs of sandals on sand behind us had ceased.

What the . . .? What happened to our captors? Are we next?

I didn't hear Kenny or Vyshinsky move. For a full sixty seconds, silence. Then the sound of a vehicle approaching made me turn my head. Not another Nissan pickup, but something with more muscle. A large truck—a diesel.

Next came the lights—even through the bag over my head, they were bright. Then multiple footsteps on the sand. A moment later, someone pulled the bag away and I was blinded by rows of floodlights. A man dressed in military fatigues stood before me.

"OSI Special Agent Maxine Decker?" he asked.

I nodded and he moved to Kenny, pulling the bag from my ex-husband's head.

"OSI Special Agent Kenneth Gates?"

"Yes," Kenny replied.

Finally, he moved to the last of us. "Colonel Nikolai Vyshinsky?"

"And you are?" Vyshinsky said with a growl.

"Major General Hassan Jafari of the Islamic Republic of Iran. I'm here to escort you to your final destination."

Jafari turned back to me. "Agent Decker, may I please have the thumb drive."

CHAPTER 54 - THE RUINS
North Africa, the Republic of Sudan

I looked around and saw at least four other military vehicles and a dozen armed soldiers. As we were being shown to a large troop transport truck, I glanced back at our two rebel captors. Both had died of a single head shot each—there wasn't a great deal of their heads left. High-caliber rounds from a silenced military sniper rifle with night vision devices are deadly and messy.

"The drive," General Jafari said. "Last time I will ask."

I couldn't think of anything else to do, except give to him. If I refused, he'd just kill me on the spot and then search me.

"Give it to him, Max," Kenny said. I guessed he was thinking the same thing I was.

I reached inside my bra, withdrew the drive, and then held it out in my open palm.

"Thank you for cooperating, Agent Decker."

One of Jafari's soldiers approached. He said something I didn't understand. And then he handed over my cell phone that he must have retrieved from the dead rebel. I reached for it, but Jafari shook his head and slipped it into his own pocket.

Now we were in the back of the truck, bumping along—Kenny beside me and Vyshinsky sitting on the opposite side. Not long after, we rumbled to a halt. The back of the transport opened and the rising sun blinded me. Strong hands grabbed my arms and guided me to the ground. When I was finally able to glance around, I saw in the distance what I was sure was a grouping of Nubian mini-pyramids from the Kush kingdom. We were somewhere near what I guessed were the ruins of the Kushite necropolis at Sedeinga—the landmark President LeClaire referred to in our call.

Jafari emerged from one of the other vehicles and joined us. "This way," he said. Without waiting for a reply, he moved off toward a large stone structure, part of the ruins, but standing apart from the others.

When we got there, we started down a set of steps beside the pyramid leading into the ground. At the bottom we entered a tunnel. I had heard rumors over the years that a network of tunnels existed below the desert connecting the ancient pyramids, but until now, I had seen no proof. The passage was spacious enough to walk through comfortably, its width about the size of a panel van. Although the walls had probably been carved out thousands of years ago, a modern lighting system made the going easy.

Fifty meters later, we came out of the tunnel into a large, bright room that turned out to be a security checkpoint. This room had not been constructed by ancient Nubian hands. Concrete walls and bright utility lighting gave the space a stark, factory feel.

After searching each of us, they led us along a concrete-walled hallway past a series of offices manned by technicians in white coats, and side rooms filled with racks of electronics. From there we walked through a large fortified steel door into an observation room. Before us was a wall of windows looking down into a cavernous space cut deep into the desert bedrock. The perimeter of the room was lined with workstations and computer terminals. A number of technicians were busy at work. I stared with fascination at the centerpiece of what I now knew was the secret Iranian lab. It was almost a mirror image of Beowulf.

In the center of the room was a chrome rectangular box big enough for two or three people to stand inside. But what overshadowed the box were the rings. Well over six meters in diameter, the rings were multicolored and resembled huge transparent donuts standing upright. They gave off a soft glow as if made of neon. Even from where I stood with the others, I sensed a low hum coming from the device below. It made me uneasy.

General Jafari came to stand next to me. "You'll get used to it," he said. "The sound makes everyone feel uncomfortable at first, but soon you hear it as background noise. Like white noise."

"What makes the sound?" I asked.

"No idea."

A man approached in a white lab coat.

"Agent Decker," Jafari said, "may I present Dr. Mostafa Moghaddam, Director of Uranium Enrichment. Dr. Moghaddam, these are OSI agents Decker and Gates. And this is Colonel Nikolai Vyshinsky."

Rather than shaking hands, we all simply nodded.

Moghaddam said, "I hope your journey was without incident."

I almost laughed but held back. He knew full well what we had gone through.

"I've had worse," Vyshinsky said.

"Now that you have arrived," Moghaddam said, "we can begin to enlighten you as to what we are doing out here in the middle of the Sudanese desert, and what part you will play in our work."

"Can you begin by telling us what that is?" Kenny said and motioned to the large device on the laboratory floor below.

"It is called the Shield," Moghaddam said.

"That doesn't tell us much."

"You will learn soon enough, Agent Gates," Jafari said. "We are on a very tight deadline."

"And what part do we play in all this?" I asked.

Moghaddam smiled. "You will bring about change."

"Change to what?" I asked.

CHAPTER 55 - ALLIES
North Africa, the Republic of Sudan

Dr. Moghaddam patted my shoulder as he turned to Vyshinsky. "Colonel, you have a relationship with Agents Decker and Gates, and you speak most excellent English, one of my deficiencies. So if I may suggest, why do you not explain our project? Perhaps your translation would be clearer to our visitors."

Moghaddam had a thick accent, but his English sounded fine to me.

Vyshinsky seemed to be taken by surprise.

"Proceed, Colonel," Moghaddam said. "I am interested in how you will present this in terms they will understand."

I noticed that General Jafari's eyebrows lifted, but he said nothing. It looked like he was eager to hear Vyshinsky's explanation, too.

"If you wish," Vyshinsky said, "but I am not a scientist—I can only explain in the simplest of terms." He still seemed uneasy.

Looking at Kenny and me, he said, "My American friends, what you observe is the result of years of research, begun even before Beowulf. Our Iranian comrades and the New Soviet Republic are partners in this project. Some refer to my employers as the Russian cabal, but I do not find that term especially endearing. It implies divisiveness, and they strive for unification, bringing home all of the Union of Soviet Socialist Republics together again—the rebirth of Mother Russia."

"Doesn't sound like a simple objective," Kenny said.

"*Nyet*. Problematic, but not impossible. Not impossible at

all. Not now. With your help."

"I can't agree to help," Kenny said. "And neither will Agent Decker."

"This is not a request," General Jafari said. "And I do not appreciate your interruption. Colonel Vyshinsky will continue or you will go to your *quarters*."

The bold tone in his voice when he said "quarters" sent a shiver through me.

"Accept our apology, Colonel," I said, not wanting to shut down the conversation and end up in a human kennel. I hoped Kenny wasn't going to shoot off his mouth again.

Vyshinsky waited a moment before he continued. "Five years ago I traveled to Tunguska in Siberia where I collected an unusual artifact. You are aware of the Tunguska event, yes?"

I nodded.

"Like your Roswell, but much earlier," he said. "We believe, as do the Americans at Beowulf, that this artifact and the ones collected at Roswell are from extraterrestrial aircraft and possess certain properties that are thousands of years ahead of our knowledge of physics. Perhaps they reflect another science that we know nothing about."

I thought "another science" was an interesting concept. But then who could conceive of what might exist thousands of years into the future?

"And so," he continued, "as directed by my commander, General Lushev, I delivered the artifact to Dr. Drozdov, who as you know was a renowned leader in the world of quantum mechanics, and in the opinions of some circles, supplementary bizarre theories. Dr. Drozdov had completed a two-decade project to develop a quantum computer. His remarkable accomplishment was kept quiet so that other endeavors would continue without attention."

"Undertakings based on the artifact?" Kenny said.

"Correct."

"But not in Russia?" I said.

"To do so would be impossible to keep secret."

"So you chose the desolate Sudanese desert and paid Iran

with currency and the benefit of sharing the end product."

A snide smile coiled around his mouth. "Not currency. Bullion. Gold. Except for the small details, your assessment is accurate, comrade."

I didn't like being called a comrade but thought disputing the moniker would only cause trouble. I thought of the *quarters*. "The cabal funded the Iranians to build this facility and carry out your mission, silencing Drozdov's crowning achievement in the process."

"You make it too simple, my friend," Vyshinsky said.

Too simple? Drozdov was on the floor of his home with a hole drilled through his head.

"Sometimes I think you do not listen. As you were told before, Drozdov's assistant was sent on ahead to prepare, but that man was greedy. The assistant is the one who stole Drozdov's recognition, not the cabal. In the assistant's hasty attempt to test the project, the original facility was destroyed."

The picture was taking form in my head. "That's why you raided Beowulf. You needed the Roswell artifacts because the Tunguska pieces were wiped out. And you took the scientists because, like the artifacts, the Iranian staff went up in smoke."

"Yes. Now you see."

"Not completely," I said. "You haven't explained exactly what's going on here. What is of such enormous magnitude that it justifies all these betrayals and deaths? This thing you call the Shield."

Vyshinsky glanced at Jafari, who nodded.

"The Shield will serve as the ultimate deterrent against aggression and war. For the new Soviet Federation, it will be the means to shift Russia from its corrupt capitalistic government back to the glory of its former self as a world superpower to be feared and respected. The Shield will need to be used only once to convince the world of the power we wield. And as part of our agreement with Iran, we will inform the world that they, too, have the power of the Shield—no one will be able to threaten or touch them, including Israel and the West. They will have the ability to protect themselves against all enemies. The only global superpowers left after the introduction of the Shield will be the New Soviet Republic and the Islamic Republic of Iran. It will end the thousands of years of war and terror in the Middle East and guarantee the Soviet Republic world supremacy."

Kenny tilted his head and heaved out an aggravated moan.

I knew that was a sign of a particular attitude Kenny got, and it was a giveaway to me what he was thinking. My ex was about to tell them to go screw themselves. I hoped he would keep himself in check.

"So what now?" Kenny said. "Let me take a wild guess. You brought me here to clean up the mess?" He heavily emphasized *mess*, transforming his statement into a subtle insult. "You killed Drozdov because he would no longer cooperate. He just didn't give a shit anymore. You stripped him of everything. You are as gluttonous as his assistant, but you stand on a rung even lower than that. You, my 'friend,' slog in the sewer with the rats."

"Feel better getting that off your chest, comrade?"

"I'm not your fucking comrade, Vyshinsky."

"But you are. You will cooperate. The definition of comrade is friend. Friends work together."

"Eat shit," Kenny said. "It ain't happening, *friend*."

"I think you are wrong," Vyshinsky said. "You see, we have something you want."

"I don't want jack shit from you."

"Are you sure?" Jafari said, planting the barrel of his gun against my temple.

CHAPTER 56 - JAFARI
Underground desert laboratory, Sudan

I held my breath as Kenny and I gazed at each other, trying to hide our fear and indecision. "Are you certain your mind is made up?" Jafari asked Kenny. "My advice is for you to give it another moment of thought. You see, if you do not cooperate, we will kill Agent Decker. She is needed but expendable."

"Don't listen, Kenny," I said. "They won't kill me."

"I do beg to differ with you, Agent." He jabbed the gun against my skull for emphasis.

Kenny crowded Jafari. "Don't do anything to her, asshole."

I bit my bottom lip. "Kenny, just back away."

Kenny looked at me. "If they lay a hand on you . . ." He faced Jafari. "Does asshole translate into Farsi or Persian or whatever the hell you speak?"

"Kenny, shut up," I said. I wanted to plunge an elbow into his side and slap my hand over his mouth before he got us killed. I suppose he figured we were as good as dead anyway.

Vyshinsky stepped up behind Kenny, twisted his arms to his back, and zipped a cable lock around his wrists. He gave an extra hard yank. Kenny flinched in response as the plastic dug into his skin.

"You think you are a super hero?" Jafari said.

Vyshinsky raised Kenny's arms behind him, straining his shoulders. Kenny threw his head back and squeezed his eyes shut in pain.

Jafari thrust a finger in the center of Kenny's chest to punctuate each sentence. "You will cooperate."

Jab.

"You will do exactly as I instruct."

Jab.

"You will use our quantum computer to unlock the thumb drive." He grabbed Kenny's head and jerked it sideways so my ex could look at me. "Imagine this beauty with a hole all the way through her head. Can you picture that? No, wait. Let me clarify so the image is clear. Vyshinsky, should we shoot through the temple, the mouth, or up from the chin? What do you think?"

The Russian didn't answer.

"If you murder her, you might as well take me out, too," Kenny said. "Kill her, you lose me. Either way, I'm not going to do a single thing for you. Not one small, minute, infinitesimal thing. How's that for clarity?"

"Good, actually. Your description is noteworthy. But I feel it only fair to tell you that after I kill your former wife, I will compel you, with my most persuasive techniques, to clean her brains and blood from the wall and floor with your bare hands. You will pick out and save the small bits of gray matter and skull fragments and put them in a receptacle. And then I will force a tube down into your belly and feed them to you. Your thirst will be quenched with her blood, and your hunger satisfied with her raw remains. Now, it is my turn. How did I do expressing myself with clarity?"

Kenny's face blanched. His bravado disappeared, replaced with fear.

"Don't listen, Kenny," I said. "He's bluffing."

"This is not a poker game. For some reason you do not seem to grasp the enormity of our mission nor our undertaking."

The room was silent for a moment. Then Jafari lowered the gun. "Do you know what, Agent Gates? You have given me another idea. I do not know why it took me so long. Ah, I am not as young as I used to be. Are not you the smart one?"

"You're going to hell," Kenny said.

"In due time," Jafari said.

195

CHAPTER 57 - BLUE EYES
Underground desert laboratory, Sudan

Vyshinsky shoved us along through the interior of the facility. At this point I was just happy we were alive and neither of us was whistling air through a bullet hole.

Kenny and I exchanged glances. He'd always been my hero. Even back when I was new at OSI, he'd been the one who taught me the inside ropes and picked me up when I stumbled. I could see the pain in his face as he understood there was nothing he could do to save me from this situation. I showed him a smile to let him know I was okay.

The colonel kept us moving with a push against our backs now and again. As we moved through the facility its resemblance was so much like Beowulf that it gave me a sense of déjà vu. We exited the main area of the building. At the end of a long hallway was a white wood door that seemed out of place in such a modern facility. Standing in front of it was a man who also seemed out of place.

His blue eyes told me he wasn't Middle-Eastern. He had short dark hair with strands of silver at the temples, and was freshly groomed and clean-shaven. His clothes also stamped an impression in my mind. He wore a stiffly-starched white shirt, a dark suit that looked expensive, and black wingtip shoes. To me, he appeared to qualify better for the cover of GQ than whatever work he was doing in this hellhole. Maybe he would be somebody I could talk to. Maybe he would be the one to get us out of here.

Blue Eyes, as I thought of him, opened the door and motioned us through. We entered what looked more like a tunnel than a corridor. With walls made of clay and brick, the passage appeared to be much older than the main structure. Instead of blazing lights like in the modern section of the facility, dusty bare bulbs hung from the ceiling, run together by outdated, exposed wiring. It was probably built during World War II when the Sudan was directly involved militarily in the East African Campaign. Perhaps it was an underground barracks or a place to store supplies and arms.

The tunnel gave me the creeps. I was sure I felt spiders and webs on my skin and heard all kinds of vermin scuttling about. The cold, dank air was laden with the choking odor of mold and mildew. I vigorously rubbed my upper arms.

About twenty meters down the corridor, Vyshinsky stopped in front of a barred room, like a jail cell. Planted in the corner was a cracked porcelain pan. Was that the toilet?

Blue Eyes extracted keys from his pocket, found the one he wanted, and opened the cell door.

"Inside," the colonel said to Kenny. He clipped the tie wraps around Kenny's wrists and my ex stepped inside.

So "quarters" was not a kennel—it was more of a dungeon.

Vyshinsky closed the door, and the clunk let me know it was locked.

The colonel stared at me for a moment. I couldn't tell if it was pity or foreboding I detected. He turned and headed along the way we had come, never looking back.

Blue Eyes opened the next cell. This one did have something like a shower curtain with metal rings dangling from a rod suspended from the ceiling. *A privacy space for toileting? A cell meant especially for a woman to suit the Islamic culture?*

The door clanged as the man opened it. My boot heel caught on the raised threshold and I faltered. Blue Eyes caught my elbow to help me reclaim my balance. A twinge pinged my ankle, reminding me that it still hadn't completely healed.

In another moment I was locked in and Blue Eyes was gone.

Curious, I looked behind the curtain. I was correct. There was an old sink, the porcelain flaking and iron-stained, and a toilet that matched the sink, blemish for blemish.

I came around and stood next to the damp concrete wall that separated me from Kenny. "Can you hear me?" I said softly. When he didn't answer right away I went to the barred door. "Kenny?

"I'm here."

"Any idea who the guy is who locked us up?"

"None."

"He doesn't look like he has a Middle-Eastern heritage. And I'd bet he's not Russian."

"It's hard to tell. Be careful around him, Max."

"Let's call him Blue Eyes."

"Wonder if he knows any Sinatra?"

I wrapped both hands around the bars. I wanted to say I love you, but stopped myself. "You're the best. No matter the situation, you know just how to make me laugh."

"Well, hell, I should. I was married to you long enough."

I looked down and leaned my forehead against the bars, remembering the good times and trying to forget the not-so-good.

"I take that back," Kenny said. "I wasn't married to you *long enough*—should have been longer."

We were both silent for a few minutes. "Kenny, you still there?"

"No, I've gone out for Chinese."

He brought another smile to my face. Maybe I would say I love you. There might not be another chance. "Kenny, I—"

Footsteps sounded in the hallway. A moment later Blue Eyes walked into view, hauling something behind him.

CHAPTER 58 - MOTORCADE
Washington, DC

The black General Motors seven-passenger limousine, known as *The Beast*, swept up Pennsylvania Avenue along with the usual escort of Secret Service SUVs and police cars. In the rear seat, President LeClaire watched CIA Director Singer speaking quietly on one of the half-dozen secure telephones built into the communications console. Despite not liking the director personally and always having to deal with his tardiness, he had to admit the man did get things done.

LeClaire glanced out the five-inch-thick bulletproof windows at the cross streets, each blocked off by police cars. He always felt self-conscious about inconveniencing the traffic flow of the city, but in the end, he had no say in the matter. It was the infamous "they" who made those types of the rules.

National Security Advisor Scarborough, who'd been checking his smartphone, glanced out the window. "I've got a bad feeling about this."

"Let's wait until we have all the facts," the President said.

"I've already heard enough to give me heartburn." Scarborough shifted his focus back to the window.

"It's not good," Singer said as he hung up the phone.

"So it's confirmed?" Scarborough placed the BlackBerry on the seat beside him.

Singer nodded. "Iran has ordered the immediate expulsion of all UN nuclear inspectors and members of the NRC. In addition, they are ordering the closure of all non-Islamic embassies and consulates. They're giving all diplomats and staffs twenty-four hours to leave Iran under threat of arrest and prison."

"So this all comes after the inspectors demanded to see a suspected weapons development site not on the list?" the President asked.

"Told you," Scarborough said.

"Thank you for that timely reminder." The President looked back at Singer. "What about the Russians?"

"Equally interesting turn of events." Singer checked the notes he had made while he spoke on the phone. "What we refer to as the cabal has apparently gone underground. The government pulled out all the stops to find them, and according to our analysts, General Lushev, Boris Ivankov, and Vladimir Butorin have vanished."

"I thought their whole New Soviet movement was gathering steam," LeClaire said.

"It was," Singer replied. "Significant portions of the population including the military were starting to come around to the Big Three's way of thinking. But Putinov dropped the hammer and ordered all hands on deck to find the three and bring them in."

"Once again, let me just point out—"

Yeah, yeah. President LeClaire held up his hand to silence Scarborough. "Let's concentrate on how we deal with these developments, shall we, and leave the gloating for later?"

The phone that the CIA Director had spoken on rang. He picked it up, listened, then hung up. "Vladimir Butorin, President of Red Star Media Group, was just arrested."

The President leaned back into his seat. "Looks like the cabal totally miscalculated President Putinov."

"Maybe," Scarborough said.

LeClaire motioned to his National Security Advisor. "Maybe what?"

"Maybe something else triggered the cabal shutdown."

"No," Singer said. "Putinov is like a great white shark playing with a doomed seal. When he's had enough fun, he goes in for the kill. That's how he ran the old KGB."

"Still," Scarborough said, "the cabal had a long way to go to pull off this New Soviet shit. Why now? What caused them to suddenly jump into the nearest rat hole?"

The President cleared his throat. "What's the latest on the status of the two OSI agents?"

Scarborough stared at him. "With all due respect, Mr. President, I can't believe you even asked that question. Considering the latest events, the two missing agents are the least of our concern."

"I agree," Singer said. "For the life of me, I can't understand your obsession with these two. The Russians are rounding up their citizens in the streets and the Iranians appear to be gearing up for a full-scale war. What is so special about a retired federal agent and a computer geek?"

President LeClaire turned to the window for a moment, then back. "Gentlemen, perhaps it's time I tell you what's really going on."

CHAPTER 59 - BURN
Underground desert laboratory, Sudan

I tried to see what it was that Blue Eyes was pulling behind him. It looked like a suitcase, not a large one, more like a kid's, or the cases that lawyers drag about when going into courthouses.

In a moment he was jangling keys and then opening the door of my cell.

"Hang in, Max," Kenny called out.

"Shh." Blue Eyes brought his finger to his lips.

He entered my cell, unzipped his suitcase, and took out a laptop, a small folding metal stool, and a projector. It took him a few minutes to get everything hooked up and plugged in, including running an extension cord to a relic of an electric outlet in the hallway. He put the projector on top of the portable stool and aimed the lens at the whitewashed back wall. Then he closed the cell door.

"Maxine, I want you to watch," Blue Eyes said.

He spoke so low I was certain that Kenny couldn't make out his words. I noted that he called me by my first name which I found oddly refreshing considering the situation.

"You don't need to say anything unless I ask. And I don't want you to turn away. Can you do that?"

"Uh huh," I said. I tossed my previous *refreshing* thought out the window. His sheer calmness and even-toned voice made me more apprehensive than if some ghoulish cinematic villain had been threatening me with an ax. The cold and sodden air in this dungeon soaked through my skin, chilling me as much as Blue Eyes.

He fired up the projector with a remote and punched a few keys on the laptop, causing a picture to appear on the wall. Imperfect as the *screen* was, the image was surprisingly clear. It was of a young boy. The color of the photo had faded with age.

I thought my visitor would say something, but he didn't. The picture remained frozen on the wall, and I continued to stare at it. Finally, I realized what he must have been waiting for me to see. It was the color and shape of the eyes. The photo was of him when he was a boy. I guessed he was around eight years old. However, there was a difference besides age. This boy was pallid and frail, with dark half-moons beneath his blue eyes, a far stretch from the robust man beside me. The boy was dressed in what I thought might be a school uniform—navy blue shorts belted over a white shirt. And a tie. So stuffy for a kid. I looked at Blue Eyes and compared him to the picture. "You?"

He nodded. "I was wretchedly frail and sickly as a boy. I suffered from severe asthma."

I picked up on a faint accent. Those few sentences gave away his nationality.

"You're Irish," I said.

"I am."

"What in the hell are you doing here?"

"Shh." The finger to his lips again.

I silently wondered why he was involved with Vyshinsky, Jafari, and the Shield project.

The next shot appeared on the wall. Again, it was Blue Eyes, but older in this photograph. Late teens, close to 20, I thought. Gone were the shorts and uniform. Gone were the dark circles. And there was meat and muscle on his bones. In this picture he was in a room—maybe a dorm room—with pictures and posters on the wall.

Blue Eyes tapped a button on the projector and the photo zoomed in.

The posters were of NFL football teams, Yankees and

Atlanta Braves baseball logos.

He zoomed closer, bringing into focus what appeared to be a blowup of a newspaper photograph of a man. "He gave me the strength. He showed me how to become the best that I could be."

I recognized the man in the picture. G. Gordon Liddy.

Blue Eyes read my expression. "Do you know how he became the man he was?"

"Yes."

The image on the screen changed again. This time it was Blue Eyes standing on a train track with an engine seeming to roar toward him. He leaned to my ear, so close I felt the breath of his words stir my hair. "Have no fear. That is the key."

The photo changed once more to one of Blue Eyes sitting on a couch with a lit cigarette pressed to the flesh of his inner arm.

"Some men can condition themselves to tolerate pain so they can endure almost anything. It training. Some men can never be made to talk."

This sounded just like a biography of Liddy, the man in the newspaper picture.

"You've fashioned yourself after G. Gordon Liddy?"

"I have. It is a valuable skill."

Blue Eyes opened his case again and took out a cigarette and lit it with a lighter. He put it to his lips and sucked in, making hollows in his cheeks and the tip of the cigarette grow fiery. He held the cigarette out toward me and expelled the smoke, without ever inhaling.

My stomach twisted into a nauseating knot, squeezing up its contents near my throat as I imagined what he was going to do. My skin went clammy.

His blue eyes skewered mine. I blinked, but he did not.

"Are you afraid?" he whispered. "Or have you done the work that I have in order to prepare yourself for anything?"

He knew the answer.

"Max?" It was Kenny's voice.

Blue Eyes shook his head and took my arm and turned it

wrist side up. "Such delicate flesh."

I squeezed my eyes shut and held my breath.
Then I smelled it.

CHAPTER 60 - SLIDESHOW
Underground desert laboratory, Sudan

Burning flesh is a sickening, charcoal-like, sweetish smell. Once experienced, you never forget.

"Open your eyes, Maxine," Blue Eyes said.

I was reluctant, afraid that I would see the skin somewhere on my body smoldering and I was just too numb with fear to feel it. Trepidation clattered through my bones, making my whole body shudder. My eyes flew open even though I was thinking I didn't want to look.

What I saw was disturbing. Blue Eyes had rolled up his sleeve and pressed the burning cigarette tip to the skin on the inside of his forearm. He wasn't even watching his flesh scorch, much less grimacing. He was looking at me, judging my reaction.

"Stop." I turned away. "You don't need to prove anything to me. You're sick. I mean—"

"Conditioned is a good choice of words."

I glanced in his direction. He'd withdrawn the cigarette and held it out to me. "Want to give it a go?"

He waited while I glared at him. He needed to be institutionalized.

"I know what you're thinking," he said, "so I'll answer. The Troubles—that's what they called the conflict in Ireland—stole my innocence. What I witnessed as a boy, a child's eyes should never see. I vowed that nothing would ever be able to hurt me. Not man, not machine, not nature. Like my hero, I often straddled the train track and dared the oncoming locomotive to kill me. Only at the last minute would I step off the track."

"That gave you a rush?"

"Conditioning, Maxine. Conditioning."

"Madness."

"You had to live my life, see what I've seen. You are too quick to judge." Blue Eyes brushed the top of my hand with his. "I should get on with business if I am to earn my wage."

Clearly, I'd been way off base thinking this man might possibly be our liberator.

The image on the wall mirrored the laptop's desktop. I watched the cursor point to a folder titled Persuasion. He clicked it open and then the slideshow presentation inside. *PowerPoint?* There was no title slide. It jumped to the first image of a metal bull. *Bizarre.*

"One of my favorites, but not very practical. I'll leave the decision up to you."

"I don't know what you're talking about."

"Give it a moment, Maxine. You will. Now, let me explain what is before you. This is a brazen bull. It is a hollow bronze bull with enough room inside for one person. It is a simple device, but so effective." He rolled his eyes emphasizing the pleasure he felt thinking about the bull. "The victim is put inside, and a fire is built beneath it. The Greeks were so inventive, don't you think? They attached a system of tubes to the bull in order to make the victim's screams sound like an enraged ox, also described as melodious bellows." He smiled. "I think I prefer the latter. The brazen bull was a superb deterrent to crime in its day. My only issue is that once the fire is ablaze, there isn't much one can do to abort the event. It is over for the victim—and often that is not what I want—or the people who contract me, want."

"I don't want to see any more." I turned away, not wanting to think about the reasons he might be showing me this.

"Turn back and look, Maxine. Or maybe you would like to test the cigarette right here." He touched my neck with his finger.

My heart fluttered a scary uneven beat. I bit the inside of

my cheek.

Blue Eyes put his hand on the side of my head and redirected it for me to look at the wall. He clicked the remote and the next slide came up.

My stomach grew sour as he proceeded through more slides of torture—breathing air with high levels of CO_2, flaying, electric shock, and horrifying devices used for painful sexual assault. The gruesome pictures seemed endless, exploding one after the other on the sweating white wall.

I jumped to my feet. "Stop! I get it. You're a demented sick fuck and I should be terrified of you. Objective met. I don't want or need to see any more."

"Excellent, Maxine. Now, as you Americans say, pick your poison."

CHAPTER 61 - COMING CLEAN
Oval Office, The White House, Washington, DC

"Roswell? Little green men?" Secretary of State Butler said. "I'm having a real hard time wrapping my head around this one. No disrespect intended, but it's just so unbelievable."

The President's national security team had gathered in the Oval Office where he had just informed them about Beowulf and the alien artifacts.

Vice President Waite stood on his long Texan legs and swaggered over to the coffee service on a side table. He poured a cup and then faced the President. "I gotta tell you, Guy, this is about the craziest thing I've heard since I moved to this town. And I've heard a whole bunch of crazy."

"I've got to agree with the vice president, sir," CIA Director Singer said. "I've listened to you explain all this Beowulf stuff and still . . . I'm not even sure where to begin. I've never seen any documentation that the Roswell incident was anything more than the crash of a secret Air Force surveillance balloon. That entire scenario has been debunked by the military. Now you're telling us about a sci-fi-type of installation called Beowulf built into the side of the Grand Canyon. I don't know. Words fail me."

"How do you know this whole Beowulf thing was legit?" said National Security Advisor Scarborough. "Have you ever been there? If it's so damn black, how do we know it even exists? With no paper trail, how can you be certain they were developing this—" he nodded to Butler "—flying saucer technology, this displacement machine?"

The President let each man have a turn at expressing his concerns. Finally, when they seemed to have run out of steam, he said, "I *have* been there—to Beowulf, that is. Twice. I knew Chaucer well and spoke to him weekly, often several times a week. We were high school classmates and fraternity brothers in college. He had two doctorates from MIT and was one of the leading experts in quantum mechanics. And he loved poetry—hence we chose the code names, Chaucer for him, and Tennyson for me. If he had told me that he created a unicorn that could fart rubies, I would have believed him."

There was a round of grumbles.

"That brings up another question," Butler said. "Who was responsible for bringing Kepner into Beowulf? How could a Russian spy gain access to a facility with security so high?"

"Kepner was brought on board back in 1993." The President tapped his pen on his desk. "All I know about Peter Kepner is that he was a former CIA counter-intelligence officer in Ankara. Now we know that somehow he was recruited by the Russians to steal the artifacts."

"So he smuggled the artifacts out of Beowulf and then arranged for the assault team to gain access to the facility?" Butler asked.

"We'll never know for sure, since Peter is dead. But that's my take."

The vice president sipped his coffee. "Could Agent Decker have killed him for just that reason? So we would never know?"

"I don't believe that."

"I still don't understand why you put so much faith in Decker and her former husband, the computer genius." Scarborough looked around the room as if trying to find support from the others. "I mean, these two are international fugitives accused of murder, attempted murder, conspiracy with foreign nationals, and flight to avoid prosecution, not to mention renouncing their citizenship and seeking asylum in a country that is a known enemy of America and its allies. Even now, they are taking refuge with the enemy in this so-called underground desert laboratory." He spread his arms in a sign of frustration. "There's nothing about this that smells right, sir."

"I brought Agent Decker into this for one reason—find the artifacts. Not only has she done exactly what I asked of her, but she's risked her life numerous times in the process, including making herself a target and surviving an airplane crash. She is exactly where she needs to be to help us. She also had Chaucer's thumb drive, which contains all the information, specs, designs, and everything about the displacement device, including information the Iranians need to finish outfitting their device. The drive is now in the hands of the enemy. Agent Gates knows how to open it using a quantum computer. These two agents didn't run and hide to avoid being sucked into this mess. Instead, they are being held under duress until the Iranian-Russian partnership has built its own device. They need Decker and Gates to do so. Those agents are critical to our surviving this situation."

"What exactly is this *situation*?" Scarborough asked. "What are you expecting to happen? Iran doesn't have missiles that can strike targets in this country. Seems to me the big threat is to Israel and our other allies in the region. What can this device do to harm us?"

"I didn't finish completing the picture for you, so I understand your questions. I need to report one more thing." The President stood and came around to prop himself against the edge of his desk.

"I explained that Beowulf was close to completing the building of the first displacement device. Chaucer had shown me prototypes. All that was left to do was the final assembly, but then the artifacts that were the key to making this mechanism viable were stolen. So far, that is all I've disclosed, and I know you're, thinking of an advanced form of propulsion that will outdo anything we have by a hundredfold. But, gentleman, there is more to it than that. This device moves objects in time and space at incalculable speeds."

"We get that," Singer said. "Someday we can use the

technology to travel to distant stars. I'm just not connecting that with a direct threat to our country."

"Consider this," the President said. "If the device can move a spacecraft across light years in a reasonable timeframe, think how quickly it can move an object a short distance—say across the globe rather than across the universe. A fraction of a second? Instantaneously? A chair. A dog. An aircraft." The President lowered his voice. "A nuclear weapon."

A pall fell over the room as the President watched each man's expression turn a few shades paler. Finally, the vice president said, "There would be no warning. No time for interception. No radar. No defense. Nothing."

President LeClaire returned to his chair. "At the moment, I believe the Kremlin is the target. But what's to make the threat stop there? I've come to believe that we face the most catastrophic threat this country has ever known"

CHAPTER 62 - POPE'S PEAR
Underground desert laboratory, Sudan

"Fuck you," I said to Blue Eyes.

He laughed. "That's not on the list, and for your information it would be a torture of another sort. A satisfying one. I am a master at whatever I take seriously. Now you know two of the fields to which I have dedicated my concentration. Perhaps you doubt me and instead of a slide show would enjoy a personal demonstration?"

"Go to hell. You're a pompous and depraved pervert. I believe you did see unspeakable horrors growing up, otherwise I can't imagine a man being so warped."

He laughed again.

"Max?" Kenny called. He must have heard the creepy laugh.

"I'm okay."

"Uh, uh," Blue Eyes said, like telling a child or dog not to do something. "No conversations." He spoke loud enough for Kenny to understand his message. "I will let you know when I want you to speak, Agent Gates."

He called me Maxine but referred to Kenny as Agent Gates. The first-name basis sent another sputter of chills through me. *Does he prefer a more intimate climate with the one he will torture?*

"You are divorced from Agent Gates? Is my information correct?"

I refused to respond.

"It doesn't matter. I am certain I have accurate facts. I suppose that is why I am confused by the relationship between the two of you." He paused, put his finger to the tip of his

213

nose as if digesting his thoughts and coming to a conclusion. After a moment, he blinked several times as his smile broadened. "This helps me immensely, Maxine. Knowing about the *bond* you and Agent Gates share has inspired me. Having someone like you, who feeds me just what I need to know, makes my decisions almost effortless. I should thank you but I fear it would fall on fallow ground."

I so wanted to give him the finger, but didn't dare antagonize this madman.

He began disconnecting his equipment and packing it up. When he finished, he unlocked the cell door.

"I wouldn't want you to get lonely," he said, closing the door. "I will return, and we shall share some quality and productive time together."

Blue Eyes brushed his suit coat so the fit was perfect and ran his fingers around his shirt collar. And then in no hurry, he headed off, pulling his rolling case behind him, and was soon out of my vision range.

Kenny must have kept a bead on him as well, because as soon as the hall door sounded and the Irishman was assumed out of earshot, my ex called my name.

"Max, did he hurt you?"

"Not yet. He did his best to screw with my head, but I had none of it." In reality, Blue Eyes had spooked the shit out of me and my mouth was so dry it felt like I'd had tasted a spoonful of alum. But I didn't want Kenny to get any more upset than he already was. After all, there was nothing he could do to help. "I'm sorry, Kenny. I should have left you out of this." I gripped the cell's rails with both hands. "You should have taken a few days after the conference to party in Vegas, not dig my butt out of deep trouble." My voice trembled as I fought back tears.

"Hey, Cry Baby, knock it off. You know there's no place I'd rather be."

He'd done it again—made me smile right in the face of adversity. "Sure. Right."

"Come on." There was a *stop-it-Max* tone in his voice.

I leaned forward and the bars were cold on my forehead. "Kenny . . . If we ever get out of here do you think—?"

The door at the far end of the hall opened and closed, and the sound of footsteps headed our way. It didn't take long for Blue Eyes to appear. He carried a hinged metal box about the size of a large shoebox. I saw him wink as he passed Kenny.

The man stopped at my cell door but didn't enter. "I am so thankful you aided in my selection," he said.

"What do you want from me?"

"Actually, I don't want anything from you. Maybe some lack of endurance might apply. But I am not certain yet."

He turned, paced to Kenny's cell, and opened it. My skin went cold.

———

"Agent Gates. You are the one I want to talk to. I am finished speaking with Maxine. I will not be conversing with her again."

Kenny glared at Blue Eyes. He wished the man's eyes were brown, the color of shit, because that's how he thought of him.

"I have something to show you." Blue Eyes paused. "Oh, excuse me, I should have thanked you for your hospitality." He opened the box. "Did you know there are several ways that humans respond to a threat? Fight and flight are the two well-known responses. But then there is another called posture. That is when someone confronts the enemy with body language and verbal taunts. Posturing is what your wife—well, technically ex-wife—tried on me, but it was not working for her.

"Freeze is another response. The victim is in shock and does nothing. And then there is the submit reaction. Fight, flight, posture, and freeze are not going to be possible in this case. Submit is what we are after."

The angle of the box lid obscured Kenny's vision of the contents. "I was truly excited to realize that you and Maxine are still attracted to one another. Sex with her is not out of the question, is it Agent Gates? In fact I think you both would find that experience quite pleasing on many levels, not just the physical. I am right, am I not?"

Blue Eyes tapped the side of the box. "And so I have taken that into consideration in selecting the perfect motivator. A *deflowering* object seemed such a natural choice. Oh, I know, deflowering does not exactly apply, but I was searching for a more delicate way of explaining. A euphemism. I am sure you understand. When I perform my task, I will be prudent and unhurried, in hopes that the desires that both of you fantasize will not become unattainable due to my undertaking. All you will need to do is submit. Agree to do what is asked of you and your yearnings may be gratified one day."

From the box he extracted a metal object shaped like a pear with a crank attached to a screw at the narrow end. He held it up so Kenny could see all of it. Slowly he turned the handle, his eyes brightening with each turn. The pear gradually fanned out, flowering, with razor edges on each petal.

Kenny's stomach soured. Terror crushed him on the inside but he didn't want to give away his fear. What man—what human—could think up such horrors? Blue Eyes was the antithesis of his appearance. He was not a gentleman. He was a monster.

"Certainly you abhor the idea of Maxine suffering the pain and destruction this lovely little mechanism can inflict. Submit is all we ask. Oh, Agent Gates, envision the exquisite pleasure of being with your wife once again. It is impossible for me to conceive that you will allow Maxine to meet the infamous, medieval Pope's Pear."

CHAPTER 63 - UNLOCK
Underground desert laboratory, Sudan

"You have made the right decision," Blue Eyes said as he walked Kenny back through the tunnel to the corridor leading to the main underground lab. Colonel Vyshinsky and two armed Iranian soldiers also accompanied them.

"Soon this will all be over, Agent Gates," Vyshinsky said. "Then you and your former bride can go home or back to Iran, or wherever you want."

"Do you honestly think I believe we'll ever see the light of day?" Kenny asked.

"Anything is possible," Blue Eyes said. He stopped in front of a large metal door and pressed in a code on a wall-mounted keypad. The door unlocked and swung open.

One of the guards shoved Kenny, and the five entered a room. Its subdued lighting mostly came from racks of electronic gear and video monitors. Kenny recognized the familiar chill and the noise of a server room. The combination of computer and air conditioning fans flooded the space with a constant hum, like being inside a beehive.

A workstation sat about three meters away. On its desk rested a keyboard, an interface computer, and a large video monitor. The monitor displayed a handful of virtual windows ready for operator input. Behind the workstation, in a somewhat similar fashion as Beowulf, a glass wall separated the rest of the room from the monolithic mainframes—all black and the size of refrigerators. There were more here than at the East Rim lab. Kenny knew the extreme cold kept those

217

monsters from melting down.

"Have a seat, Agent Gates," Blue Eyes said.

Kenny pulled out the operator's chair and did so. He wiped away the sweat that had formed on his forehead. How was he going to get himself and Max out of here alive? He'd do whatever they wanted, if they would leave Max out of it. What was going to happen once he broke the code to the thumb drive? Were he and Max as good as dead?

"Here you go." Vyshinsky handed him Chaucer's thumb drive. "Perform your magic."

Kenny searched the outside of the interface computer and located a bank of audio, video, and data input connectors. One was a USB, and that's where he inserted the drive. He then sat and studied the various windows on the monitor until he decided which to highlight with the cursor first. After doing so, he entered a basic command asking the machine to identify the available input devices. A list appeared. Kenny recognized one as the label for the thumb drive. He hesitated a moment, wondering if there was some possible way he could bluff or destroy the contents without endangering their lives even more. He chose the thumb drive and the screen changed to a new input window asking for the access password.

"This may take a while," Kenny said, trying to stall while he figured out what he could do.

"I thought you did this part once already," Dr. Mostafa Moghaddam said.

Shit. With the noise in the background, he had entered the room without Kenny noticing.

"I have, but it takes time to figure out how the interface works on this machine as opposed to the computer at Beowulf. Each interface seems to be proprietary."

"Learn fast," Blue Eyes said. "Delaying the process will only cause discomfort to Agent Decker." He and Moghaddam turned and left.

"You need to leave me alone if I'm going to get this done," Kenny said to Vyshinsky. "I can't think with you hanging over my shoulder like a vulture."

"You're playing with fire, my friend." The colonel started to leave. "Two guards will remain here to see that you do not doze off."

Kenny returned to studying the interface. The Iranians and Russians had him so on edge he was afraid he was going to make some kind of horrible error and they would be so infuriated that he and Maxine would be executed within the hour. He had to think—had to take his time and focus. To get this done, he needed to put Max and fear out of his mind until he was finished.

Kenny rubbed his eyes with the heels of his hands, then rested his fingertips on the keyboard. He recalled the time at the Beowulf computer, concentrating on the series of commands he had typed. Slowly, some of them started coming back to him.

Thirty minutes later, Kenny looked away from the monitor at the guards. "Go tell Moghaddam I've unlocked the drive."

CHAPTER 64 - THE CALL
Underground desert laboratory, Sudan

We were kept in the dark of our cells after Kenny accessed the hidden partition on the thumb drive. Tired as we both were, we talked through the bars.

"We're going to be okay, Max. Keep positive thoughts."

"I'm trying, but I don't see any way out of this. They kept me alive with the threat of torture so you would do what they asked. And you did. So what's to keep them from killing us now?"

"They're done with me. But maybe not with you. I'm guessing that now I'm the 'guarantee' that *you'll* do something they want."

"What can I do? Neither of us is any use to them."

We were quiet for a few minutes.

"There has to be something else," Kenny said, "or we'd be dead by now."

"You know, there were plenty of times in my life I thought I was going to be killed. There were even lots of ways I figured I'd get killed. But this wasn't one of them—especially after I retired. I had finally found some peace when I quit OSI. Everything changed in the middle of the night when Kepner came to my door."

"Maxine, you sound like you've resigned yourself to the idea that we are going to die. Don't give up. It's not over, yet. We're both still alive for some reason."

"What do you think is going to happen now that they have access to the drive?"

"All hell is going to break loose."

———

Twenty-four hours later, after a fitful brief sleep, they gave us some juice and bread, then brought us to the observation control room where we watched while the technicians below worked at a frantic pace to finish the big donut-shaped device. I wondered what the rush was. Why were they in such a frenzy to get it completed? They scurried about the lab, shouting directions to one another. It seemed they dropped tools often because they were too hurried. Tempers flared at times. They had to be trying to meet a deadline, but neither Kenny nor I had any idea what that was.

I had to admit, the device looked impressive. Standing upright, the glowing rings were about seven meters tall, dwarfing the chrome and glass enclosure that intersected them at the bottom of the donut. When Moghaddam joined us, I said, "I understand there was one of these alien donuts prior to this one. What happened to it?"

He scoffed at my donut comment. "Professor Drozdov's assistant, who headed up the advance team, became a little too anxious to test the displacement device. Rather than sending the cargo package to a predefined location a few miles from here, he accidently displaced the entire facility to the jungles of the Amazon. He and about twenty-five of our staff and military, along with close to a hundred million dollars of advanced electronics, disappeared. Fortunately, the location in the jungle is so remote that there is little chance of anyone ever finding what is left."

Cargo package? This revelation slammed into my brain like a head-on collision. So this thing wasn't an advanced propulsion system—or at least that wasn't what they intended to use it for. It was being built to *send* a cargo package somewhere. I finally understood what we were dealing with—the displacement, this Shield as they liked to call it, was intended to deliver a WMD without the chance of being intercepted or even detected. Iran could bring down the *Great Satan* in the blink of an eye. This was the ultimate weapon, something out of a science fiction novel. I felt nauseated as I turned to Kenny. His expression confirmed my worst fear that something terrible was about to take place.

I struggled to keep my voice calm. "How do you know it won't happen again?"

Moghaddam started to answer when we heard a commotion near the control room doors to the observation deck. He spun around, stiffened, and his face turned to marble. Armed soldiers entered and positioned themselves around the perimeter of the room. They were followed by Iranian General Hassan Jafari, whom we had first met in the desert, and Russian General Yuri Lushev, one of the big three and the man who blew Drozdov's brains out in the Moscow suburb. Finally, a handful of Muslim clerics walked in, followed by the Iranian president. We had met him twice during our highly publicized press events after we *sought* political asylum. He wore his customary black suit with a white shirt and no tie. An Islamic Republic of Iran pin on his lapel reflected the overhead lights.

Moghaddam took a hesitant step forward. "Mr. President, we did not expect you—"

The president paid no attention to the scientist, but came to me with outstretched arms. Taking both of my hands in his, he gave me a smile. "So good to see you again, Agent Decker." Moving to Kenny, he shook his hand in turn. "And you, Agent Gates. I hope the accommodations have met with your expectations."

I wanted to say something sarcastic, and I knew Kenny did, too. We nodded instead.

"And Dr. Moghaddam, how are we progressing?"

"As you can see, Mr. President, we are on the verge of completion." He motioned to the gleaming donut on the assembly floor and the portal container inside. "We are working through the night, and I predict we will carry out the launch on schedule."

"So the additional data from the thumb drive was useful?"

"Very much so, sir. It completed the puzzle."

The president turned to Kenny and gave him a nod. Looking to Moghaddam, he said, "Tell your staff I'm proud of them all."

One of the clerics stepped forward and said to the president, "It is time. The American president will soon address the nation and a joint session of Congress."

The president's gaze fell back on me. "And now, Agent Decker, it is your turn. Time for you to live up to your end of the arrangement. Keep in mind that whether your former husband lives or dies is entirely in your hands."

General Jafari reached into his pocket and pulled out a cell phone—my cell phone. He handed it to me.

"You are about to make the most important phone call of your life," the president said. "Here is what you will say."

CHAPTER 65 - SITUATION ROOM
The White House, Washington, DC

The room commonly referred to as The Woodshed fell silent. President LeClaire had just informed his national security team and cabinet officials that an act of war against Iran was essential and imminent. He instructed them not to say anything from a knee-jerk perspective, but rather to allow his assessment a moment to settle.

During the lull, while the others contemplated what they had just been told, the President's thoughts turned to his children. He was proud of his boys and daughter, and wondered how they would remember him years from now. What was the legacy he would leave them? He'd accomplished great things, but from today on, the world was going to change. War always claimed innocent lives, and he knew that would forever weigh on him. Still, there was no other choice. If he didn't act swiftly with maximum force, it would be too late, and the consequence was not what he envisioned bequeathing his children or anyone else's.

LeClaire's calculations swam briefly through his head as a last-chance check to make certain he had come to the right decision for resolution of the crisis with Iran and the Russians. It was imperative he stop the production and use of the displacement device. Neither Iran nor the Russian cabal could be permitted the opportunity to use it. He was told the Iranians referred to it as the Shield. But what it would shield would be a weapon meant to destroy the West, the reigning Russian government, Israel, and any nation in the world they chose. There would be no protecting the United States from nuclear attack. It had to be terminated.

"Mr. President," CIA Director Singer said, breaking the quiet and making LeClaire abandon his thoughts. "You are certain we have undeniable proof that there is such a device in Sudan and it is near or already completed?"

"No doubt." He reviewed the solemn faces of the men and women who sat at the long conference table. "I have shown you what we've recovered from Beowulf, and we have all the intel from Agents Decker and Gates. I have tried to reach Agent Decker, but thus far have not been successful. But we continue trying to get in touch with her for one last confirmation. We will, however, carry out our attack whether we reach her or not. If the Russian cabal–Iranian group launches against Russia, the next targets are most assuredly the United States and Israel. The world will have no alternative but to stand by and watch. One strike is all it will take, and they own the globe."

National Security Advisor Scarborough massaged the top of his balding head as if his brain was clawing at it. "They'll take us out in a heartbeat."

"We can't wait any longer," LeClaire said. "It's not worth the risk. There is no reasoning with them. Everything is in place. The moment I finish addressing the joint session and the American people, our attack will commence. The facility in the Sudan will be annihilated."

There was a tap at the door, and a member of the secret service popped his head in. "Sir, the limos are coming around in five minutes."

LeClaire nodded. He glanced about at those at the table. His eyes burned with weariness. "Are we ready, ladies and gentlemen?"

The vice president gave an affirmative nod as did the rest. "Congress and all the others have started to assemble in the House Chamber."

A beep came from the conference phone. The line dedicated to critical calls was blinking. LeClaire stared at it as if it was a scorpion ready to strike. If he answered, he might be stung. Everyone in the room stared at it, too.

The President leaned over the table and pushed the speaker button so all could hear. There were no more secrets to hold back from his inner circle. "Yes, what is it?"

"I'm sorry to interrupt, Mr. President." He recognized the voice of his personal secretary.

"What have you got?"

"Sir, there's a call." She paused and took in a breath. "The caller is asking for Tennyson."

CHAPTER 66 - SWEET HOME MONTANA
The White House, Washington, DC

"Agent Decker, I've got you on speaker," the President said. "Are you all right?"

"Yes."

"And Agent Gates?"

"He's here, and fine as well."

"Did the Navy SEAL team arrive?"

"I'm afraid not, Sir. But we did find a secure location."

"Why are you calling?"

"I have some good news. Mr. President. The *Shield* has failed. The information on Chaucer's thumb drive was incomplete or corrupt. The end result is that the displacement device does not work, and the Iranians have decided to abandon its development. The missing data needed to finish it cannot be accessed from the alien artifacts. There's nothing left to do here but close up the laboratory. I knew you would want to hear this as soon as possible."

LeClaire listened carefully to her voice for signs that what she was saying was rehearsed. Her voice did sound tremulous, but considering what Decker had been through, and the urgency of the message, that could be expected. "Of course. And that is wonderful news. Maybe we can all take a breath now. Things have been tense here, as you can imagine."

"I'm sure they have. Mr. President, I understand that you have called for a joint session of Congress to address the nation. Sir, I am respectfully proposing that you announce in your speech that the United States is standing down. There is no need for a preeminent strike now that the whole *Shield* project is dead."

LeClaire tried to read into her hesitation. He wasn't certain what she was trying to communicate. "You're absolutely sure of this?"

"Yes."

LeClaire watched the expressions on his teams' faces. They appeared relieved.

"And the cabal?" he asked.

"We have been told that the Russian government has rounded up all involved and shut them down."

"I couldn't have asked for any better news. You can't believe how close we have come to disaster. There is no winner in war, Agent Decker. Thank you, again. We will start immediate diplomatic procedures to bring you and Agent Gates home safely."

"That's all I want, sir. Just to sit on the porch of my Montana cabin and see the stars and the moonlight on the water. To see the sun rise over the lake and the fish jumping. I so want to be home again."

"I'll make it happen."

"Then you'll tell the nation that there's no more threat? You'll cancel the attack on Iran and the lab?"

"Yes. We leave in just a few moments."

There was another short pause. "Mr. President, do you understand what I've told you?"

LeClaire felt a clutch in his chest. "I do, Agent Decker. Thank you for your service to your country."

A collective calm swept through the room.

As LeClaire put his finger to the phone button he heard Agent's Decker's frenzied voice. "Mr. President, don't—"

There was a sound of a scuffle and the phone went dead.

"What happened?" the vice president said.

"I don't know," answered the President. "Someone stopped her from talking to us. We should all pray that Agent Decker is okay."

"Guy, are you really going to call off the attack? How do you know she's not lying?" the vice president asked.

LeClaire started for the door. "She *is* lying. Her cabin is in Colorado, not Montana."

CHAPTER 67 - DESTROYER OF WORLDS
Underground desert laboratory, Sudan

"You said too much, Agent Decker." The Iranian president took my cellphone and tossed it to General Jafari. Then he slapped me hard across the face.

My tooth bit into my lip and I tasted blood.

Kenny started to rush forward but Vyshinsky grabbed his arm.

"You have just sealed your fate," the president said.

A thrumming noise and additional activity on the lab floor captured everyone's attention. Iranian soldiers were pushing a metal handcart toward the donut. They stopped and stood back as technicians approached. On the cart was a box the size of a hotel room mini-bar. It had a series of control knobs, meters, and a keypad on the top. A digital readout, big enough to see from where I stood, showed all zeros. The technicians began opening various compartments on the sides of the box and checking components against paperwork on their clipboards.

At the same time, the soldiers were gathering the Beowulf staff together, forcing them at gunpoint out of the lab.

"Where are they being taken?" I asked.

"With the additional data from the thumb drive," Dr. Moghaddam said, "they have outlived their usefulness. Our staff is now fully trained to take over the duties of the Americans."

Distant muffled sounds of multiple gunshots erupted. I squeezed my fists tight at my sides. The Beowulf staff had

230

been executed. No, murdered.

Rage roiled inside me. I wanted to strike out—to pummel and bloody Moghaddam and his rabble. Rabble was a good term for them, I thought. The lowest form of people. Not one had a shred of conscience or human principles. If I lived and had the chance, I would find a way to take them down—down to hell.

I turned to stare at what the soldiers had wheeled in on the cart. Suddenly, I realized what I was looking at. The cargo package.

"Here is my gift to you, Dr. Moghaddam." The president started to turn to leave.

"What is it?" I asked with a weak voice, afraid I already knew the answer.

"When Robert Oppenheimer built the first one," the president said, "he declared that he was 'Death, the destroyer of worlds'. We have no intention of destroying the world, Agent Decker. Instead, we will use it to reshape the world in the name of Allah. And you will live just long enough to witness it."

General Lushev added, "Soon we will see the rebirth of the great Soviet Union."

The Iranian president paused and faced Lushev. "I almost forgot to tell you. There has been a change of plans."

CHAPTER 68 - THE TARGET
Underground desert facility, Sudan

General Lushev looked as if he had been told he had terminal cancer. Then his eyes narrowed. "What did you say?"

The Iranian president faced him full-on. "We have made a critical decision to redirect the package to a new target."

Lushev grew stiffer as his face reddened. "What target?"

"Relax. It is for your own good and ours."

"What target?" The words came from deep in his throat.

The president raised his hand and smiled as if disciplining a child. "You must calm down, General, or I will have you removed."

I wondered what exactly he meant by *removed*.

Lushev seemed unable to speak. I worried that a heart attack was seconds away. From the corner of my eye, I saw Colonel Vyshinsky move a step closer to the general. The Russian soldiers who had accompanied us from our cells also appeared to tense, as did their armed Iranian counterparts.

"Have you forgotten who is funding this?" Lushev was finally able to speak.

"And we are eternally grateful. But you have to understand, General Lushev, we must consider what is best for us all."

"What is best is for you to adhere to our agreement and finish the task at hand. The rebuilding of the great Soviet Union depends on it."

The president laughed out loud. "That is never going to happen. The only reason Putinov has not arrested you and put a bullet through your brain is because you are here and not in

232

Russia. Carrying out your ill-conceived plan to blow up the Kremlin would only result in the destruction of hundreds of years of beautiful buildings, nothing more."

Lushev wiped the sweat from his brow. "I ask again, what is the target?"

The president motioned to Moghaddam, who picked up a remote and turned on a flat-screen TV mounted above the control-room windows. A woman appeared—SNN Senior Correspondent Cotten Stone on a split screen. On the other side of the image was a night shot taken by a helicopter showing a line of vehicles, some with emergency lights flashing, moving along Pennsylvania Avenue. The caption read, "President Guy LeClaire on his way to the Capitol to address a joint session of Congress and the nation."

My legs went limp. I'd tried to warn the President to cancel the meeting—not to go—but they'd stopped me before I could. I wrapped my arms around my middle as if keeping my insides from exploding. I'd failed. I could only hope that he'd picked up on the location of my cabin being incorrect and deduct that all I had said was a lie. I prayed the attack on the Sudan facility was imminent and would be carried out before the Shield could be launched, even though it would kill Kenny and me in the process.

The president pointed to me. "Let us hope you convinced LeClaire to stand down and tell the American people that we pose no threat. That is the only reason we have spared your life until now."

Until now? It came as no surprise. And Kenny was alive only to make sure I'd follow through. I knew what was next for us.

The president pointed to the TV. "Watch, Agent Decker. You are about to witness the destruction of your government."

CHAPTER 69 - COUNTDOWN
Underground desert facility, Sudan

Everything happened within a few seconds—coming at me in bursts of flashes, images, shots, and blows.

Colonel Vyshinsky drew his automatic and aimed it at the president of Iran.

Kenny shoved me hard to the floor.

Moghaddam lunged forward and ran for the doors.

An Iranian soldier aimed his assault rifle at General Lushev. Vyshinsky shot the soldier dead.

General Jafari shouted an order, and the Iranian contingent rushed to surround the president and push him out of the room.

Moghaddam tripped and fell.

An Iranian soldier smashed the butt of his rifle into Moghaddam's head. The scientist screamed.

A Russian guard fired into the group of exiting Iranians. One of the clerics collapsed.

An Iranian soldier turned and fired twice. One bullet blew out a window over my head. The second shot hit Lushev. The general dropped to his knees.

Vyshinsky shot the soldier in the forehead sending him sprawling backwards.

Protecting their president, the Iranians disappeared into the hallway.

The fortified doors to the control room slammed shut.

Smoke from the gunfire filled the room.

My ears rang, and for a moment, I couldn't hear.

I scrambled to my feet, ran to the dead Iranian soldier, and grabbed his assault rifle.

Lushev fell forward onto his face, probably dead.

Vyshinsky pulled the general's pistol from his holster and tossed it to Kenny.

The colonel called out an order to the other Russian soldier, who aimed his AK-12 at the doors.

It was then I noticed Blue Eyes coming through the door. As I raised the rifle, a blast from the weapon Kenny held filled the room. Without hesitation, he had scored a headshot, dead center of the sadist's forehead.

Moghaddam moaned and tried to sit up.

I moved to the window and saw the Iranian technicians lift the package from the cart and place it on the floor in front of the enclosure's portal doors. The donut rings began glowing brighter and spinning as the large numeric display on top of the package counted backwards.

Time remaining: 4:56.

"We've got less than five minutes. We have to stop it!" I yelled.

I started climbing through the shattered window.

CHAPTER 70 - JOINT SESSION
United States Capital, Washington, DC

"Mister Speaker, the President of the United States."

There was a scattering of polite applause as President Guy LeClaire entered the back of the House chamber. A few members of congress reached to shake his hand or offer an encouraging pat on the shoulder as he walked down the center aisle. The fast-growing tension between the U.S., Russia, and Iran had darkened the mood of congress. With public knowledge of the ramping up of the military for war, everyone knew this was to be a somber speech.

The President slowly made his way up the steps to the podium. He shook the hands of the vice president and the speaker of the house, then turned to face the gathering. A hush fell over the assembly as all sat, eyes focused on LeClaire.

He opened his notes, a duplicate of what appeared on the teleprompter. Taking a deep breath, he said, "Mr. Speaker, Mr. Vice President, members of Congress, Justices of the Supreme Court, Joint Chiefs, dignitaries, guests, and" he looked straight into the TV camera, "my fellow Americans. I come before you tonight with a heavy heart. For at this moment in our nation's history, we face the gravest of threats, the result of an advanced technology that may very well have originated from beyond our world."

He heard a slight uneasy shuffling of members in their seats along with a few whispers and clearing of throats.

"A small but extremely powerful group of Russian oligarchs

has funded, with the assistance of Iran, a secret underground laboratory in the desert of Sudan. At this laboratory, Iranian scientists have developed a new system that can deliver a weapon of mass destruction inside the most secure and sacred centers of our government and those of our friends. We believe the attack can be carried out in the blink of an eye, that there is no defense against it, and no advanced warning."

More nervousness swept through the chamber. This time the whispers grew to voices that LeClaire heard. A few calls came from the gallery accusing him of losing his mind, lying to the public, leading the country to war needlessly.

"Beyond our world? You mean aliens? Are you insane?"

"You're lying to us and the American people. This is incredulous!"

"It's just a ploy to attack Iran. We can't allow for this!"

As the noise grew louder, he raised his hand for quiet and waited until he could be heard. "I don't blame any of you for questioning what I have said. I didn't believe it either until the information brought to me became undeniable. What we are dealing with, my fellow Americans, is a tipping point in the history of not only our country, but our planet. For the first time in human history, we are facing a technology that is beyond our control. A technology that originates from an intelligent life form thousands, if not hundreds of thousands of years ahead of us. And that technology is now in the hands of those who hate us most."

SUDAN

From the blown-out window I could see below that there was a large cabinet sitting against the lab wall. I realized that was my way down to the main floor of the lab. I climbed over the ledge and hung for a second before dropping to the top of the cabinet, then down to the floor. I glanced back to see Kenny and Vyshinsky follow.

The handful of technicians spotted us, and worked frantically to finish moving the package through the portal into the enclosure. Another stood outside the donut in front of a podium-style control panel and punched in a series of commands, starting a second countdown clock.

An Iranian guard came from across the lab and aimed his assault rifle at us.

"No!" Moghaddam screamed from the window I had just passed through. "Don't shoot! You'll hit the device or the weapon."

Vyshinsky fired and took the guard down, causing the technicians to bolt. Another guard came from around the big donut but hesitated to fire because of the package. It cost him his life.

I ran to the portal doors. Kenny and Vyshinsky were right behind. The control panel clock displayed fifty-two seconds while the nuclear package readout showed fifty-four. The package would detonate two seconds after it was displaced. The control panel also displayed a set of coordinates—38.53.26.62N, 77.00.31.80W.

The target.

WASHINGTON, DC

The once hushed crowd became agitated to the point of drowning out the President. The speaker of the House banged his gavel, calling for order. It took a couple of minutes for the crowd to settle back down.

A member of congress called out, "Do you really think we believe this nonsense?"

The President held up his hand. "I don't blame you for doubting. We have come to a point in the history of the human race where we now know we are not alone. But before we can address that revelation and the life-altering changes it will bring, we must first address the immediate threat facing our nation." He paused for a second but this time, no heckling could be heard. He knew each one present, along with the millions watching around the world, wanted to hear every word of what he was about to say.

SUDAN

Kenny and I maneuvered through the open portal doors into the enclosure. We shoved the box hard, trying to push it back out through the doors. The doors were slowly closing and the countdown clock continued to tick off seconds.

A half-dozen soldiers rushed into the lab. One fired at the colonel, hitting him in the leg. He fell in front of the portal.

Moghaddam screamed again for everyone to hold his fire.

Kenny and I continued heaving the package. Wounded, Vyshinsky still managed to grab a handle on the front of the weapon, tugging the package back out the portal's doors. He pulled and we pushed. Together we worked it halfway out. The portal doors closed against the package, grabbing its sides. We shoved harder, but it wouldn't move.

The Iranian guards turned and ran back through the lab entrance as if getting a few meters away from a nuclear detonation would save them. If they could run thirty kilometers from the underground facility in the next few seconds, they might have a chance of survival. Otherwise, they were about to be vaporized. So were we.

Wedged between the doors, the package's weight made it almost impossible to slide.

Through the partly opened doors of the portal I saw Dr. Moghaddam climb down from the window to the top of the metal cabinet. He jumped, then rose and ran to Vyshinsky. The scientist started kicking the Russian, trying to make him release his grip on the package. They struggled—Vyshinsky pulling on the package, Moghaddam trying to stop him.

WASHINGTON, DC

"Therefore, based upon the undeniable evidence brought to me by not only our intelligence gathering organizations, but first-hand accounts from inside the laboratory, I have taken steps to bring our military to full battle readiness. I now consider a state of war to exist between the United States of America and the Islamic Republic of Iran.

"I have ordered our warships and submarines stationed within striking distance of Iran to arm their weapons with nuclear capability. These weapons are to be targeted at all military and government facilities inside Iran. In addition, our fleet of stealth bombers, already en route, will seek out and destroy the secret underground Iranian facility in the desert of Sudan.

"As of now, I am declaring a state of war to exist—"

SUDAN

Colonel Vyshinsky slammed his gun across Moghaddam's face, sending the Iranian sprawling. Blood flowed from his nose and mouth. Then Vyshinsky turned, his face contorted. He gave the package one great tug while I sat on the floor inside the enclosure and shoved against it with my feet. Beside me, Kenny let out a heavy grunt and pushed.

It slid past the threshold.

The glass portal doors closed.

I took in a deep breath, knowing we had stopped the package from being sent to its target.

Then it hit me that we were trapped inside the displacement device. I reached for Kenny's hand.

The control panel display clock showed two seconds.

Vyshinsky once told us he only worked for winners.

My eyes met the colonel's. He mouthed, "You win."

WASHINGTON, DC

LeClaire froze in midsentence. In the same fraction of a second, the standing-room-only chamber became silent. With a collective gasp, all eyes fell on a spot just in front of the chamber podium.

A man and a woman appeared. They looked haggard and exhausted—like they had been living on the streets. Both had bloodstains on their clothes.

The woman looked up at LeClaire. With a labored smile, she said, "Good evening, Mr. President. Or should I say, Tennyson."

Slowly, a grin spread across LeClaire's face. "Good evening, Agent Decker. Agent Gates. You arrived just in time."

CHAPTER 71 - KICK BACK
Big Bear Lake, Colorado

I sipped Johnny Walker as I gazed out over the dark water of Big Bear Lake. The flat, polished surface reflected the final colors of the day fading behind the mountains. Kenny was next to me, both of us occupying a couple of antique rocking chairs I'd picked up in town a few months back. Not much of a whisky man, my ex worked on a bottle of Coors.

"Nice to finally kick back and relax," he said. Our slow rocking gave off comforting creaks from the old pine chair rails.

"I love this place." The clean smell of the Douglas firs mixed with the last breath of autumn and filled my senses with what I liked to think of as *heaven's scent*.

"What's not to love?" He lifted his bottle in a toast to the view.

We sat in silence for a long time just listening to the sounds of the forest and our rocking. Finally, Kenny said, "What was it like for you?"

"I know it only took a fraction of a second, but I remember feeling suddenly chilled. Colder than ever. And floating, like there was no gravity. I was dizzy, too. And a bit nauseated. But only for a short time after we *landed*. How about you?"

"Similar. Except the dizziness hung around for a few minutes."

"That's because you're such an old man." I followed that with a smile. "Course, I've always been fond of older men."

"Next thing you're going to say is I robbed the cradle."

I shrugged. "Maybe back when we first got married. Probably wouldn't hold up in court today."

"I don't think I'll ever forget the look on their faces when we appeared right there in the Senate chambers in front of congress and the President. Not to mention the millions watching on TV. The only thing that would have made it better is if I'd pulled a rabbit out of my hat."

"Oh, I think that would have been anticlimactic," I said. "Popping up out of nowhere was more than enough to get their attention. I still get a chuckle out of the White House calling it a hoax. That a hacker broke into the network feed."

"Still, everyone present in the chamber knows they saw something. They just don't know what."

"They'll be analyzing those few seconds of video for years."

"Like the Zapruder film."

"Exactly. I'm just thankful they were quick to pull the networks feed."

"And whisk us and the President out of there."

"Bottom line," I said, "it's not our problem anymore. Clever how the White House put a different spin on it and chalked up the detonation in the middle of the Sudanese desert to the Iranians testing their first nuclear weapon. That'll cause enough distraction to take the spotlight off us."

"The only light I want to see is the moonlight on you."

I reached to hold Kenny's hand.

There was another long pause as we watched the night roll in across the water and wrap itself around my cabin.

I took another sip of my scotch. "Never thought I'd say this, but I kinda miss Colonel Vyshinsky."

"Maybe it's because he kinda saved our skins."

"The man was ruthless, and yet he had a small space in his heart that was good."

"You had to dig deep to find it, but I agree." Kenny took another pull from his longneck. "So how did you know the President would understand your signal?"

"I didn't. It was a shot in the dark that he would remember my cabin was not in Montana."

"Is that when you came to finally trust him? Chaucer had told you not to trust anyone."

"I never trusted him. I just figured at that point there was nothing to lose."

"So saving the world from nuclear war all came down to the difference between Montana and Colorado?"

"Just another day at the office. The big gamble was that the Iranians didn't know the difference."

"At least you got your wish to meet Cotten Stone with that exclusive Satellite News Network interview."

"She's a very cool lady. I didn't realize there are a number of books written about her. First order of business is to read them all."

After another pull from his Coors, Kenny said, "Did anyone ever say what they intend to do with Beowulf? I wouldn't mind getting my hands on that quantum computer again. Oh, the things I could do."

"Get a hold of yourself. The place is locked down tighter than Fort Knox. The world still doesn't know what's there, and that's the way the government wants it."

"Speaking of the government, do you think the FBI director is serious about building a special task force around you? You know that if you accept, you'll have to move to Washington. Hey wait, that's where I live. You wouldn't even have to rent an apartment. *Mi casa es su casa.*"

"Thanks, Zorro. But moving back to the city is not in my future. This is where I want to be." I motioned to the lake and the dark forest beyond. The first of the brightest stars were making their presence known. "No more shootouts, no more plane crashes, no more Blue Eyes, and no more alien donuts."

"You won't even listen to his offer?"

"I'll listen, but . . ."

"At least the President swore he wouldn't call on you again unless it was a dire emergency."

"He's got a whole bunch of folks to call on before he gets down to the bottom of his list where my name's at."

"Maybe you should block his phone number."

"That would only bring the black helicopters."

We both leaned forward in our chairs. The unmistakable thump-thump of rotor blades echoed off the nearby mountains and drifted across the water.

"You've got to be kidding." I stood and tried to see the source of the sound in the darkness. My iPhone vibrated. I pulled it from my flannel shirt breast pocket and stared at the collar ID.

"Who is it?" Kenny asked.

"Tennyson."

CHAPTER 72 - JALAPEÑO
Near the Brazil-Peru border

The sniper was known as Jalapeño, not only because everyone believed the guy thought he was a hot shot, but also due to his expert marksmanship. The name stuck, and his given name had long been forgotten.

The sniper had bedded in a self-constructed platform in the trees overnight. At first light, he gathered his gear and hit the jungle floor ready to go on his mission.

Jalapeño panned the jungle, noting its lush greenery hanging like living curtains, often so heavy in the canopy that it blocked the sun. At least the thick plants and trees provided brief midday relief from the heat for the natives of the area.

The sniper lowered the binoculars. The air was rich with the scent of decaying vegetation, yet tempered with a mix of aromas from manioc, banana, annatto, and papaya, a concoction of smells that Jalapeño had not breathed before. He also detected cook-fire smoke nearby. A good sign.

He heard static and pressed his hand to his ear, adjusting the earpiece so it was snug.

"Target?" the voice said in his ear.

"Not yet, but close," Jalapeño whispered, knowing his throat mic would pick up his low voice.

He tracked the odor of the smoke, presuming it would lead him to the remote village.

A moment later, Jalapeño abruptly stopped. In the distance he picked up the faint sound of voices. Gibberish to him, a strange language, but still, human voices. He crouched and whispered again. "Within range."

The sniper checked his watch. The helicopter would return in 38 minutes. The chopper wouldn't land for lack of open space, so he was to go to the riverbank where a military spec roll-up ladder would be used to extract him.

He crept on toward the direction of the voices until the forest became sparser from frequent beating down by foot travel. Jalapeño dropped to the ground, high-crawling even closer to the voices. Finally, he halted again, and through the binoculars he could clearly make out the small primitive village and the nearly naked brown natives.

A noise to his left made him look that way and he eased, as if in slow motion, to the earth. He could barely make out two figures in the distance. Again, he raised the binoculars. Two natives stood side by side and appeared to be laughing. One would reach out, touch something, then pull his hand back while the other man laughed. They seemed to be taking turns.

Jalapeño focused on the object of their attention. "Jesus. What the fuck?"

A voice came through his earpiece. "Got something, Jalapeño?"

"It's a keyboard," he whispered. "A goddamn computer keyboard that's melted into a tree stump. I'm in the right spot for sure."

"Keep looking."

Jalapeño observed the two natives poking at what to them had to be a total aberration of their natural environment.

Just as that thought passed through his mind, he saw something on the ground a few meters in front to him. *Glass?* He crawled forward. The object was an irregular puddle-like solid piece of glass. As if sand had been super-heated and turned to glass. But there was no sand here. Just dirt. As he looked around, he noticed there were several more pieces.

Looking ahead, Jalapeño saw something metal in the grass. He inched forward and picked it up. It looked like a long metal thermometer, like one used in a science lab, but it was grossly misshapen, with most of the numerals gone.

"What else are you seeing?"

"Evidence is everywhere."

"But you haven't found it yet? You need to hurry. Time is running out. The chopper is on its way back to extract you."

"Yes, sir."

Knowing he was within meters of the village, Jalapeño leopard-crawled closer. At last he had a good location for viewing. Lifting his head, he spied through the binoculars to see several natives going about what appeared to be nothing more than daily chores. All except one, who sat cross-legged on the ground, wearing vibrant bird plumes fastened to a headband and armbands. Red streaks striped his cheeks and black smudges circled his eyes.

Jalapeño zeroed in on the man, zooming and sharpening the focus. He examined the native, concluding he was nobility, like a chief or shaman. Several necklaces dangled from the native's neck.

Jalapeño studied what looked like human toe bones, drilled stones, and other ornaments strung on a worked leather necklace. A second necklace brought the sniper's observation to a sudden halt.

Woven inside what he assumed was fine sinew or fiber cordage was a piece of material he could only describe as off-white ceramic or porcelain, about seven by four centimeters.

Jalapeño dropped the binoculars, raised the CheyTac M200, and peered through the scope.

A satisfied grin played on his lips. He said softly, "Got it. It's around some honcho's neck, but it won't be a problem retrieving it. I've got a clear headshot."

The voice in the earpiece came again.

"Take the shot."

NOTES FROM THE HISTORICAL RECORD

THE TUNGUSKA EVENT

On the morning of June 30, 1908, a bizarre and ferocious explosion occurred forty miles north-northwest of Vanavara, Siberia, in the remote region of Stony Tunguska. The explosion was so forceful that tremors of earthquake proportions registered as far as 3000 miles away, including Moscow, Germany, Indochina, and Washington, D.C., dwarfing the atomic bomb blasts at Nagasaki and Hiroshima by 1,000 times.

Even though the event took place in 1908, it wasn't until 19 years later that the site was explored. The first attempt at scientific expedition, led by Leonid Kulik, the chief curator for the meteorite collection of the St. Petersburg museum, was foiled by the inhospitable conditions of the Siberian outback. Finally, in 1927 he organized another expedition that was successful.

When he first questioned some of the locals, they refused to speak of the incident, believing the blast was the result of the god Odgy who came down, felled the forest, and killed the animals.

The more Kulik explored, the more evidence he found of the horrific event. Eight hundred square miles of forest had been destroyed. Approximately eighty million trees were flattened, radiating out from the epicenter. At ground zero, the trees stood upright, though the bark and branches had been stripped away by the shock waves.

The pillar of fire was probably visible for hundreds of miles. It is said that the night skies glowed so brilliantly that people living as far away reported they could read their newspapers at midnight. The thunder-like claps could be heard from five hundred miles away and those who were the closest were deafened.

In Kansk, 375 miles south-southwest, the people experienced wind gusts that rattled windows and doors, followed by shock waves that threw their horses to the ground. Ominous dark clouds rose for twelve miles. For hundreds of miles around, the earth was showered by *black rain*—dirt and debris that had been sucked into the vortex of the explosion.

Curiously, there is no crater, no evidence of impact, which means it was a mid-air explosion. Mainstream science has assumed the Tunguska explosion was due to a meteorite, which entered the atmosphere and detonated in the sky. The debate continues as to whether this hypothesis is true. There are those who believe this explanation has never been satisfactorily resolved. Some eyewitnesses described a cylindrical-shaped object that glowed a blinding bluish-white, which descended from the sky for approximately ten minutes just before the blast. The trajectory is also not consistent with a meteorite, comet, or other natural object.

To date, there has been no collection of meteorite or comet fragments that can be positively identified as such.

Outlier theories conclude the object that exploded over Tunguska was an extraterrestrial craft.

The mystery continues.

THE ROSWELL INCIDENT

The Roswell incident has remained such a point of interest and controversy for so long that fact has entwined with conjecture and fiction, forming a braid that seems impossible to separate. Even the exact date of the supposed UFO/balloon crash is unclear.

The following is a compilation of fact and opinion offering the best description of what likely happened as can be determined by the authors.

The night in early July 1947 was laden with thunderstorms over the Foster Ranch in Corona, New Mexico, 75 miles north of Roswell, New Mexico. William "Mac" Brazel, the foreman of the ranch, heard what he described as an explosion strong enough to rattle the windows in the house. The same noise was heard on another ranch miles away. Thunderstorms were frequent in the summertime around Roswell and were often intense. Brazel, like the other residents, was familiar with the sounds and sights of such storms, and the sound he heard that night was more like an exploding bomb.

The following morning, he rode out to check on his sheep and to see if he could find just what caused the loud explosion. What he found in one pasture took him by surprise. He discovered a large amount of odd wreckage, the debris spread in a fanned-out pattern. He noticed that the sheep would not cross the debris field in order to get to their water source. He had to lead them around the rubble.

Mac Brazel had seen the remains of balloon crashes on the Foster Ranch before, but what he saw this day was nothing like he had seen. He gathered up some samples and went to the sheriff, who also could not determine what the items were. Sheriff Wilcox, in return, contacted the Roswell Air Field. Colonel Blanchard, the SAC base commander, asked Major Jesse Marcel, the base intelligence officer, to see what Brazel had brought to the sheriff. Major Marcel was also responsible for nuclear weapons housed at the base.

When the major inspected the debris, he concurred that the material was out of the ordinary. After reporting back to Colonel Blanchard, Marcel was directed to accompany Brazel back to the ranch to see for himself. Joining them was Captain Sheridan Cavitt, a counterintelligence agent.

After surveying the bizarre debris field, which was estimated to be three-quarters of a mile long and a hundred feet wide, Captain Cavitt returned to the base. Not certain whether samples had been collected, Major Marcel lingered and gathered more. On his way back to the base, he stopped at his home to show his family a portion of the strange material. He presented his wife and son with what appeared to be a unique type of foil, broken pieces of plastic-like fragments of a what looked like a phonograph record without grooves, and small metal beams resembling I-beams. The I-beams had undecipherable hieroglyphic-style writing on them in two colors.

Major Marcel demonstrated how the foil was much stronger than the common cooking foil found in the kitchen, and it was extremely light in the hand. With a burnished appearance, it had less of a shine than household foil. When he bent or folded the foil then released it, it returned to its original shape. He and his family searched the box of debris for wiring, tubing, condensers, resisters, or anything associated with electronics, especially radio components. They also searched for staples, fasteners, and rivets. None of these types of elements were found.

When the major returned to the base, some military personnel examined of the larger pieces of foil. After a sledgehammer bounced off it, leaving no dent or deformity of any kind, they pronounced it indestructible.

On July 8, 1947, Lt. Walter Haut, RAAF public information officer, finished a press release Blanchard had ordered him to write, stating that the wreckage of a crashed UFO had been recovered. Local newspapers and radio stations were given copies, and by that afternoon the story had hit the Associated Press wire.

Calls began pouring into the base from all over the world. Meanwhile, Lt. Robert Shirley observed the wreckage being loaded onto a C-54 from the First Transport Unit.

Blanchard sent Major Marcel to Fort Worth Army Air Field to report to Brigadier General Roger M. Ramey, commanding officer of the 8th Air Force. Marcel later reported that he had brought debris to show Ramey, but the Brigadier General was not in his office. He displayed it on Ramey's desk for the general to examine upon his return.

Ramey was intrigued and asked Major Marcel to show him the exact location of the find on a map down the hall. When they came back after checking out the map, it was reported that the wreckage on Ramey's desk was gone and the remains of a tattered weather balloon, which Ramey did not recognize, was spread on the floor.

The original press release was rescinded and a second press release was issued the next day saying it was all a mistake. There wreckage found on the Foster Ranch was not a UFO but rather the remains of a crashed weather balloon.

There have since been many versions of what happened that night near Roswell, New Mexico, the latest of which concluded that what crashed in the desert was part of a top secret operation called Project Mogul. In the fall of 1994, the Air Force proposed that Mogul Flight #4 was the source of the wreckage found on the Foster Ranch. Project Mogul involved microphones flown on high-altitude balloons to detect sound waves generated by Soviet atomic bomb tests. The project was carried out between 1947 and 1949, then was replaced with less expensive seismic detectors and air sampling. Originally, the balloons used had been clusters of rubber balloons, but they were soon replaced by balloons made from polyethylene, because they were more durable and leaked less helium.

Issues still remain with the Project Mogul explanation. Even though Mogul Flight #4 is explained to be the source of the crash, Mogul Flight #4 does not exist in Mogul's records because it was cancelled due to cloudy weather, just as were Flights #2 and #3, for the same reason. Some records indicate that Flight #5, launched on July 5, was the first Mogul flight in New Mexico.

As for the historical records, they are rife with memoirs, firsthand accounts, records, diaries, interviews, secret documents, theories, and fanciful interpretations. There seems to be as much evidence to suggest that the crash on the Foster Ranch was that of a UFO as there is to imply otherwise.

KINCAID'S CAVE

On April 5, 1909, the *Arizona Gazette* published a front-page article detailing the discovery by explorer, G.E. Kincaid of a great underground citadel located in the Grand Canyon. Mr. Kincaid was described as a lifelong explorer and hunter.

According to Kincaid, he was traveling alone down the

Green River in a wooden boat in search of a "mineral." When he was about 42 miles up the river from El Tovar Crystal Canyon, Kincaid claimed to have noticed stains in the sediment of the east wall of the canyon gorge about 2000 feet above the riverbed. Being an excellent climber, he scaled the wall, but with great difficulty, until he reached the entrance to a cave. This entrance was above a shelf that hid it from view from the river, and it was also 1480 feet down a sheer rock from the surface.

Kincaid noted that there were steps extending down from the entrance approximately thirty yards, to what had been the level of the river thousands of years ago. Intrigued by chisel marks on the rock he saw inside the entrance, he took his gun and went inside. He reported that he gathered several relics and then traveled down the river to Yuma, where he shipped them to Washington D.C. along with the specifics of his discovery. It is assumed that the shipment was sent to the Smithsonian.

According to the *Gazette* article, he teamed up with the Smithsonian, which financed expeditions under the direction of Professor S.A. Jordan. The details of the discoveries boggle the mind. Described was a long main passage leading to an enormous chamber with numerous passageways radiating out from it like spokes on a wheel. These passages led to hundreds of rooms with oval entrances, which were ventilated by air spaces between the passages. Kincaid stated that a hundred feet from the entrance was the cross-hall, where in the center was an statue resembling Buddha.

There were other remarkable findings as well—artistic vases, urns, cups of gold and copper, and enameled and glazed pottery. Also unearthed was gray metal, much like platinum, which scientists could not identify. And scattered all over were yellow stones, cat's eyes as they were called, each engraved with a head. Yet another hallway led to granaries, one standing at least twelve feet high.

Carved over each doorway and on the urns and tablets were engravings similar to Egyptian hieroglyphs, which Kincaid believed the Smithsonian would decode. The explorer also came upon another large chamber that contained tiered shelves of mummies and grave goods (items buried with the dead) of copper cups and portions of broken swords.

Kincaid commented on the uniqueness of another cavern so dark his light couldn't penetrate the blackness, which emitted a foul "snaky" odor.

It is interesting to note that areas surrounding the location of Kincaid's cave have names such as Osiris, Isis, Shiva, Buddhist and Horus Temples, Towers of Set and Ra, and Cheops Pyramid. When David Childress, author and owner of Adventures Unlimited Press, a publishing house established in 1984 that specializes in books on unusual topics such as ancient mysteries and unexplained phenomena, inquired about the names, he was told by the state archaeologist at Grand Canyon that the early explorers just liked Egyptian and Hindu names. He also confirmed that the area with these names was off-limits to visitors and even to most of the park personnel. The reason given was the existence of dangerous caves. Conspiracy theorist John Rhodes claims to know the location of the cave and states that the site is guarded by a soldier carrying an M-16.

To date, there remains debate as to whether or not G.E. Kincaid in fact, existed. The Smithsonian contends that neither Kincaid nor Jordan were ever employed by the Smithsonian Institution, nor do they have records that either existed. Is there a possibility that Kincaid worked under another name? "G.E. Kincaid" reported that he was traveling the Colorado River in search of a "mineral," which is probably a euphemism for gold, due to the fact that on January 11, 1908, Theodore Roosevelt had established the Grand Canyon National Monument out of the existing Grand Canyon Forest Reserve, which prohibited any new mining claims. Did Kincaid use another name while working with the Smithsonian?

Also, interestingly, there are many reports that a recently discovered ancient manuscript described a voyage taken thousands of years ago by an Asian group visiting a city built within "The Canyon of Light," for the purpose of visiting a holy man or shrine. The descriptions given indicate that this destination was located within the Grand Canyon.

Is the story of G.E. Kincaid's cave true? Is there, indeed, a cavern hewn from rock in the sheer wall of the Grand Canyon containing incredible artifacts that have been conveniently lost because the evidence contests our current conception of history? Perhaps that question will never be answered.

ABOUT THE AUTHORS:

Lynn Sholes has worked as a writing trainer for Broward County Schools and Citrus County Schools in Florida. Before writing thrillers her interest in archaeology led her to write historical fiction under the name Lynn Armistead McKee. Lynn is a member of the International Thriller Writers, Mystery Writers of America, and The Authors Guild.

Joe Moore is a former marketing & communications executive and two-time EMMY® winner with 25 years' experience in the television postproduction industry. Joe is the president emeritus of the International Thriller Writers. He writes full time from his home on the banks of the Blackwater River in Northwest Florida.

ALSO BY LYNN SHOLES & JOE MOORE:
THE BLADE
THE PHOENIX APOSTLES
THE GRAIL CONSPIRACY
THE LAST SECRET
THE HADES PROJECT
THE 731 LEGACY
BAM! JUST LIKE THAT (short story)

ALSO BY LYNN SHOLES WRITING AS LYNN ARMISTEAD MCKEE:
WOMAN OF THE MISTS
TOUCHES THE STARS
KEEPER OF DREAMS
WALKS IN STARDUST
SPIRIT OF THE TURTLE WOMAN
DAUGHTER OF THE FIFTH MOON

AN EXCERPT FROM
THE BLADE
LYNN SHOLES & JOE MOORE

PUBLISHED BY STONE CREEK BOOKS

"And Abraham stretched forth his hand,
and took the blade to slay his son."
~ Genesis, 22:10

CHAPTER 1 - BETRAYAL
Three years earlier, North of Kirkuk City, Iraq

I lay flat on the ground beside the five-thousand-year-old Assyrian settlement wall and watched the smuggler through my night vision goggles. My partner, OSI Special Agent Aaron Knox, was concealed among the ruins fifteen meters to my right.

"Maxine, what's he doing?" Aaron's voice whispered in my earbud.

"I'm not sure," I said. "Looks like he's fumbling with some boxes in that van."

Just moments earlier, the smuggler had emerged from the farmhouse, glanced in my direction as if he sensed my presence, then headed toward an old panel van twenty meters away. With it parked facing away from me, I had a back view of him as he opened the cargo doors. He kept looking toward the road a hundred meters to the east, probably anticipating the arrival of the transfer truck any moment.

A faint odor of cattle manure drifted from a nearby dusty pasture as I turned my head to the left. A ridgeline ran at an angle across the back of the property, making a perfect hiding place for the Iraqi National Police commandos waiting there.

I shifted my focus back to the van. The smuggler, a twenty-year-old Sunni Kurd, remained at the rear by the open doors. At such a young age, he had already made a name for himself on the black market as part of a smuggling ring that pilfered Iraqi artifacts out of the country through the neighboring Sulaymaniyah Province. Recently, he'd gotten his hands on a few of the valuables looted from the Baghdad National Museum during the chaotic start of the war back in 2003. Our intel said the treasures included several small Sumerian relics and a number of gold and silver pieces dating back to 2000 BC. The smuggler's take would be hundreds of U.S. dollars, but as the goods moved up the food chain to the ultimate private collectors, they could be worth millions. Because the artifacts were believed to have been originally stolen by U.S. Air Force personnel, the Office of Special Investigations had sent in Aaron and me.

"Truck." The voice in my earbud was now the Iraqi police captain.

I heard it before I saw it. Through the night vision goggles, its headlights glowed green—a ghostly image of a lumbering farm truck appeared over the crest of a hill and headed toward us along the old Kirkuk highway. The Iraqi police would perform the actual apprehension. The two of us were there to observe and assist in the recovery and identification of the artifacts. Nothing more.

I glanced back at the van. "Shit!"

"Max, what's wrong?" Aaron asked.

"He's gone." The van doors stood open like a gaping mouth, but the smuggler had vanished.

I swept the space between the van and the house. Empty.

Back to the van. Dark interior. No movement.

"Maxine?" Aaron's voice was louder.

I looked in the opposite direction and spotted our target hauling ass on foot toward the road. "The little prick is bailing!"

I saw the blurry image of the smuggler running across the flat, barren space toward the highway at a full sprint. He gripped the straps to a bulging backpack, and I realized he had duped us with the cargo van full of cartons. Instead he had all the goods on him. Chances were, nothing of value would be in the van.

"Agent Decker?" The captain was waiting for my signal.

"Hang on." I spotted my partner running behind the

smuggler. He was within a meter of being able to tackle the target.

But something wasn't right.

I stood and signaled to the Iraqi commandos to begin their assault.

"Aaron," I called, "Take him down! Stop the bastard!"

My earbud filled with orders from the captain shouting to his men. They were already swarming over the ridge.

Shots came from the van. Someone had been hiding inside. The shooter seemed to be ignoring the commandos and instead was firing at me. *What the hell?* I dropped behind the ancient wall and pulled my SIG Sauer.

Pieces of clay burst from the wall as slugs slammed into my hiding place. *How do they know my exact location?* I heard the Iraqis yelling. More shots. Within seconds, the sound of automatic weapons was everywhere. The guy in the van was relentless.

Crouching low, I maneuvered around the wall toward where my partner had been positioned. New shots fired. I popped up my head for a second and determined they were coming from the farm truck. It had stopped beside the highway, and at least four men were firing at the commandos from the truck's canvas-covered bed.

Whoever was still in the van was spraying bullets across the top of the ruins to keep me occupied. Then I saw him jump out and start to make a run for the truck before the commandos got to him. I moved to the end of the wall, rose, and fired three shots at the gunman. He dropped and didn't get up.

Several Iraqis swarmed the house while the rest headed for the farm truck, their tracers lighting up the night. I took off running to back up my partner but immediately caught the attention of someone in the truck—bullets were now coming at me. The commandos had to seek shelter behind the van as the men in the truck laid down cover fire for the smuggler's escape.

"Aaron, get down!" I yelled into the mic. He was running in

the open area. I felt my belt to make sure I had a fresh clip ready before racing along the perimeter of the pasture. I had to help him before he got himself shot.

The smuggler veered off the direct course toward the highway to avoid the line of fire, with Aaron right behind him. They left the open space of the pasture and weaved through the ruins. I took advantage of their detour and sprinted straight toward them for an intercept.

Just before they emerged from the last ancient clay structure, they charged right into me.

I aimed my gun and the smuggler froze. Aaron bent over, hands on his knees catching his breath.

"Aaron!" A voice shouted above the gunfire coming from the truck.

It was American. Not Iraqi.

I ripped off my goggles and glared at my partner. "Who's that? How does he know your name?" The smuggler sidestepped. "Freeze!" I ordered. "Aaron, who's that in the truck?" I had to shout for him to hear above all the racket. "What's going on here?" The pieces were coming together and I thought I already knew the answer, but I desperately wanted to be wrong.

"This has nothing to do with you, Max. Just turn around and walk away." Aaron straightened. "This is my ticket out."

"Have you forgotten that you're a federal agent?"

"Just back off. You're not supposed to get hurt. That was part of the deal."

"Deal? What deal? I'm not backing off. This isn't going to go down. Not like this." Bullets pelted the opposite side of the structure protecting us.

The voice from the truck roared out my partner's name again.

Aaron still hadn't caught his breath, and his words came in a staccato rhythm. "Don't make me do it. I don't want to shoot you."

The truck engine revved.

"Maxine, I'm sorry—"

As he brought his gun up I fired twice.

He collapsed.

"You bitch!" The scream came from the direction of the truck, but closer.

The American. Without my goggles, he was nothing but a dark form rushing at me.

The smuggler took off.

Then a flash.

The bullet struck my side just below my vest. Another slammed into my right thigh. The pain was white hot.

I dropped to my knees and fell forward.

The odor of the cattle manure seemed stronger this close to the earth.

Or was it the smell of death?

CHAPTER 2 - THE VISITOR
Present day, Big Bear Lake, Colorado

As I crested a hill, half a kilometer from my cabin, I spotted a Jeep in the distance. For an instant, the last orange from the setting sun glinted off its shiny paint even as it sat partially hidden in the shadows of the Douglas firs below.

Quickening my pace, I slipped along the path, protected from view by the Gambel oaks and mountain mahogany. I wanted to get a better look at the vehicle.

The Jeep might belong to hikers or wilderness lovers fancying a view of the Rockies in springtime. But this area was not a popular spot, which is one reason I had chosen the location—for solitude. And the signs declaring private property were hard to miss where the dirt road to my place turned off the county blacktop. The Jeep either belonged to a lost soul or to someone looking for me. The latter made me nervous.

The trail leveled off as I came down to the southern end of Big Bear Lake. The path hugged the lake's perimeter in a sweeping arc. Tall blades of grass and sedge kept me partially concealed. Combined with the onrush of night and my dark clothing, I was just a shadow.

I came to the edge of the clearing that cascaded from my cabin down to the lake. Crouching behind a thick fir tree, I poked my head around and scanned the rear of the cabin. That's when I saw him.

The guy was dressed in jeans and a heavy jacket with a baseball cap pulled low over his forehead. Dark hair. Maybe six foot one. Trim. Between 160 and 170 pounds. He walked slowly along the back porch. Judging by the way he moved he was agile and I bet fit beneath the bulk of the jacket.

At each window, he paused to peer in. As he reached the back door, I instinctively went for my sidearm, but the SIG Sauer had long been replaced with a five-inch hunting knife and a Maglite. I hadn't touched a gun since I shot Aaron Knox.

Time to improvise.

I waited until he cracked open the door and entered. Keeping low, I moved through the grass and took advantage of an occasional tree to evade the clearing until I made my way to the side of the cabin. With extra care, I eased open the storm door and slipped into the basement.

It was pitch-black and dank smelling—I'd had every intention of cleaning and reorganizing it, but it was still down near the bottom of my to-do list.

I kept my flashlight off. Moving blind, I felt my way around boxes, tools, and general junk. A rattling thud came when I bumped my shin on an old bedframe. "Damn!" *Had he heard both the collision and my curse?* When I found the thick supports of the wooden stairs, I slid underneath and waited.

The soft creaking of the floorboards told me he was in the kitchen. His steps were slow and light, obviously exercising caution as he searched each room. With my old F150 parked out front and the back door unlocked, it was no mystery that I was home or not far away. Since he wasn't ransacking and rummaging, I concluded that he was not there to burgle. That left one alternative, and I didn't like it.

Narrow slits between the floorboards lit up as the intruder swept his light around each room. He approached the door to the basement.

At the sound of the door hinge squeaking above me, I pushed back against the wall.

He took the first step on the stairs, and his light beam came to rest on an old refrigerator sitting next to a workbench. The Frigidaire didn't function, and the tools on the bench were worn and rusted, left behind by the former owner.

The second step creaked and then the third, slow and easy. A dark leather hiking boot settled on the step level with my face. The next step down, I grabbed his boot laces and he flew forward, head first. With a grunt, he hit the dirt floor hard. I ran out from under the stairs and before he could move, I had my knee planted firmly in his back at the base of his neck and the butt end of my Maglite pressed into his skull.

"Move and you're dead." I stabbed the Maglite against his head for emphasis, hoping it felt like the real thing.

"Maxine, sweetheart, is that any way to greet your long-lost love?"

THE SHIELD

CHAPTER 3 - KENNY GATES
Big Bear Lake, Colorado

"What did you expect me to do, Kenny? You broke into my home and sneaked around like a burglar. We've got electricity up here in the backwoods. Next time, ring the doorbell. Or call first."

I leaned against the porch railing with my arms folded and watched him baby a cut on his forehead with a Ziploc bag of ice. He sat in a high-back rocking chair and glanced up at me with his apologetic hazel eyes.

"Knocked at your door. No answer. Car was here. You live way out in the middle of bum-fuck Colorado. Anything could have happened to you. I was just checking the place out to make sure you were okay. Of course I loved the extra element of surprise. "

"I'm sure you adored your little perk of scaring the hell out of me."

"So you were going to blow me away with a Maglite?"

"If I had to. It was locked and loaded with double-As."

Kenny smiled as he shifted the plastic ice pack to a new position on his head and looked at the lake in the distance. The stars and fireflies were coming out. "Nice place, Max. You've done good."

He was right. This was what I needed after the long recovery and rehab from my gunshot wounds in Iraq, not to mention the additional hell of going through endless grilling by the Inspector General's Office on the shooting of Aaron Knox. The actual gunplay took a few seconds—the inquiry

267

seemed to go on forever. It didn't take much to push me over the edge. I decided to retire after being shot at three times during my eighteen years as a special agent with the OSI.

The first time was an airman who stood in the parking lot of the Eglin Base Exchange and decided to shoot his girlfriend and any other females within line of sight. I was three cars over. He got the girlfriend and my driver's side window.

Second time, I was conducting an interrogation at MacDill on an officer caught smuggling stolen Peruvian artifacts out of Florida. He came to my hotel room and knocked. When I asked who it was, he fired three bullets through the door. One grazed my arm. I went to the hospital and he went to prison.

The first two weren't anything like Kirkuk. There was also the mental and emotional wrecking of having shot my partner and friend. To make things worse, I was then under suspicion of involvement in the smuggling operation. That nailed my decision to leave the OSI. I didn't just retire, I fled. I *needed* to get out. And I needed to go someplace and be alone for a long time. Big Bear Lake was perfect.

Kenny and I had a long history. We'd met when I joined the OSI. I was only 23 and green. Kenny, on the other hand, was an experienced agent and a good one. While others let me flag and flounder, Kenny found time to coach me through the maze of my new job. He was my personal mentor, even though our fields were different. He was an OSI Computer Crimes Investigator specializing in computer forensics, while mine was the antiquities black market. If a crime was committed by military personnel, we were usually called in to investigate. Kenny had to deal with everything from kiddy porn to falsifying documents, while I dealt with stolen art objects and smuggling.

"Must be boring up here." He put down the ice pack and took a long pull from the Coors.

"Not when I've got people sneaking up on my place and breaking in." I took a drink from my beer. "And why did you park your Jeep up the road? You're lucky I don't like guns anymore."

"My intent was to happily surprise you. But when you weren't around, I got worried. I screwed up, okay? So sue me."

I shook my head. "And people wonder why I got out of the military."

"What do you do up here all day?"

"Well, I do some painting. Lots of reading. And I've started writing—"

"Really? What kind of writing?"

"Fiction. I've got a few ideas for a novel. I write longhand, then type my work into my laptop. It's fun. They say everyone has at least one book in them."

"Am I in your book?"

I resisted a smart reply and zapped him a *give me a break* look.

"Just asking," he said.

"And I fish. There's some decent trout fishing in the lake. A boat came with the house, so I go out on the lake once in a while. I like being around nature. As a matter of fact, I was coming back from checking on a litter of foxes about a kilometer from here when I saw your Jeep. The mother's been missing for a few days, and I was worried about the kits. But mom showed back up today, although she looked the worse for it."

"Probably a slut fox.

"Or a battered wife."

"Touché," Kenny said, hoisting his bottle.

"So, now that we've had the obligatory idle chitchat and the complimentary beverage, why are you here?"

He set down the beer, rubbed the dark stubble on his chin, and let his face go serious. "We want you back."

I stared at him, wondering if this was someone's idea of a joke. "Back? Back to what? Kenny, there is no back. There's only forward. I'm moving forward with my life. This is my life. Look around you. What could be better than this? There's nothing the government could possibly offer that would entice me to return to active duty."

"Max, you're living in downtown boredomville. OSI is in

your blood. You've had your R&R. Now it's time to get back to work. Catch some bad guys. Find an ancient relic or two. Do your magic. I know you."

"Well, for once, you're wrong. This *is* me. And I like me." I walked a few paces away and turned toward the lake, now only a dark mass under a brilliant, star-filled sky. I rubbed my upper arms, enjoying the brisk Colorado mountain air before turning to Kenny. "There's nothing that could bring me back."

"Don't be so sure."

I didn't like the way he said that. He understood me well enough to know what blew my skirt up. Maybe he was just playing with me. He had an annoying habit of doing that. "What do you mean?"

"We think we've got a line on the Blade."

I felt a tingle in my belly and my pulse quickened. Suddenly, that old rush of the chase shot through me. Just to clarify, and with a great deal of anticipation I asked, "What blade?"

"The Blade of Abraham."

CHAPTER 4 - THE ROAD
Austria, 18 months earlier

"Debbie, check this out," she heard her boyfriend call out.

"Where are you?"

"Over here." She looked toward the sound. He was waving at her from among the deep shadows of the forest. He stood in knee-high brush about twenty paces from the remote mountain hiking trail.

"What've you got, Scott?" It took her a few moments to make her way through the brush. "And why did you have to come this far just to take a leak?"

"Took advantage of the moment to see what the woods are like off the trail." He stooped and lifted the edge of a large piece of metal off the ground.

"So what's your big discovery?"

"I found this underneath some brush and ground cover." He pulled the plate up so she could see the bottom. The faded lettering was barely visible among the rust and corrosion. "What's it say?"

Debbie stared at the words. She'd learned German from her mother and maternal grandmother. It was her interest in her heritage and Scott's graduate studies in history that had inspired their summer backpacking trip through central Europe.

"It's German," she said. "Basically says to turn back, that if you go on you'll be shot."

"Turn back from what?" He glanced about at the dark forest as it followed the curve of the mountain. "There's nothing here."

"Well, nothing *now*," she said. "But by the looks of its condition, the sign must've been around for years. Chances are the only reason it's still here is because it's made of metal rather than wood." She leaned forward. "Hang on a sec." Bending, she gave the sign a closer inspection. "Hold the edge up higher. There's something else near the bottom." She brushed away the dirt and caked-on debris. "Wow!"

"What?"

"I'll hold it while you take a look." Tilting the heavy metal plate upright, she waited until he came around. "See it?"

"A swastika. I'm not surprised. The Nazis took over Austria in 1938. Near the end of the war, Hitler had a plan to make a last stand in the Alpine areas of Austria, Bavaria, and northern Italy. They built a number of heavily fortified bunkers to house the army. When that didn't work out, some say they used them to hide all their looted treasure."

Debbie dropped the sign. "I wonder if we're close to one of those treasure bunkers?"

"Plenty of the stuff stolen by the Nazis is still missing. But it's not likely we've found anything after nearly seven decades. Let's get back on the trail or we won't make it to the next hut by sundown."

"Now it's my turn to have to pee." She waved with both hands, motioning for him to turn away. "I'll just be a minute."

Debbie headed for an area a few meters further into the woods. Coming to the top of a slight rise, she looked down onto what she thought was an irregularity below. The brush there was less dense, less lush, and it seemed to form a pattern, like a trail through the thick forest. "Scott," she called out. Her voice sounded small among the thick oaks and sycamore maples.

She ambled down the slope. Kicking at the brush and vines, she noticed the ground felt especially hard and rugged beneath the scrub here. Ripping out some of the plant growth revealed a swatch of cracked and pitted pavement.

"A road," Debbie said. "An old road." So that was why the

brush was less dense. It struggled to survive atop pavement.

Looking around, she saw more evidence of crumbling pavement riddling the area. The remnants of the road continued through the forest up a gradual incline to the left until it curved out of sight.

She wondered if Nazi transport trucks loaded with gold bullion or rare art objects had once traveled along it. A scrabbling sound and a grunt caused her to turn.

Scott had lost his balance as he came down the embankment and landed on his butt.

"That was graceful."

"What are you doing?" He brushed off the dirt before resecuring his backpack. "All of a sudden I turned around and you were gone."

"Look what I found." She gestured like Julie Andrews on the mountaintop in *The Sound Of Music.*

"What?" Scott said, eyeing the surroundings.

"This." She pried loose a piece of the pavement and held it up. "A road. It must date back decades. Certainly hasn't been used in a long, long time."

"That's impressive. Now can we get back on the trail? The hut is hours away. We're losing valuable time."

"But don't you think this is so cool? You found the old Nazi sign, and now I've discovered a hidden road. Think where it might lead. A German treasure bunker could be right around the next bend." She turned, adjusted her backpack and started walking. "Come on, let's explore a little."

"Not a good idea."

"Why? It's headed in the same general direction as the trail. If we get bored, we can work our way west and jump back on."

Reluctantly, he fell in beside her. "We're going to wind up sleeping on the ground, mark my words."

"Where's your sense of adventure? Everyone takes the trail. We're the only ones following this."

"It's just an old road."

"Yes," she said, picking up the pace, "but one with a Nazi warning that beyond this point we'll be shot. You won't find that kind of adventure on the trail."

They followed the road through the forest as it wound around the side of the mountain. After a couple of miles the trees thinned enough for them to see the rugged incline of the mountain.

"I still don't think we should have taken this side excursion," Scott was saying when they rounded a bend and came to an abrupt halt.

What was left of the pavement seemed to run right into the side of the mountain—at least right into a large pile of rocks and debris.

"Landslide?" Debbie asked.

He shrugged. "If it was, it happened a long time ago. No wonder the road isn't used anymore—it doesn't go anywhere."

"So it went somewhere but there was this landslide and now it ends here."

"Now that we've solved the mystery of your phantom highway, can we try to work our way back to the trail? If we move fast, we might be able to make the hut before nightfall."

"Do you think it continued on past the rockslide?" she asked.

"It doesn't look like there's anything beyond the rocks." He walked to the far edge of the debris pile. "I don't see any road beyond. My guess is that it ended right here."

"That makes no sense," Debbie said, heading over to the opposite side of the slide. "Why build a road that dead-ends on the side of a mountain?"

"Deb, we really need to get a move on."

Ignoring him, she passed the base of the rockslide and wandered into the trees and underbrush. She didn't have to look back to know Scott was following her. His grumbling was loud and clear.

"Why are you obsessing over this place?"

"I'm curious, that's all." She climbed over an outcrop by pulling herself up using low hanging branches. "Don't you think it odd?"

"What? That someone a long time ago built a road that

274

dead-ended into the side of a mountain?"

"That's just it." Standing on a rock, she turned to face him. "I think the road runs *into* the mountain."

"You mean like a tunnel?"

"Maybe. Why would the Germans threaten death to anyone who came up here if they didn't have something to hide? We could be right on top of your treasure bunker."

"So what are you looking for?"

"What's the one thing you need if you're in a bunker inside a mountain?"

"I don't know. Flashlights? Schnapps?"

"Air."

Scott stared at her for a moment before nodding. "So you think if there's a bunker, there might be some kind of ventilation?"

"Maybe. It shouldn't take too long to find out." She started climbing over the next grouping of rocks.

He looked at his watch. "You might as well take your time, now. There's no way we're going to make it to the next hut. We'll sleep back down on the road and head over to the trail tomorrow."

"Be looking for some unusual feature."

They spent the next twenty minutes investigating, climbing, parting vines and weeds, searching the landscape for some anomaly. At last, just as she was ready to give it up, Debbie spotted something. "Over there," she said pointing and heading toward her sighting.

Scott climbed to join her.

"Look at this," she said, pushing the undergrowth aside to expose a man-made stone and mortar slab. "I should be a detective rather than an engineering major." Protruding up from its center was a metal tube about thirty inches in diameter with a cone-shaped lid mounted on top. The lid sat at an odd angle, having been the victim of wind, rain, rust, and more than one falling rock.

Looking inside the small space between the cone lid and the tube, Scott saw a layer of straw and twigs from generations of bird nests. "Well, I've got to admit, you were right. Somewhere inside is a tunnel or bunker, and this probably leads to it." He looked at his girlfriend. "But finding it isn't enough, is it? You're still not satisfied, are you?"

She slipped her backpack off and tested the strength of the cone-shaped lid supports. "Of course not. Now we go inside the mountain."

CHAPTER 5 - EBAY
Big Bear Lake, Colorado

"You're kidding!" I stared at Kenny as I recalled the first time I'd seen the Blade of Abraham. When I was a teen my family took a vacation to Egypt. During our visit to the Cairo Museum, one exhibit especially intrigued me. I remember standing transfixed and staring at the age-worn twelve-inch-long knife with its simple wood and leather-bound handle that rested in a wooden box. I was drawn to it because of the dramatic story it told, one I'd read as a child in Sunday school. Unlike the cold stone statues and endless rows of pottery in the museum, this simple knife suddenly became a direct connection for me to an event over four thousand years ago.

It was the tale of ultimate faith—how Abraham obeyed God's command to sacrifice his son, Isaac. Only at the last moment did God send an angel to intervene. It had a profound effect on me as I stood there staring at the relic in the exhibition case. Throughout my life the Blade of Abraham was my personal symbol of faith and sacrifice.

Not long after our family vacation, I read that the relic was stolen. I suppose that's what helped lead me to pursue my profession. I started following news accounts of other ancient artifacts being stolen and sold on the black market. After I graduated from college, one of my professors told me of his time in the military as an agent in the Air Force Office of Special Investigations. When I found out they needed an archaeologist and welcomed civilian agents, I joined up. But no matter how fulfilling it was to solve hundreds of cases over the years, I never lost my hope of someday finding and recovering that simple blade: the Blade of Abraham.

"We've been down this road before," I said. "Always a dead end, or the piece turns out to be a fake. What's different this time?"

He set the empty Coors bottle on my porch deck. "When was the last time it showed up on your radar?"

"There were rumors of it surfacing in Damascus five years ago and then a year later in Istanbul." I handed Kenny another cold one from an ice chest at my feet.

"Thanks." He twisted off the top. "And nothing since?"

"Right."

"Until last week. You'll never guess where it popped up. eBay."

I almost spit out my beer. "Are you shittin' me?" Wiping my mouth on my sleeve, I decided to drop into the companion rocker beside Kenny. "What kind of moron would auction a priceless religious relic online?" I looked at him. "And a stolen one at that."

"It appeared under the Holy Land Antiquities category. The auction lasted one hour before it disappeared."

"Any bidders?"

He shook his head. "By the time we got wind of it, the listing was gone. Turns out someone hacked the seller's account to post it."

"I can't believe someone would use a public internet site to try to sell a relic like the Blade. Had to be a hoax."

"That was my reaction at first."

"And they actually called it the Blade of Abraham?"

"Takes balls."

"I'll say. What makes you think it was the real thing?"

"We had eBay send us the cached images, which we forwarded to the Cairo Museum. The pictures were high res, so it was easy to compare to what they had on file. Interestingly enough, it was actually the container the Blade was displayed in that gave the most proof. One of the guys at the museum confirmed a small identifying mark on a corner of the wooden box that matched their records and photos perfectly."

"I remember that box from when I first saw it years ago. So the big question—why is OSI involved?"

"The hacked account belonged to an Air Force officer."

I stared at the starlight reflecting off the dark lake, wishing it had gone that easy for me after... My cat suddenly appeared, winding around my ankles and purring. I put him in my lap, stroking his head and back. "Another of my simple pleasures."

"I never knew you were a cat lover."

"After all these years? Surprise, surprise." I hesitated a moment. I was being bitchy and decided to let it go. "Even as a kid I wanted a kitty, but Mom and Fran were allergic. Now that I'm retired and live alone, I tend to indulge myself. So I got a cat. Named him Nanki-Poo. Nank for short. From *The Mikado*."

"Speaking of Fran, how is your sister?"

"Still a free spirit with a big heart. She took off a few months ago on a humanitarian mission to Haiti after the earthquake. They say twins act and think alike, but I never got her wanderlust. She's with a UN-sponsored relief organization. After her work in Haiti, she headed to Cuba to help out with the victims of the hurricane."

I rocked for a few minutes, petting Nank, enjoying his attention as much as he seemed to enjoy mine, and deeply missing my sister. "I have to admit I'm interested."

Kenny gave me that "I know you so well" grin, the one that had rankled me so often over the years—mostly because he did know me so well, and he knew it. But just for an instant, I felt an old cold trail turn warm, maybe even hot. Then the distant sound of a fish jumping out on the black water and the memory of what I'd done that day three years ago in Iraq near the Assyrian ruins brought me back to reality.

"Despite your tempting news, I'm going to have to pass, Kenny. I wish you luck, but I gotta tell you, I'm perfectly happy right here." I leaned back in the rocker and inhaled the fresh mountain air, clearing my head.

"Come on, Max. What's put out that spark in you? Get

back on the horse, as they say. You aren't afraid. Of that I'm sure. The only thing I've ever known you to fear is heights. So why not?"

He wasn't going to quit, and I could feel the fire of my temper flaring. My posture stiffened, and I glared at Kenny. "It's not about fear. How could you even ask me such a thing knowing what I went through after Iraq?"

"Look, Max, I've put my neck on the line for you."

"Maybe that's what you should have done three years ago."

"You're right. I should have. But that's Monday morning quarterbacking. I was wrong. I've told you that before. But I can't change that."

"No, you can't."

"Time and distance make us see things more clearly. I'm not trying to make up for anything. I'm just trying to do what's right."

There wasn't much I could say to that. Yes, he should have done more in my defense and not let me get beat up so badly with the investigation. But looking back, I realize that at the time he was angry. Interesting that I wasn't as bitter anymore. Maybe a tinge of sourness still rose up now and again—that accounted for some of my snippiness with him. Tangled, tangled webs we weave.

Kenny paused a moment, then continued. "You know, at OSI there's still a black cloud that hangs over the name Maxine Decker. People get all weird when your name comes up. Just so you know, when I suggested bringing you in to help with this case, not everyone got excited. I had to remind them that there was never a shred of evidence that you were involved in that smuggling plot, and that killing Aaron had nearly killed you—emotionally. No way would you have shot your partner without just cause. Oh, they agreed that you were the best one suited for this job, but there was resistance in getting you involved. I pushed hard to turn them around. They relented, and I volunteered to come out here and recruit you. They don't have anyone with your level of expertise. You're it, Max, and if you don't say yes, I guarantee they won't get to the bottom of the Blade issue."

I looked away, lowered my head and rocked a few times before I spoke. "Sorry, Kenny." I faced him again, looking into his disappointed eyes. "I just can't. After the Aaron incident, I was severely depressed and I about lost my sanity. It's been a long road back. I finally get out of bed in the mornings instead of finding no reason to get up, take a shower, or get dressed. And I don't think about hurting myself anymore."

He stared into the night for a long time. "I'm so sorry you had to go through all that, Max. I can understand why even a chance at finding the Blade isn't enough to bring you back. No sense in discussing it any further." He stood. "I hope you have a nice life in your mountain hideaway. I'll just be running along. There's no reason to tell you the best part."

I stared up at him and saw a hint of a smile playing at his lips. God, he could be exasperating. "What best part?"

THE BLADE is available in e-book. For more information on Lynn Sholes & Joe Moore, and their thrillers, visit www.sholesmoore.com and follow them on Facebook at www.facebook.com/sholesandmoore